"Don't be af
Rafe murmu
away the tears on her face.
"Look at me...."

Carrie looked at him, hating him and herself. "What?" The word came out as an angry, bitter snarl.

"You're hurting, and it's my fault." His gaze caught hers. It was impossible to look away from those expressive amber eyes. Eyes that were full of remorse, and an expression she could easily have mistaken for love. "You're angry at yourself. You're asking yourself how you could have made love to a drug dealer and murderer. You're not that kind of woman."

The fact that he understood exactly what she felt struck her deeply, somewhere around her heart. "Apparently I am."

He shook his head. "No, you're not. And I'm not the man you think I am."

She swallowed hard, but couldn't help but answer honestly. "Maybe not. But you're a hell of a man."

Dear Reader,

Merry Christmas, Happy Holidays of all sorts and welcome to another fabulous month's worth of books here at Intimate Moments. And here's a wonderful holiday gift for you: *Captive Star,* the newest book from bestselling, award-winning and just plain incredibly talented author Nora Roberts. The next of THE STARS OF MITHRA miniseries, this book has Nora's signature sizzle and spark, all wrapped up in a compellingly suspenseful plot about a couple on the run—handcuffed together!

We've got another miniseries "jewel" for you, too: *The Taming of Reid Donovan,* the latest in Marilyn Pappano's SOUTHERN KNIGHTS series. There's a twist in this one that I think will really catch you by surprise. Susan Sizemore debuts at Silhouette with *Stranger by Her Side,* a book as hot and steamy as its setting.

And then there are our Christmas books, three tantalizing tales of holiday romance. *One Christmas Knight,* by Kathleen Creighton, features one of the most memorable casts of characters I've ever met. Take one gentlemanly Southern trucker, one about-to-deliver single mom, the biggest snowstorm in a generation, put them together and what do you get? How about a book you won't be able to put down? Rebecca Daniels is back with *Yuletide Bride,* a secret child story line with a Christmas motif. And finally, welcome brand-new author Rina Naiman, whose *A Family for Christmas* is a warm and wonderful holiday debut.

Enjoy—and the very happiest of holidays to you and yours.

Leslie J. Wainger
Senior Editor and Editorial Coordinator

Please address questions and book requests to:
Silhouette Reader Service
U.S.: 3010 Walden Ave., P.O. Box 1325, Buffalo, NY 14269
Canadian: P.O. Box 609, Fort Erie, Ont. L2A 5X3

STRANGER BY HER SIDE

SUSAN SIZEMORE

Silhouette®

INTIMATE™MOMENTS®

Published by Silhouette Books

America's Publisher of Contemporary Romance

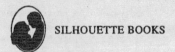

SILHOUETTE BOOKS

ISBN 0-373-07826-9

STRANGER BY HER SIDE

Copyright © 1997 by Susan Sizemore

Printed in U.S.A.

SUSAN SIZEMORE

hates winter, but lives in Minnesota anyway. She can't remember a time when she wasn't making up stories. The only things she loves nearly as much as writing are books and movies. All sorts of books and movies. Her hobbies include collecting art glass and traveling whenever she gets a chance—especially getting away from those cold Minnesota winters! Her first effort at writing romance was a story she wrote as a present for a romance-reading friend. That effort led to the discovery that she loved writing romance, and also led to a Romance Writers of America Golden Heart Award and a career as a professional writer.

For Mary Schultz,
who convinced me I could do it.

Prologue

"His name's Rafael."

Carrie kept her voice equally low when she leaned over and replied, "He doesn't look like an archangel to me."

"More like the devil himself," Juana agreed.

Or a stalking panther, Carrie thought, but kept the comment to herself. Lord, but the man's body was gorgeous. She couldn't take her eyes off him as he walked to the bar. He moved with the fluid grace and the dark intensity of a stalking cat. Silence slashed in his wake. All eyes were turned toward the black-clad newcomer. Black suited him. In fact, the shadows seemed to gather around him, almost obscuring him even though his presence seared across the room like dark lightning.

She hadn't gotten much of a look at his features as he'd gone by, just a glimpse of a strong jawline and a masculine column of throat as he tossed shoulder-length ebony hair away from his face.

It had been enough to excite more than casual curiosity.

Her fingers were firmly wrapped around a tall glass of luke-warm beer, but they were itching to brush through the stranger's silky mane.

There was something elemental about her instant reaction to this man, Carrie realized. She wanted to reach out and touch him, to make tactile contact, to know him by feel, the way she did with the hieroglyphs on the temple walls. Which was ridiculous. She had reasons to be passionate about her work interpreting the Mayan language. She had no reason to feel anything toward this man.

"It would be a sin if his face didn't match his body," she whispered. And she really, really wanted to know what this fallen angel, Rafael, looked like.

"He's no stranger to sin," Juana said.

"Amen to that."

"Be good, *chica*," Juana warned. She briefly touched Carrie's hand. "Remember what I told you?"

Carrie sighed as a group of men gathered around the newcomer. It did not look like it was going to be a friendly meeting. "There are only two kinds of men in Oro Blanco," she repeated Juana's warning. There were the farmers who worked for Señor Alvarez and the crew who worked for her at the temple dig. And then there were Torres's men. The first type were respectable, honest folk. "And he's obviously the other kind. Pity. Doesn't mean we can't enjoy the view, though."

The two women exchanged an amused look and went back to drinking their beer. From the table in the darkness at the back of the room, Carrie continued to surreptitiously watch the broad-shouldered stranger. She didn't glance at her friend for fear they'd break into a fit of nervous giggles and call attention to themselves. If there was one thing she'd learned in her time in Oro Blanco, it was to keep a low profile, especially while visiting the community's only bar. The place always smelled of beer and old sweat. Now with Rafael's entrance, there was also a sudden aura of impending danger.

To get up and leave might be more chancy than staying put and Carrie didn't want to be noticed if there was some sort of drug deal going on at the bar. This wasn't Newport or Brook Run, where she could just call the police. This was Oro Blanco, where many of the *federales* worked for the drug dealers, for Torres.

"Nice women should not be in Maquiero's," Juana firmly pointed out, not for the first time. "Not with men like Rafael in town."

"I'm not a nice woman," Carrie replied, feigning a nonchalance she did not feel. "I'm a foolish *gringa*. Besides, I like bars."

She'd been raised in one after all. Well, not in, but over the neighborhood bar her parents owned in Newport. Of course, her family's establishment was a lot cleaner than Oro Blanco's only bar, and the clientele was a great deal friendlier. Robinson's Roost was a haven to enter; Maquiero's was a challenge. Even though she'd grown up to be an archaeologist working in a setting far away from Rhode Island, Carrie Robinson found the environs of a tavern, even Maquiero's sleazy dive, comforting when she suffered a bit of homesickness. Though she had to admit that coming in here today, no matter how tiring a day it had been out at the dig, had probably been a bad idea.

"You don't look like a *gringa*."

"Looks can be deceiving," she answered and nodded toward the magnificent male animal at the bar. The men who flanked him had a dangerous, feral quality about them; they radiated tension. Rafael seemed almost relaxed as he slouched forward to speak to a much shorter man. If what she saw as he bent was the hint of a gun beneath his jacket she didn't want to know what it was doing there.

"Looks can be deceiving," she repeated.

"Angels and devils can look alike," Juana reminded her. "That's how devils started out, remember? As fallen angels."

"Wonder how far he had to fall? And how is it a nice woman like you knows anything about this Rafael—if he's that kind of man?" she asked.

"He's my nephew from Los Angeles. Rafael Castillo. The son of my brother who lives in California."

Carrie recognized the contempt in her friend's voice and gave Juana an understanding look. Carrie knew all about outsiders who came back to exploit their Mexican roots and impoverished relations. In a way, she was one herself, or so she'd been accused. Torres must find someone like Rafael Castillo invaluable.

He was certainly fast with a gun.

The observation came with a bolt of blood-freezing terror as hell broke loose in Maquiero's. Rafael Castillo was not the first man by the bar to pull out a gun. He was the first to fire. Blood blossomed on the front of a man's dirty shirt. Rafael whirled, his hand curled around the butt of a 9 mm pistol as someone else raised a weapon against him.

Shock kept Carrie in her chair for the first moment after the initial shot roared out. Before the second gun spoke, she'd grabbed Juana's arm and hit the floor. They were cowering behind the overturned table by the time the gun battle was blazing in full.

Her sense of self-preservation shouted for her to keep hidden, to keep her head down and pray. Some other sense urged her to *do* something. Everything was noise, a horrible, unforgettable cacophony. Men cried out in anger and in pain. Furniture creaked and crashed as it was overturned, and bodies fell with a heavy thud, stirring up dust from the floor. Glass cracked and shattered as bullets ricocheted around the room. Maquiero's had never been a haven; now it was hell.

The devil had indeed walked in the door.

It had to be the devil that urged her to lift her head above the vague safety of the table's edge. Some primal urgency drove her to look for Rafael Castillo as he swirled and ducked amid flying bodies, bottles and bullets. The shout that burst out of her came straight from the heart as she saw a gun lifted toward Rafael's back.

Whether he heard her warning or not, she didn't know. She *did* see him drop to his knees and spin around in one fluid movement. The man who had been about to shoot him was the one who went down, a bullet in his shoulder. Then Rafael was on his feet again. He was the only man in the room who was. All the rest were too wounded to rise, or too afraid.

He turned with the speed of light to face her.

Carrie gasped as the black steel gun barrel centered on her forehead. Her heart forgot to beat. She was going to die, but she looked her executioner in the eye.

The Devil and Death were one and the same. His name was Rafael, and he had amber eyes.

Chapter 1

The dream could go two ways.

Sometimes he fired the gun, put a bullet between those lovely brown eyes and they closed forever. Sometimes he made love to her. In the dream, he pinned her against the wall, felt the swell of her full breasts pressed against his chest, kneed her thighs open and entered her in one smooth thrust. In the dream, she cried out his name like a hungry lover.

Either way, whether he dealt death or passion, Rafael woke up aroused and covered in sweat.

"She doesn't even know my name," he muttered as he threw off the sheet. He didn't know her name. It was better that way because the ugly truth was that a man who didn't know the difference between dealing out death and making love didn't deserve a woman like her. But it didn't stop him from wanting her.

Knowing that it was foolish hadn't stopped him from asking his aunt who she was. It had taken all his considerable willpower not to pursue the subject further when Aunt Juana told him that scaring the *chica* nearly to death had been more contact than the poor girl needed. His Aunt Juana had had a lot to say about his life, how he was going to die and how he was going to roast in hell. And all of it was true.

So he'd kept away from any more inquiries about his aunt's companion, kept away from Oro Blanco and temptation since the shooting. But that didn't stop the dreams or the pounding need that came with them. The need ran counterpoint to the guilt. Despite all the shooting, only one man had died in the gunfight, a stranger to Oro Blanco and a very bad man indeed. It had been kill or be killed, Rafe knew, with not just his own life at stake.

The knowledge didn't stop the regret for what he'd done. And yet the guilt didn't eat away at him so badly that it overrode his thoughts of the angel who'd called out the warning to him and left him aching to touch her.

"I'm going to have to get myself a woman," he told himself. "It's just been too long, that's all."

He sat up very carefully, waiting for his body to calm down. The faint glow that came in from the window set high up on the wall told him it was near dawn. Torres always got up early. Rafael made it his business to be up before the boss. His job was to show rock-solid loyalty to his *compadre,* to be there when Torres wanted something done. He tried not to think too much about any of it.

He didn't sleep much, either. When he did, it was alone and with a gun under his pillow.

No police had investigated the incident in Maquiero's; no witnesses had been interrogated. Torres saw to it that his people weren't bothered by the authorities. When he told Torres about the fight, Miguel Torres would think him mad not to have guaranteed the woman's silence. Worse, he would have thought Rafael was weak and sloppy. And there was no room for those qualities in this business.

Rafael rubbed his hands across his eyes, then combed his fingers through sweat-soaked hair as he rolled tense shoulders. While his sleep had not been restful, he was alert, with his gun in his hand the instant he heard the tread of a foot outside his door. He did not feel like a fool when a heavy knock came on the door a moment later.

"Rafael," Manolo called jovially before he eased the door open, "wake up. Torres wants you."

It was better to be found naked with a weapon in his hand by a friend than to be found unprepared. Rafael made himself answer the cheerful Manolo with a laugh. "He's up earlier than usual. I'll be right down," he added.

"Good. There's an errand he wants us to run." Manolo closed the door he'd barely opened.

Rafael waited, gun in hand, until he heard Manolo walk away. Then he went and took a shower.

"Look at this nose," Carrie said to Beltrano. She held up the small jade carving as she turned her face in profile. She pointed from the figure on the stone to herself. "Note the resemblance."

"That's quite a hooter," Beltrano agreed grudgingly.

"Honker." Carrie pointed toward her bosom. "These are hooters."

Beltrano grinned. "They certainly are."

She returned his smile. "And here I thought I was improving your stock of politically incorrect English expressions."

He folded his arms. "What you're trying to do, Dr. Robinson, is distract me."

She put the carving back on the table. "If I wanted to distract you, I would have drawn attention to the more attractive parts of my anatomy sooner."

"No, you wouldn't have. You're not the kind of woman who uses her body like that. Besides, your nose is very attractive."

"It's Mayan."

"No, it isn't."

She liked Beltrano. She liked him a lot, admired him, even. They'd had several interesting conversations since she'd begun the Chalenque excavation. Admiration aside, he was still her adversary. There were actually three kinds of men in Oro Blanco. Along with the good men and the evil ones, there were also the political men, who were a little bit of both. Having survived an encounter with the worst kind, an encounter she couldn't get off her mind, Carrie felt capable of dealing with the likes of Beltrano. She just wished she didn't have to.

"Listen," she told the native activist, "I'm not trying to steal your heritage."

He pointed behind him, toward the open tent flap. "Then why are you loading artifacts into that truck?"

It was raining, as it always did this time of day, putting a thick veil of water across her view of the camp. Rain forests could be depended upon for the regularity of the weather. The Yucatán Peninsula was a hot, steamy, lush, beautiful, but disgustingly moist part of the world. Personally, Carrie wasn't sure why a culture as advanced as the Mayan had settled on such soggy, overgrown real estate. But this was where they'd built their magnificent cities, and where anyone who wanted to study them had to come. That didn't mean she couldn't be grateful that she needed to take some of her finds away at the end of the digging season to study in a drier atmosphere. At home it was spring. Here it was the beginning of the rainy season. It was time for her to go.

Not just because of the rain, but also because a man had turned a gun on her. She had to get away from the primal emotions that coursed through her whenever she remembered those few moments when time stood still and her life belonged to someone else. No matter how hard she tried, it was a memory that couldn't be banished as long as she stayed in Oro Blanco. She needed to sort out her emotions someplace where the heat didn't keep her awake and restless in her bed all night. Some place where she had something more to do than see a hunter's amber-colored eyes watching her whenever she closed her eyes.

"I'll be back in October." She said the words as much to reassure herself, as well as Beltrano, that she would return. "My work's important to me." I'm not going to let him frighten me off, she added to herself.

"Your work is important to my people," Beltrano said. "There's no reason you can't continue it at the University of Yucatán during the rainy season."

"Except that this archaeology dig is not affiliated with that university. My grant, paltry though it is, is from Jefferson University. That's where the labs and specialists needed to analyze this season's finds are located."

"And where the artifacts that belong here will remain on display when you're finished with them."

"That won't happen."

He gave her a thin smile. "Won't it? Isn't that what always happens?"

"Not these days. Jefferson has an agreement with the Mexican government to return all artifacts."

"An agreement that will become void with the payment of a small fee to the right officials of the so-called government."

She and Beltrano almost had to shout to be heard over the hammering of raindrops against the taut canvas of the tent's roof. She knew they were both trying hard not to have this meeting turn into a shouting match that had more to do with emotions than the volume of the rainfall outside. Neither of them was succeeding very well.

Carrie stood up slowly and took a few deep breaths to try to stay calm. She leaned forward and put her hands on the cluttered table between them. They'd been speaking English. Now she spoke slowly and firmly in the regional Mayan dialect. "I won't let that happen. Chalenque is *my* project." She pointed, not at the truck in the near distance, but at the temple mound that rose out of the jungle beyond it. "I found it, I'm excavating it, and I'm going to protect it for the Mayan people."

"Why?" Beltrano's condescending smile returned. She hated that look, having seen it far too many times in her life. "Because it's part of your heritage, Carolina?"

Carrie came around the table and stood by the tent entrance, trying very hard not to show her fury at his attitude. "We don't have anything more to talk about, Señor Beltrano. It's time for you to leave."

He stood. He was a medium-size man, square built and powerfully muscled. She knew that he had been educated at both the National University of Mexico and at the University of Southern California. She had no idea why he'd ended up as spokesman for a small group of local separatists. She just knew that she wanted him out of her campsite.

He strode toward her. "The bones of my people are not leaving Mexico."

His size and closeness did not intimidate her. "We have nothing further to discuss," she informed him.

He tilted his head to one side and gave her his annoying smile once more. He called out a name. A moment later, two men crowded into the tent behind her. She was grabbed by the arms and pushed backward until her spine hit the edge of the table.

Beltrano didn't carry a weapon. Carrie couldn't help but

notice that both his friends had rifles slung across their
backs.

"I take it," she said to Beltrano, "that the conversation
isn't over until you say so."

He stepped next to her. "That's right, Carolina."

"Bring me the archaeologist," Torres had told him and
Manolo. "Take the Hummer," he'd added.

Rafael knew about the temple excavation from cousins
who worked there. He knew that it was underfunded, un-
derstaffed and run by some foolish woman. It was also
fifteen miles down a muddy, half-flooded excuse of a jungle
road from the outskirts of Oro Blanco. That Torres sent
them in the Hummer four-wheel-drive vehicle was an indication that he wanted to see the foolish woman as close
to immediately as possible. Torres wanted everything instantly these days.

Since he was living on borrowed time, Torres was a man
with good reason to be in a hurry. Rafael knew better than
any man in the organization just how tenuous Miguel
Torres's hold was on power—and life. It had been a bad
quarter, which meant the loss of millions of dollars. Torres
always looked and acted calm and in control, but Rafael
sensed he was on the verge of some desperate, maybe even
fatal move. Torres was smart, though. He might find some
way out. Rafe had to be careful never to give any hint of
his own machinations, or it would prove to be very terminal. Rafael Castillo wasn't ready to die yet.

Not until he'd had the dream woman for real.

The thought was unexpected, as was the tightening in his
groin that came with it. He closed his eyes for a moment,
helplessly caught in the longing to taste the sweat on her
satin-smooth skin.

"There's the camp."

His eyes started open. He was shocked at the loss of

concentration, angry at abandoning his focus for even a moment. Worst of all, it was because of a woman. Beautiful as she was, no woman was worth the risk. It was ridiculous to be so haunted by a woman he'd seen for no more than a few tense seconds.

"This is bad," he grumbled as he brushed a heavy fall of hair away from his face.

Manolo laughed. "You look hot. You've spent too much time in air-conditioning lately, Castillo."

He was sweating, more fever hot from desire than the sticky heat of the day. Getting himself under tight control, Rafael replied to the other man's comment with a nod. He stared ahead. Rain flowed like a waterfall down the narrow windshield. It took all his concentration just to make out a clearing with a group of tents, tarpaulin-covered mounds and two trucks up ahead.

Manolo stopped the Hummer in front of the largest tent. When they got out, several people looked up from loading one of the trucks. There was recognition in those faces of what they were, if not who; nobody came over to ask their business. Manolo waited by the Hummer. Gun drawn to prevent any argument about a visit to Torres from the lady archaeologist, Rafael walked into the tent.

To find there were already people with rifles inside.

Their backs were to him. The rain on the tent roof blocked out any sound of his entrance. The only light was centered over a table on the opposite side of the tent. Nobody looked his way, so Rafael took a moment to study the situation. The woman was taller than the gunmen who flanked her, but Rafael's view of her was blocked by the wide shoulders of the man in front of her. He caught only a tantalizing glimpse of wavy dark hair backlit by the lamp, and of long fingers curled tensely around the edge of the table.

"I'm not intimidated by this, you know."

Three men stood between Rafael and the woman who'd spoken. Her voice was deep and rich, but she sounded younger than he'd expected. And she sounded scared despite the confidence of her words.

Carrie hated the fact that her voice shook. She hated that Beltrano's smile only widened at her bravado. "Leave," she told him, "and I won't report this to the authorities."

"You're the one who's going to leave, Carolina. I'll drive you to the airport in Mérida myself, if you like."

"I'm not leaving without my—"

"She's leaving," another voice interrupted from the doorway. "She's coming with me."

Beltrano turned. His men reached for their weapons. Carrie ducked past Beltrano. She ran toward the doorway and her rescuer. She was grateful that her foreman must have decided to look in on her at last. Now she had to get them both out of here before somebody got hurt.

"Varo, I'm so glad you—"

The man blocking the entrance was not the foreman. He was the image from every lurid nightmare she'd had in the past few weeks. His eyes were just as intense as she remembered them—tawny, and glowing like a hunting cat's out of the dark. She was just as caught by them as before. He was bigger than she remembered, though, his broad shoulders filling the doorway.

He still had a gun in his hand.

This time, she was certainly going to die.

"Oh, hell," she said as he grabbed her wrist and pulled her out into the rain.

"What the devil is going on here?"

Despite her angry tone, he could see in the woman's eyes the fear of a shallow grave in the rain forest. He didn't show that he shared that fear. What did Torres want with her? And would it get them both killed? The last thing he'd expected was to find that the woman from his dreams was the archaeologist.

With the rebels pouring out of the tent behind them, he didn't have time to think about the future. The present was quite dangerous enough.

Manolo fired a burst of bullets from his AK-47 just barely over the heads of the rebels. It served as warning to bring the men to a halt.

"Go," he ordered. Beltrano and his men headed to their vehicle, well aware of the drug dealer's superior fire power. "Into the car! Drive!" Rafael told Manolo once the men were gone.

The other man reacted to the snap of command in Rafael's voice. Manolo slid quickly behind the wheel. Rafael shoved the woman in ahead of him. The Hummer was heading out of camp by the time he had the door slammed shut after him.

There was plenty of shouting, but no fear of being fired upon by the site workers as the rugged four-wheel-drive vehicle drove away. One danger was over and nobody had gotten hurt, but Rafael didn't congratulate himself on having averted trouble. He knew that the real danger waited for them back at Torres's fortified compound.

Carrie wanted to scream. She wanted to claw at the man who'd just kidnapped her and fling herself across him to get out the door, but she refused to give in to hysteria. She wanted to get away and yet she was also perversely grateful for his rescuing her from the tent. Her stomach was curdled with terror, while her blood raced with awareness of the man who held a gun in one hand and her wrist with the other.

She was well aware of the dichotomy of her reactions. He was big and male and dangerous, and for some stupid, primitive reason her body seemed to think that mating with this particular monkey boy was the best idea evolution had ever come up with.

Fortunately, the brain attached to the body clearly realized that the situation was dangerous, probably terminal. He hadn't come looking for a date, but to eliminate a witness. At least that was the only immediate reason she could come up with for his sudden, saviorlike appearance.

"If I'd known you were coming, I would have gone with Beltrano."

If I'd known it was you, I wouldn't have come. He turned from watching out the back window to look at her. The woman's wet white T-shirt clung to her like a second skin. The warm scent of her skin mixed with the fresh smell of rainwater. His dreams hadn't exaggerated her beauty. Adrenaline pumped through him, and Rafael knew that if they'd been alone, he would have kissed her. If he kissed her, he'd be tempted to do far more.

"Where are you taking me?"

Their gazes met. The hot flash of temper in hers warmed his blood. "What do I call you?" he countered. "Doctor? Professor? Carolina?"

His voice caressed the word and sent a shiver through her. It wasn't even her name, she reminded herself sternly. "Why would my murderer want to know my identity?"

He put his gun away, then flicked a strand of wet hair away from her face. Every movement was feline, thoughtlessly graceful. "I haven't killed you yet. What's your name?"

"Carrie Robinson," she answered. "What do you want with me?"

Rafael thought the important question was, what did Torres want with her?

She was far too beautiful for her own good. Torres had an eye for beautiful women. Torres was restless. Maybe he was looking for something hot in his bed for a diversion. Carrie Robinson looked hot enough to divert a dead man.

"What's a beautiful woman like you doing in this god-forsaken place?"

She sneered. She was trembling. He could feel her terror, communicated at all the points where their bodies touched. Her fear didn't keep her from retorting, "That's the worst pickup line I've ever heard."

It had been a serious question, even if he'd phrased it stupidly. Even Manolo took his attention off driving long enough to roll his eyes at Rafael and laugh.

"Let Torres ask the questions," Manolo advised.

Fresh terror ripped through Carrie's guts as the driver gave another low, dirty laugh. "Torres?" She looked wildly at Rafael. "What does he want with me?"

He looked away rather than respond to the plea in her eyes. *I wish I knew, chica,* Rafael thought. For both their sakes. He considered his options, and some odds. He didn't answer Carrie's question and refused to speculate anymore about it himself. He was going to have to let the situation play out for now.

The silence throughout the rest of the trip had not been reassuring. Being abducted from would-be kidnappers had not been reassuring. And watching the gates of Torres's walled compound close behind the Hummer was the most unnerving thing Carrie had ever seen. No, the second most. The first time she'd looked into Rafael Castillo's eyes had been the first. This wasn't much better, though.

The air was utterly motionless. The rain had stopped and the soggy heat was more oppressive than usual as Rafael pulled her out of the vehicle. Carrie could barely drag the air into her lungs as she stood in the concrete courtyard before the mansion. There were too many men about and all of them were armed. This was the last place she'd ever wanted to be.

Standing wasn't all that easy. She was so scared that her legs felt like half-melted butter. Somehow she didn't think leaning on Rafael's strong shoulder was a very good idea. He stood by her as a guard, not to lend her strength.

"This is all your fault," she muttered to him as he cupped her elbow with one hand and urged her up a flight of shallow steps.

"I know," he replied.

She gave him a quick glance and saw a flicker of amusement disturb his set features for a moment. Then the main door of the house opened. A smiling man came toward them, hands outstretched in welcome. Rafael's attention was instantly on the other man, and every bit of humanity disappeared from his face. The grip that had been gentle turned harsh. She was surprised when he let her pull away.

She turned her attention to the newcomer. "Hello, Miguel," she said as the drug lord took her hands in his and one by one kissed them. "How nice to see you again."

Even though the door was shut between them, Carrie's attention still focused on Rafael Castillo. A look of sharp suspicion had flashed across his face for one split second after she greeted Torres. Not just suspicion, but something almost unreadable that had seemed very like betrayal. Then he had gone back to being the stone-faced errand runner and hired-gun. Torres had told him to wait for them and led her into his office, chatting amiably like anyone greeting an old friend.

She'd heard the soft tread of Rafael's steps behind them the whole way down the long hallway. It had seemed like she could feel his shadow at her back, as well. Now she almost wished that at least Rafael's shadow could have followed her into the room with Torres.

She hated the thought of being alone with the most powerful man in Oro Blanco. The few times they'd crossed paths before had been at social occasions with no bodyguards or any other hint of his profession to mar the illusion of his being a civilized being.

"Drink?"

Whether Carrie hated it or not, she was alone with Torres. She made herself concentrate on him and not the man on the other side of the door. She smiled. It wasn't a very convincing smile, she was sure, but at least her facial muscles obeyed her that much.

"Sure."

She stepped forward and dropped into the nearest chair. She counted the movement as another victory of willpower over fear. Air-conditioning dried the sweat on her skin, and she rubbed her arms to drive away sudden goose bumps. Torres handed her a glass of something clear and full of ice. She took a drink but tasted nothing, possibly because what he'd handed her was a glass of water.

"You look like you expected to be poisoned."

He sounded so amused that her answering smile was almost genuine as he took the chair opposite her.

"I never poison my guests," he went on. "Business associates, perhaps, but never guests."

"Don't be charming, Miguel," she said. "I'm too freaked out to deal with it. You could have called or sent a note if you just wanted to have me over for a drink."

"You've refused before," he reminded her. "Besides, I'm in a hurry."

She did not like the sound of that. She cocked her head to one side. "Oh?"

He set his glass on the low table between them. He looked more than serious when his gaze met hers again; he looked evil. "I have a problem," he said softly. "And you're going to help me solve it."

Oh, *hell.*

Carrie responded by putting down her drink, then folding her hands in her lap. She was colder than the ice in the glass. Cold with a fear stronger than she'd experienced the instant Rafael Castillo turned his gun on her. That had been a life-and-death situation, yes, but she suspected this could be equally as dangerous. Miguel Torres wouldn't make a statement like that if he didn't intend to pull her into something far worse than a threat to her life. Miguel Torres was a practicing Catholic, she'd seen him in church, but he had no qualms about destroying anyone's soul.

She didn't bother with any protestations that she was an honest woman. She didn't attempt any outraged bravado. Why bother? When he told her what he wanted, she would say no. Nasty things would probably happen to her when she continued to refuse. Eventually, someone would put a bullet in her brain or she'd do what Torres wanted. The best she could hope for was that she had enough moral fortitude to wait for the bullet. Fortitude was supposed to be part of her New England upbringing.

It wasn't as if she could exactly call Rafael for help. In fact, Rafael would probably be the one to—

"You look like you're about to faint."

Carrie blinked. She swallowed hard and swiped a hand across her forehead. "I feel like it."

Torres sat back and casually crossed his legs. "Good. I'm glad you're frightened."

"Thanks for your concern, Miguel."

"I like your sense of humor, Carrie. Have I ever told you that?"

"Yes."

"And the fact that you're a realist. You understand the seriousness of your situation, but you probably underestimate it."

"I beg your pardon?"

He gestured toward a large framed photo of the Chalenque temple that hung on one wall. It was beautiful enough to be a tourist poster. "I've been following your work. You have sixteen people working for you this season."

"Yes," she agreed. A cold shiver ran up her spine. "Why do you mention that?"

"Because I want you to know that you have more to fear than just losing your life," he went on. "You see, if you don't run a little errand for me, I will let you watch while I have everyone who works for you at the Chalenque dig killed."

Carrie could only stare. She was numb with the horror of the threat. She knew he'd do it. She'd been prepared for her own death. That other people would die if she didn't cooperate changed everything.

There was nothing she could do—except everything Torres wanted.

While she tried to think of something to say, Torres pressed an intercom button. "Come in, Rafael. I want you in on this. Don't worry," he said to Carrie as she heard the door open behind her. "Rafael will take very good care of you."

Chapter 2

Waiting outside the door had been something like torture. Rafe hadn't known whether he was more worried for the woman or for himself. A rush of dark emotion had gone through him the moment he found out that Torres and Carrie Robinson were on a first-name basis. He told himself it was suspicion, survival instinct, kicking in. He suspected that it was, in fact, raging jealousy for a woman who wasn't his, wasn't going to be his, and certainly didn't need to be his. Instead of exhibiting his usual statue-still patience, he had stalked the hallway back and forth like a caged animal.

When Torres called him inside, he had to pause at the door for a moment to make sure the mask he lived in was firmly in place. As he entered the room, the first thing he heard was his boss saying, "Rafael will take very good care of you."

He gave a brief, acknowledging glance at Torres, but his attention swiftly turned to the woman seated in the high-backed leather chair. Worry for her instantly returned when he saw that her fingers were tensely clutching the chair arms, and her face looked unnaturally pale. His gut twisted at the sight of someone so vibrant looking so cowed.

But when she spoke, the impression Rafe got wasn't so much of fear, but of pent-up fury. She answered Torres's comment, but her hotly angry gaze lifted to meet his. "I'm *sure* Rafael will take very good care of me."

Her contempt was scalding, but Rafe didn't let the burns show. He addressed Torres instead. "How am I going to take care of the lady, boss?"

"Have a drink," Torres invited, "and I'll explain it to you both."

Rafe nodded, then snagged a cold bottle of beer from the bar, careful not to make the slightest flicker of response, though the other man's attitude set off alarms in his already alert senses. He didn't like it when Torres sounded so affable. Torres was not naturally a nice man. He was a bully and a brute, but he tended to put on a show of friendliness when he knew he had someone completely at his mercy. Someone like Carrie Robinson.

Or maybe Torres was just trying to impress a beautiful woman with a show of sophisticated charm. No, Rafe knew from looking at Carrie's tense body language, that his employer hadn't been turning any charm on his guest. The screws, perhaps, but no charm. The question for Rafe wasn't so much what was going on between Torres and the woman, but how he was going to get her out of it. He was used to only having to worry about himself, of concentrating on his own survival and doing his job. This new burden disturbed him in more ways than he dared to examine.

Or maybe the false friendliness was aimed at him. Perhaps Carrie Robinson had told Torres all about what she'd seen in Maquiero's bar. Though was it really possible that she knew the reason that Rafe had had to kill a man? He was certain that only the Colombian courier, who had by chance been at the wrong drug deal in the wrong bar at the wrong time, had known who he really was. Rafe had seen the look of recognition in the man's cold eyes in the instant before guns were drawn, but no words had been exchanged.

The small-time dealers who'd set up the buy with the Colombian to impress Torres were long out of the country and in custody. Drug buys went bad all the time, and Torres's organization had been having a run of bad luck that way. Rafe was responsible for it, but Torres didn't know that, or that Rafe was an undercover DEA agent. Rafe was cautious, maybe even paranoid after being under for so long, but he doubted the lady archaeologist was any likely threat to him.

His body tightened at a sudden, unbidden flash of remembered dream, and he almost laughed. No, she was a threat all right. If he let her be. No, he reprimanded himself, the threat came from within and she wasn't responsible for the need she fired in him.

He forced himself to look at her as he sat down on the opposite side of the room from her. He put all the indifference of the cold killer he was supposed to be in that look. From the blush that darkened her too pale cheeks when their gazes met, he didn't think he succeeded.

Torres's bark of laughter punctuated the moment, and Rafe made himself concentrate on the boss. "What am I supposed to do with the lady?"

"Not what you look like you want to do," was Torres's answer. "I want you to guard her body, but that's all."

Rafe took a sip of beer. "Sure. No problem."

"It better not be."

Rafe gave an indifferent shrug.

Carrie squirmed in her chair as the men discussed what Rafael was supposed to do with her body. She tried to ignore the crude implication of their byplay and made herself concentrate on Torres rather than on the henchman who sat across from her. She found the way Rafael Castillo looked at her bad enough, but her own response to the gaze he turned on her had triggered not only anger, but the primal response that did its best to grip her every time she looked at the man.

What she'd seen in his eyes was a cross between arrogant indifference and arrogant need. The two emotions should have canceled each other out; the arrogance should have been all she had to deal with. That shouldn't have been too difficult. Arrogant males were a dime a dozen down here. All she wanted to do was to get out of this part of the world; leave men like Rafael Castillo behind. She definitely wanted her hormones to stop sizzling every time the man was near. She knew she'd be lucky to survive this, and she had no time for primitive responses when she was going to have to use all of her intelligence to endure Torres's trap.

"Just what is it you want me to do?" she asked him.

Torres nodded. "Down to business. Good. She's a practical woman, Rafael. She won't give you any trouble."

Rafe kept his opinion on that subject to himself. "What do you want her to do, boss?"

"Make the American pickup."

Rafe was glad he wasn't taking a drink when Torres spoke. He might have choked on it. As it was, he had trouble keeping himself from protesting that this innocent bystander was the last person he wanted in on that deal. Rafe had his own plans for the American operation well laid. It took all his years of role-playing to merely nod at Torres's words. Then he took a long gulp of beer.

"American pickup?" Carrie asked. "You want me to smuggle drugs from America?"

Torres chuckled. "You won't be going anywhere near any drugs, Carrie. I wouldn't let you get your pretty hands dirty like that."

Carrie glanced at her hands. They were work roughened,

with grime under the nails from her morning's toil on the temple staircase. She also noticed how tightly she had them clenched and deliberately made her muscles relax. "You're so thoughtful, Miguel."

"I know." His gaze turned dangerously serious once more. "Do you know the term 'mule,' Carrie?"

"Couriers used in the drug trade," Carrie answered promptly. "People who aren't otherwise involved with the business."

"So discreet, Carolina," Rafe couldn't help but say. The taunt came from his assumed persona. It was the sort of comment Torres expected him to make. It wasn't his persona that was raked by her acid look, however. He shrugged, then set the empty bottle on the floor. "Honesty is better than discretion about some things, Carolina." The way he pronounced the name made it sound soft and sultry and very sensual.

"My name is Caroline."

He smiled. "I'll remember that." This was no time to tease her, but he couldn't help it. "Carolina." It wasn't his persona that spoke this time.

"Carrie, if you must." She wished she hadn't even bothered to respond to his taunt. She wished she hadn't been maneuvered into inviting him to use her name. Never mind what she wished. "What sort of mule do you want me to be?"

Many mules, she knew, were otherwise honest, upstanding citizens, businesspeople, students, grandmothers... archaeologists. People with legitimate reasons for traveling, no police records, no ties to the drug cartels; people whom the dealers bribed to carry all sorts of illegal substances concealed in all sorts of ingenious ways. Many were outwardly respectable people whom inspectors didn't look at twice when they came through Customs.

"There's a pickup I need made in Washington," Torres

told her. "You're on your way to Washington. No one will notice you. No one will suspect you. You're going to bring your artifacts to Jefferson University, but before you settle in to do whatever you do with all those old stones you collect, you're going to pick up a suitcase for me and bring it back to Oro Blanco."

"A suitcase? What kind of suitcase? Where? What's in it?"

"There'll be a letter sent to your house in Brook Run," Torres answered.

Brook Run was a Virginia suburb of Washington, where she lived and the university was located. She didn't remember mentioning this to Torres, but this was hardly the time to recall the content of their few conversations.

"That's it? I'm just supposed to fetch this suitcase for you without any more instructions than that?"

Carrie almost shot to her feet, but managed to hold her indignation in check and not make any swift movements. She'd seen Rafael draw a gun once before. She didn't want to give him any excuse—such as trying to stop a furious woman from attacking his boss—to do so now.

The only gesture she made was to stab a finger toward him. "Why not just send him? If he's going to Washington with me, he might as well get your suitcase instead of me."

"Because Rafael and Manolo are only going to accompany you as far as the airport in Mérida, then wait there for you to return. You'll be on your own in Washington."

Carrie shook her head in confusion. "Why?"

"Because my pretty face is known by the gentlemen who want that suitcase for themselves," Rafe answered. Carrie found herself looking at him as he went on, his intense amber gaze boring into hers. "In fact, lots of people who want that suitcase know my face."

"The authorities," she interpreted.

Again he gave a slight, offhand shrug. "Them, too."

"I wish I'd never seen your face." Her voice was low and intense, the words not really meant for anyone but herself.

"No, you don't." His answer was just as low, but the tone sent flames shooting through her.

This time, she did surge to her feet. As she tore her gaze away from Rafael Castillo's, she was aware of him gracefully rising from the chair opposite her. She concentrated her attention on the smirking Torres. "I'll run your errand. Let's get this over with."

Torres put a hand lightly on her shoulder. She froze. She would much rather have shaken it off. "You can leave, Carrie," he told her. "Any time you want. Right now is fine. But Rafael goes with you."

"Don't touch me."

Rafe cocked an eyebrow at Carrie Robinson, but let his arm drop back to his side. He'd only put his hand out to help her down out of the high door of the Hummer. He'd had her ride in the rear seat on the way back from the compound, with himself and Manolo in front. It had seemed for the best. Except that he kept glancing in the rearview mirror and getting glimpses of Carrie Robinson. The faint sheen of sweat gave her skin a deep copper shine, while the swell of her bosom beneath the plain cotton fabric of her shirt kept drawing his eyes. So did the taut muscles of her thighs when he caught the movement as she crossed her legs or shifted to keep her balance as they bounced along the road.

Their eyes had met once in the mirror, and he'd gone hot all over as he read in her gaze that she knew just what he was looking at—and that it wasn't for him. He hadn't read hatred in that gaze, though he merited it, nor had it been the contempt a murdering drug dealer deserved, but her look definitely warned him off.

Now she wouldn't even take his hand. He stepped back and let the good Dr. Robinson bounce down all by herself into a patch of mud churned up by the tires. She didn't even notice the dirt that splattered her legs when she got out of the Hummer. Rafe guessed she was used to it. When she headed for the tent where he'd found her confronting the rebels, he hurried after her.

Carrie wasn't sure what she expected once they reached the dig, but it certainly hadn't been to have Rafael Castillo follow close on her heels to her office. Even though she didn't turn around to look, and he moved so quietly that she didn't actually *hear* him, she could *feel* his presence—large, masculine and alert—right behind her.

She stopped at the tent door to confront him. "Do you *mind?*"

He came inside, forcing her to move backward to keep from having him run into her. When they were in the center of the tent, he smiled, ducking his head and looking up at her through the thickest eyelashes in the world. "Mind what?"

The devastating part about his smile was that it was so boyish, so full of life. How very incongruous it looked on the face of a killer, she told herself sternly. "I have work to do," she told him. "If I don't get some work done right now, we won't be getting out of Oro Blanco any time soon. Which will delay your boss getting his suitcase, and you don't want that."

Rafe opened his mouth to tell her that her little project was canceled, that getting out of here and picking up Torres's package was all that mattered in her life right now. He saw the tenseness in her, the desperation deep in her eyes, and kept the words to himself. What Carrie Robinson could use for the time being, he decided, was some semblance of normalcy. He sensed that just beneath the surface she knew very well that her life was in shambles, that what

she was doing was just a rearguard action to try to gain
some control over what was happening to her. If pretending
that her archaeological dig was her primary focus would
help her cope, he'd give her that out. For now.

Carrie waited for the thug to sneer, drag her out to the
already loaded truck and tell her that they were leaving
immediately. Instead, he said, "Then you'd better do whatever is necessary. We leave in the morning," he added. He
stepped aside and let her go to her worktable.

He didn't go away, however. Carrie sat down and tried
to ignore him. She opened her laptop computer and began
to type up some handwritten notes, but how did one ignore
a panther in the same room? By concentrating, she supposed, and only allowed her glance to shift from paper to
small computer screen. Didn't everyone who worked the
Chalenque dig joke that she could lose herself for hours at
a stretch bent over one piece of ancient carving? Hadn't
there been one incident when she'd been timed—and there
had been bets placed on how long it would take her to
surface—as spending twenty-three hours deciphering a recently uncovered inscription, mostly by lantern light in
drizzling rain? In fact, her co-workers had decided that the
Mayan tale she'd so laboriously translated must be one rip-
roaring dirty story to keep anyone that interested for so
long.

And her co-workers—the people whose lives were in her
hands—had been absolutely right, and she hadn't blushed
at admitting it. Of course, it wasn't the salacious content
of the writing that was important. It was the context of
where it fitted in the culture of the people who'd built the
temple complex. Theirs was a culture that had fascinated
her all her life, a lost world about which she was determined to uncover a few more bits of knowledge. She'd
loved the Maya ever since her mother first told her of the

forgotten places that had once been her people's home. In a way, Chalenque was Carrie's home.

A home she was frightened she couldn't return to after Torres—and Rafael Castillo—had destroyed her sense of safety. They'd stripped from her the invulnerability and objectivity of being a scientist. She'd been blind, reckless, and they'd easily made her their pawn. How did one continue even in a life one loved after something like this? She almost laughed at herself for assuming she was going to get out of this alive. She also supposed the most important thing *was* to get out of this hellish situation in one piece and then worry about rebuilding her life.

Her resentful thoughts led her inevitably to look up to glare at Rafael Castillo. Only he wasn't anywhere in sight. Time had passed, the tent had darkened but for the light of her computer screen. She almost couldn't see him when she looked wildly behind her, but his presence was hard to miss. Big, motionless, he stood in back of her chair, his hands at his sides. She hadn't heard him come up behind her, hadn't heard him breathing, hadn't felt his body heat radiating from him. She hadn't been aware of him for a long time, but suddenly she was all too aware of him, of every subtle dark-on-dark nuance from his clothing to his silky hair to the shadows across his face.

Carrie promptly turned her back to him. He put his hands on the top of her chair, not touching her, but very close. "How long have you been reading over my shoulder?" she demanded.

"Not long. Was Jade Butterfly really the name of the warrior king who ruled this place?"

He'd been reading longer than he claimed. She'd mentioned the name only once, several screens back. She had no idea why a murdering drug dealer would ask her such an academic question. She also had no idea why she answered him. "The last ruler, yes. Evidence suggests that he and his wife were sacrificed by invaders from another city state.''

"Sacrificed? As in *human* sacrifice?" He sounded surprised.

She nodded. "Our ancestors were a bit on the ruthless side that way."

His hands drifted up from the back of the chair to her shoulders. The warmth of his palms radiated into her tired, tense muscles. She should shake him off, but she went very still instead. "*Our* ancestors, Carolina?"

"I know your aunt," she told him. "I know that your family's from here originally. That you grew up in Los Angeles, but that you came back here to work for Torres."

She felt like an idiot and the worst sort of fool the instant the words were out. Knowing details about this man's life was dangerous; letting him know she knew those details was suicidal. The last thing he needed or wanted was one stupid semi-*gringa* who had not only witnessed him commit a murder, but knew far too many other things about him.

His hands tightened on her shoulders.

Rafe felt her skin grow cold beneath his touch. He wasn't surprised when she said, "You're going to kill me, aren't you?"

If he was really who she thought he was, he certainly wouldn't let her live past the pickup job. That he wasn't who she thought he was was something she had to know. Did he dare tell her now? With Manolo nearby? This close to Torres and all his men? No, as much as he wanted to reassure her that she was safe, she really wasn't. Not until he got her out of the country. If he told her now, she might make a wrong move or comment in front of Manolo. He didn't want to have to kill Manolo, and it might come down to that. He never wanted to kill anyone again. He was so tired of the violence, the threat of violence.

He hated the fact that Carrie Robinson was living under a threat of violence from him. She couldn't know for the present that the threat was a false one. He was also, foolishly, pleased to know that she'd bothered to ask his aunt about him.

He began to massage her shoulders. Or rather, he noticed that he was already massaging her shoulders. He didn't know how long his fingers had been working on tense muscles, trying to return some of the soft suppleness he dreamed about to her chilled flesh. He couldn't bring himself to take his hands away, though he didn't think his touch was doing her any good.

"I'm not what you think I am," he told her. She jumped at his words, her nervous reaction rippling beneath his hands. "I'm not Mayan," he hurried on before a more important truth could get a chance to slip out. "My father's family settled Oro Blanco when the Spanish came. Didn't my aunt tell you that about our family history? She's quite proud of it. The bloodline on the Castillo side is pure Castilian to the core. My *mamacita*'s pure barrio East L.A. Chicana."

And I'd like to take you home to her, he thought. *Even if Aunt Juana did tell me to stay away from nice girls like you.* Of course, Aunt Juana was right. Even the real Rafael Castillo wasn't the kind of man any sane, sensible, respectable woman should get mixed up with. He forced his hands down, then stepped back.

"I'm not going to kill you." He desperately wished he didn't have to say it. She needed to hear it, and he gladly gave her as much reassurance as he could.

Carrie was on her feet so fast she knocked the chair over. She wanted to run from the tent. She whirled to face Rafe instead. "Not tonight, you mean."

"Just drop it," he answered. "Don't think about it."

"Don't think—"

"It's late. Time we went to bed."

For some stupid reason, his words made her look at her watch, only for her to discover that it was indeed late. She had no idea where the hours had gone. She had a dim memory of being dragged off to meet with Torres some time in the morning. Now it was past midnight. What was she doing up past midnight? She had to leave in the morning. Whether this goon here was with her or not, she had a shipment of artifacts scheduled to be aboard a chartered cargo plane three days from now.

It was only after several seconds of recalling her real life that another implication of what he might mean by "Time we went to bed" struck her. She gave him a startled look.

Rafe responded with a soft chuckle and waved a hand at her. "Not tonight, Carolina, I have a headache."

Oddly enough, she thought he was telling the truth. With a certain amount of bravado, she opened the lid of the blue plastic tackle box that sat on one side of the table, then tossed him a bottle of aspirin. As he caught it one-handed, she said, "Save some for me."

She did not fail to notice that his other hand held a gun. She blamed herself for startling him by making a fast, unexpected move, made a mental note not to do it again and pretended not to notice as he slipped the 9 mm pistol back into whatever spot on his large person it had been concealed.

"That was my fault," she conceded after the gun was out of sight. She kept her tone matter-of-fact though she struggled to keep her knees from buckling. He *knew* she was afraid. There was no reason for her to do something silly, like faint.

He frowned. "Your fault?"

"One should never make sudden, unexpected moves around gunfighters," she explained. "I'm almost tempted to apologize."

"Don't bother."

"I won't. Take your aspirin," she added. She walked to the tent entrance, attempting to make her legs do something as outrageous as saunter past him when they didn't even want to hold her weight.

He came up behind her and took her by the arm, walking out into the night with her. It was actually lighter outside the tent than inside. While they were enclosed all around by the heavy rain forest canopy, the clearing around the temple and dig site gave a clear view of the sky overhead. A nearly full moon rained down light that cast a silver glow on the world outside the denseness of the trees. The temple reared up before her, its shadows darker than usual in contrast to the pale light.

Beside her, Rafael Castillo's features were as mysterious, as carved of dark and light, as the ancient Maya temple she'd made it her life's work to explore. Just like the stones of the temple, he was a far more substantial presence than the contrasts of shadow and brightness would suggest. Unlike the massive stillness of the great stone edifice, he radiated restless energy.

"Where do you sleep?"

Carrie stiffened. "Why do you want to know?"

He sighed. "We've been through this already. I don't plan to ravish you."

She couldn't help but arch an eyebrow at him. "Ravish?"

"At least not tonight."

She was sure her blush added to the ambient temperature of the clearing. "I was referring to your use of such an old-fashioned term." What she wished she could do was just shut up. She had no business playing word games, or any other sort of games, with this man.

"I'm very old-fashioned." He pointed toward a row of tents. "Where do you sleep?"

"In a nice, comfortable bed at your Aunt Juana's house. Normally," she added. "I like my creature comforts when I can get 'em."

"Then we have something else in common." His voice was a rich, deep purr.

Carrie let the comment hang in the still, dense air for a moment. If he expected her to protest that they had nothing in common—a killer and a scholar—she didn't rise to the bait. She yawned instead, and his grasp slipped away from her arm. Even when he was no longer touching her, her skin remained sensitized to the feel of him.

Carrie turned and walked toward the tents. She didn't hear the cat-graceful Rafael follow, but she was well aware that he was behind her. "I always stay in camp the night before leaving," she conceded as she reached her tent. She turned her head to glance at him before unzipping the entrance flap. The tent where her luggage was stored held one narrow cot. "This is where I'm sleeping. I think I heard your friend snoring in the Hummer. I'm sure he wouldn't mind sharing a seat with you."

Rafe shook his head. "I'm not leaving your side."

"You're not coming in my tent."

"For modesty's sake?"

For sanity's sake. She could not deal with the idea of sharing sleeping quarters with this man. Not after some of the wild dreams she'd had about him since the gunfight in the bar. Never mind the dreams. She needed some privacy. She hadn't had a moment of it since Beltrano had walked into her office to issue the first threat of the day.

Her shoulders slumped. "My world's upside down," she confessed. She hated giving this man the truth, but it was all she had. "I've got to be alone for a while to get my head together or I'm not going to make it. I'm a little close to the edge here, Mr. Castillo."

The back of his hand brushed across her cheek. She

wished he wouldn't touch her, but found an odd comfort in it. She was glad there were no tears there for him to wipe away. "I thought letting you work would help."

"It did." She hated that it was easy to admit such weakness to him. She hated the gratitude. She did manage not to say thank-you. She unzipped the entrance and didn't complain further as he followed her into the darkness inside.

He immediately bumped into her one suitcase. Carrie, well aware of every inch of the small tent, made a successful dive for the cot. As she settled into it, she said, "Good night," adding, "watch out for spiders when you lie down." Then she turned her back—on Rafael Castillo and the whole situation.

Chapter 3

Carrie Robinson's soft-sided luggage made a comfortable enough pillow. Rafe might like his comforts, but he coped with roughing it when he had to. He could sleep anywhere, and did, though his dreams were anything but restful. He didn't dream about making love to Carrie Robinson. He didn't dream about killing her, either, but he did dream about her.

In the dream, they'd had at least two children.

It was the most impossibly realistic dream he'd ever had, and it made no sense. It certainly did nothing for his mood to wake up and find that it wasn't true. Not that he wanted dreams of domestic bliss to be true, he told himself. It was just that he hated waking up grimy and covered in sweat on the canvas floor of a tent in the middle of the forest. He came awake to the sound of rain and to awareness of Carrie Robinson's soft breathing very near by. His internal clock told him it was just past dawn. His aching muscles told him it was time to get up, stretch and get moving.

He got up, but he didn't move far. Though the growing light was dim, there was enough of it for him to see the woman sleeping so peacefully on the narrow camp bed. This was a luxury he had no business indulging in, but he couldn't help it. There was no harm, he told himself, in looking. All he was going to do was look. He wasn't going to touch, even though her shirt was scrunched up under her magnificent breasts, revealing the smooth, flat surface of her stomach. He wondered what it would be like to lay his palm across the warm expanse of skin, or to inch his hand up and cup the underside of her breast.

Rafe let out a long, frustrated breath, but kept his hands at his sides. His gaze moved up to her face. She looked peaceful, the tiredness and tension of yesterday drained away.

It was easy to imagine her smiling. Even easier to imagine what she would look like waking up in his arms. He could fantasize all he wanted, but when she woke up she would want nothing to do with him. That was all right. That was how it should be. He let her go on sleeping a little longer than necessary, a gift of respite from the nightmare he'd help make of her waking world. Eventually, he allowed himself to touch her—a brief, brusque shake of her shoulder.

"Time to get up."

Carrie woke to his touch, the sound of his voice, and she smiled. She didn't know why, because she was instantly aware of where she was and with whom. She recalled everything that had happened, everything that was supposed to happen, and yet she still had a brief surge of pleasure at knowing Rafael Castillo was nearby. It was ridiculous, some sort of sleep-induced hallucination, but for a moment she felt comfortable in the man's presence.

She shouldn't have slept well, maybe not at all, knowing that he was sharing the tent with her. She should have shook with dread or something all night long. Instead, she'd been asleep almost as soon as her head hit the cot. No bad dreams haunted her night. She'd slept quite peacefully. In fact, she had a vague memory of briefly waking for a few moments when some animal noise had come out of the jungle. The sound had startled her, but hearing the quiet breathing of the big man had brought instant comfort and reassurance. Not quite awake, she'd quickly gone back to sleep.

Her subconscious, she decided as she opened her eyes and sat up, was a trusting idiot. Fortunately, she was awake now and on her guard against Rafael Castillo. She pushed her tangled hair out of her face, rubbed her eyes and glowered at him. His shoulder-length hair was mussed. He needed a shave. His clothes were rumpled. But he still looked better than a man who'd slept on the ground had any right to. He also looked better than any hired gunman had a right to. He basically looked just too damn good for any woman's peace of mind.

"Get out of here," she ordered irritably. "I want to get dressed."

Rafe was glad that Manolo had sensibly insisted they pack for the trip. If Rafe had had his way, they would have left Torres's yesterday and made the drive straight to Mérida without bothering to stop. The point was that Dr. Robinson was supposed to look like she was going about her ordinary business, and that included hauling a ton or two of artifacts out of the jungle. He almost wished his and Manolo's arrival yesterday hadn't frightened off the rebels or they might have stolen the inconvenient truck. But here they were, still in Oro Blanco. At least he had a change of clothes and a shaving kit in the Hummer.

"Hurry up," he told Carrie after they'd stared at each other for a while for no reason Rafe could fathom.

"You leave, I'll hurry."

"I'm going."

"Go."

Manolo was leaning against the driver's-side door of the Hummer when Rafe approached, an eager look on his face that told Rafe the other man wanted details of the night he'd just spent in the archaeologist's tent. Rafe expected teasing, but what he got was a good-natured slap on the shoulder. "You make a nice couple," Manolo said, "but I think she's the marrying kind."

"She has a body," Rafe answered gruffly. "I was guarding it. Nothing happened."

Manolo laughed. "Sure." Then he turned serious. "I think I believe you. Torres wouldn't want you messing with his mule, and you wouldn't do anything Torres didn't want."

Rafe nodded. "That's right."

"Too bad," the other man said. "I think you two make a nice couple."

Manolo, Rafe recalled, was married. He had daughters, lots of them. He worked for Torres because he wanted to give his wife and daughters a better life. Rafe liked him. He's one of the bad guys, Rafe reminded himself sternly. Manolo was perceptive, tough as nails and as loyal to Torres as Rafe supposedly was. If Manolo knew what Rafe really was, *compadres* or not, Manolo wouldn't hesitate to kill him. That's just the way it was. Business.

Bringing Torres down was Rafe's business. That meant Manolo came down, too, despite his wife, his daughters and the personal feelings Rafe had for him. He'd been taught that when an undercover agent started identifying more with the bad guys than with the job, it was time to surface. Rafe knew it was more than time. He felt as if he were drowning and the surface was very far away.

Manolo opened the door and tossed Rafe his bag. He

pointed across the compound. "There's a shower over there."

Rafe was not surprised to discover that the bathing facilities involved canvas curtains and buckets of rainwater, along with a portable toilet. Carrie Robinson was just finishing brushing her teeth as he approached. She spit on the grass at his feet as he came up to her.

"Charming," he said. He took a step closer to her, then gave a critical glance around. "And primitive."

She frowned at him. "We all live in town most of the time."

His fingers moved of their own free will to push a stray lock of hair out of her face. The back of his hand lingered on her cheek as their gazes met. He couldn't keep from teasing, "I was referring to your personality."

The amused gleam in Rafael's eyes did nothing for Carrie's mood. Nor did his touch. She refused to utter the retort that popped into her mind. She was clean. She wanted coffee. She wanted her pulse to slow down and wished he would stop looking at her in a way that made her want very much to be kissed. For an instant, the temperature around them grew hotter, her world narrowed down to just the awareness of him, and she forgot to breathe. He bent his head forward.

This was ridiculous.

Carrie took a quick step backward. Then another. She turned her back on him. She wanted to get in her truck and drive away from this whole awful situation. She tossed her head and walked determinedly toward her office, telling herself that she was imagining his gaze on her as she went to fetch her laptop.

But she didn't imagine her reaction—the slight extra sway to her hips, the stirring of her breasts or the tingling heat deep inside her. That her body felt his presence didn't mean he was actually looking at her. It only meant that her body had a mind of its own, and it was focused on pure gut lust that had nothing to do with the way her mind worked or what was really going on. Once inside the tent, she stayed there and gave her body a firm lecture until she'd gotten the visceral, tactile awareness of the panther-graceful, panther-dangerous male outside under control.

When she came out of the tent, she couldn't help but look around with a sense of nostalgia. She very carefully didn't look for Rafael. She concentrated on saying goodbye to this small corner of the world. No matter how badly this season was ending, she hated leaving Chalenque. The fact that she might never see the place again brought on a deep sense of melancholy as her gaze took in the many-stepped temple, the covered trenches and digging pits, the tents her crew would come to break down later in the day, the metal-roofed storage sheds that had flowering vines crawling up their sides. The world around the site was green and wet and noisy with all manner of life. The sky above the thick forest canopy held gray clouds, gathering for the second of the day's downpours. Wisps of white mist rose up from the warm jungle floor and twisted across the clearing. It was exotic, yet utterly familiar. Not quite home, but a place she very much loved. The Lost City of Chalenque.

"Lost again," she said, and sighed dramatically. Then she laughed at her own morose pronouncement and stepped away from the tent entrance.

She'd only gone a few feet toward the waiting truck when Beltrano stepped off a footpath that led into the rain forest. He hurried toward her. He was alone. He didn't seemed to be armed. He looked determined. Carrie stood her ground and waited for him.

"I'm sorry about yesterday," he said when he reached her. "It wasn't my idea to frighten you."

"Threaten me, you mean."

He shrugged. "Threaten," he conceded.

"It might not have been your idea, but you did it."

"My associates aren't quite as interested in negotiating as I am. They see their heritage being stripped away, and force seems like the only alternative they have left."

Carrie listened with growing impatience. "Maybe what I do helps save the culture. Trying to stop me isn't helping your cause."

He vehemently shook his head. "You're taking bits of our soul to a foreign land for the sake of your own career." The intensity of his expression told her that it was useless to argue. He put a hand on her arm. "I can't let you do that."

She shook him off. "Oh, yes, you can."

Carrie realized that she wanted to explain to Beltrano that she had no choice but to leave, that she was trying to protect some of the people he claimed as "his." But that would just have been an excuse. She had every intention of taking the artifacts back to Jefferson University whether she was threatened by drug dealers or not. She didn't need to make excuses for her perfectly legitimate study of the Mayan culture.

When she started to walk away from Beltrano, he stepped in front of her. Having been threatened by men far more expert in it than this scholar-turned-revolutionary, Carrie was more exasperated by his posturing than she was frightened. "Oh, for crying out loud! Will you leave me alone?"

Rafe saw Carrie confronting the man he'd rescued her from yesterday and almost laughed as she shouted angrily at the stranger. Rafe saw from the look on her face that Carrie Robinson was about to give the man a piece of her mind. He would have happily stood back and let her, but the stranger had had friends with guns yesterday. Rafe obeyed the urge to protect this woman even though he thought she was pretty good at taking care of herself in most situations. But whether she was good at it or not, she'd been threatened by men with guns far too often lately. She deserved some looking after.

Besides, it was past time to get out of Oro Blanco.

"We're leaving, Beltrano," Carrie said as Rafe came up behind the man. "But I promise you that those artifacts will be shipped back within the year."

"I don't believe you."

"It doesn't matter what you believe, friend," Rafe told Beltrano. He gently nudged Beltrano in the spine with the barrel of his 9 mm Smith & Wesson for emphasis.

Rafe had looked the other man over as he approached. Beltrano didn't seem to be armed. Rafe knew that *he* wouldn't look armed, either, at a casual glance, and he was anything but weaponless. He'd drawn a gun as he approached, on the theory that it was better not to take any chances. Besides, it was best to assume that Beltrano's armed and dangerous *compadres* were lurking somewhere in the cover of the nearby rain forest.

"Turn around," he ordered, "and we'll have a little talk. Slowly." Rafe took a step back, but kept his gun level as Beltrano obeyed him. Rafe gestured to Carrie. "Come over here." She moved quickly to join him.

The man's expression was contemptuous as he looked first at Rafe, then at Carrie. "You know who this man is? What his kind are doing to our country?"

Carrie gave a sad little laugh that twisted Rafe's heart. "Of course I know what he is."

Rafe hadn't felt shame in years, but the way Carrie spoke of him to Beltrano made him shrivel inside. He wanted to make excuses, explain himself. Then he saw Beltrano give a self-righteous smirk, and any interest in justifying his existence quickly faded.

"What is he doing here?" Beltrano demanded. "Why did you go with him yesterday?"

Rafe suspected that he heard a hint of jealousy along with the righteous anger in Beltrano's voice. It seemed Dr. Carrie Robinson was a very popular woman among all the armed and dangerous men in the area. He doubted Carrie even knew it. Before he could answer for her, Carrie said, "I didn't 'go' with him as you very well know. It was a choice of being kidnapped by him, or threatened by you. I didn't have any involvement in the decision-making process." That she hated her helplessness was even more evident to Rafe than Beltrano's interest in her.

Beltrano stabbed a finger toward him. "He works for Torres. Why is he here?" he asked Carrie again.

"I'm here because Torres wants me here," Rafe answered.

Beltrano ignored him while still glaring at Carrie. "What's Torres got to do with your archaeological dig?" The look on the man's face was hard and suspicious. "What game are you playing with the drug dealers?"

Carrie fought the urge to justify her actions. She fought the urge to ask for help. What was she supposed to do? Ask Beltrano's people to protect her staff from Torres's threats? Call in the rebels' guns against the drug lord's guns? How ridiculous, how wasteful. She was a civilized person. If she did what she was told, maybe nobody would get hurt. Besides, she wasn't letting Beltrano have any advantage over her. He'd want her artifacts as the price of his help, and that was one thing she was feeling way too stubborn about giving in on. She'd done far too much paperwork to get permission to take her finds out of the country.

"We're leaving," she said to Beltrano. "I suggest you leave, as well. In the opposite direction."

He shook his head. "You're going with this man? Under Torres's protection?" His expression once again became contemptuous. "Smuggling drugs along with my people's heritage. I'm disappointed," he said coldly.

Carrie lifted her head proudly. What Beltrano accused her of was galling. "You have nothing to be disappointed about. Nothing." She threw a look first at the revolutionary and then the drug runner that should have boiled their skins off if there was any justice in the world. But there wasn't and looks couldn't kill and she wasn't going to stand here and be verbally abused one moment longer. "You've got the gun," she said to Rafael. "You want him to go, make him. I'm going to the truck."

She didn't know quite what she meant when she spoke to Rafael. Not that a mere woman's wishes mattered in their hairy-chested scheme of things. Maybe she was just tired of watching these men play their macho games. She didn't want anybody getting hurt, but if they insisted on preening and threats and even gunplay, there wasn't exactly anything she could do about it. Except get in her truck and drive away.

"Wait for me, Carolina," Rafael called after her.

She hated the reminder that she could drive away, but that she'd be taking her troubles with her.

Beltrano also shouted after her, "You're not the only one who can call on the drug gangs for help. You've raised the stakes in this game, Dr. Robinson, and you'll pay for it."

Beltrano's words frightened her, but she didn't stop walking. At least he hadn't called her Carolina.

Once Carrie was gone, Rafe stepped closer to Beltrano, his gun very carefully leveled at the man's chest. "Don't threaten her," he said quietly. "Don't ever threaten her."

Beltrano sneered. "Or you'll do what?"

"I think we both know. I also think I told you to leave."

The sneer turned into a dangerous, arrogant smile, but Beltrano didn't say anything. He turned around and disappeared back the way he'd come. Rafe didn't put the gun away and walk across the clearing himself until Beltrano was long out of sight. As he passed the truck, he saw Carrie sitting behind the wheel instead of in the passenger seat. That was to be expected, he supposed. She was very protective of her bits of ancient stone. He went over to where Manolo lounged by the door of the Hummer and told him about Beltrano.

Manolo nodded. "As if we don't have enough trouble from people like Enrique Munoz and Estaban Quarrels." He named the leaders of rival organizations. "Now we'll have to be on the lookout for these stupid separatists." He spit. "I wish I'd never left El Paso."

Rafe shrugged. "That's why Torres pays us the big bucks."

"Not big enough. I've got two girls in college. I'm getting too old for this, man." Manolo got into the Hummer. "I'll drive point." He gave Rafe a sly smile and an encouraging wink. "You go with the girl."

Rafe had every intention of riding with Carrie. He nodded to Manolo, then went and got into the truck. "Let's go, Doc."

Carrie was at the point where she would have hit him if he'd called her Carolina, but Doc was almost worse. She sighed with exasperation, but didn't bother to ask the man why he couldn't just call her by her given name. She started the old truck, put it in gear, then pulled out after the Hummer. She resisted the urge to look back one more time as they left the looming Mayan temple behind them.

An hour passed without a word being spoken. Wet heat boiled in the air around them, along with growing tension. Carrie concentrated on driving. She was good at it, and even if the dirt track wasn't in very good shape, it wasn't as if she had to battle a lot of other traffic.

Rafe sat back and tried to enjoy the ride. He was free

from the constant strain of being near Torres. He couldn't afford to relax, but just being away from the drug lord's compound was enough to bring his stress level down to something that was almost bearable. He would be so glad when this assignment was over. He glanced at Carrie Robinson—he couldn't keep from glancing at her—and anticipated how relieved he was going to be to get her out of the country and in protective custody once they were in Washington.

After a while, she took her gaze off the road long enough to glare at him. "What are you looking at, Castillo?"

He found himself brushing his hand across her thick dark hair. She swatted him away. He almost apologized, but how could he say he was sorry for something he hadn't meant to do? Besides, he wasn't sorry. He only regretted that he couldn't touch her as much as he wanted to.

"Well, I guess that answers my question," she grumbled as he drew his hand back. "You want to stay on your side of the seat?"

He might have been more convinced of her annoyance if her head hadn't swayed ever so slightly toward him when he touched her. She liked being touched by him, then, though she didn't like liking it. He liked touching her, though she was way off-limits. He didn't know what the hell they were going to do about it.

"I was looking at you," he belatedly answered her question.

"I know that."

"You want to know why?"

She had a death grip on the steering wheel. "No."

"It's your name."

"Oh, please, not that again."

"Not your first name. Your last name."

"What about it?"

"Robinson." He looked her over carefully, from her

dark wavy hair and fiery brown eyes that darted a fresh glare at him to the creamy-coffee tips of her fingers as they circled the steering wheel. "You don't look like a Robinson. Your husband's name?"

"I'm not married."

Rafe was surprised at the tension that drained from him when he heard this. He sternly reminded himself that her marital status was no business of his. "That's good," he found himself saying anyway. He touched her cheek. "You're too beautiful to be a wife. A rich man's mistress, maybe."

She spared an instant to roll her eyes and make a derisive noise. "That's the most ridiculous thing I've ever heard."

"Yeah," he agreed. "Call me an old-fashioned, sexist pig, macho kind of guy."

"You're worse than that. And stop telling me I'm beautiful—too beautiful." She snorted. "What a load of—"

"It's an honest observation." Her sharp crack of laughter was punctuated by a bounce as the truck hit a deep hole in the road. He was surprised when her arm shot out in front of him, automatically protecting him from falling forward. He couldn't resist the temptation to brush a kiss across the back of her hand as she snatched it back. "Beautiful *and* caring," he murmured.

"I baby-sat too much in high school. And keep your lips to yourself."

"No children of your own, Carolina?"

"No. And my name's Caroline. Carrie. I think we've been through this already."

"I'm a slow learner. You look like a Carolina." He drew the next words out slowly, seductively. "A very beautiful Carolina."

She gave the name its flat American pronunciation when she responded, "Carolina's a state."

"A state of grace?"

Her reaction was another sharp laugh. "If you say so. What I am is a reasonably attractive, healthy female with a slightly oversize, but elegant, proboscis."

He studied her profile and decided that the high-arched length of her nose was indeed elegant. He resisted the urge to stroke his index finger along the length of it. Instead, he continued to indulge in his wayward curiosity. "But how did you get to be Caroline Robinson?" It was none of his business, but he really wanted to know.

"It's something my parents put on my birth certificate at the hospital."

"And this hospital was where?"

She sighed. "Rhode Island. Providence, Rhode Island. I'm not from the Yucatán. I'm from New England. And it's Caroline Beatrice Robinson to be precise. I'm as WASP as they come on my daddy's side."

Why on earth was she telling him this? The man had no real interest in her or her life. Maybe her death, but certainly not her life. She was just Torres's mule to him. She didn't discount the possibility that he might want to sleep with her, but he had no reason to care about her as a person. Besides, her life—the life he was probably going to end—was none of his business.

Her stomach knotted and her hands clenched on the steering wheel once more as a moment of panicked terror clutched at her. She forced it down. She couldn't look at him, but she kept her voice calm. "If we must make small talk," she said, "I think we should change the subject."

"Okay." He glanced out the window, back along the way they'd come. The road was narrow and the rain forest encroached closely on both sides and overhead. There wasn't much to see behind them, or ahead. He disliked the enclosed atmosphere. He knew how easy it was to drive into an ambush in this countryside. With that in mind, he said, "Tell me about your friend Beltrano."

Carrie realized that the man wasn't making small talk anymore. He was checking out the territory, looking for trouble, though their truck and the Hummer up ahead were the only vehicles on this miserable excuse for a road. He was preparing for an assault. The man wasn't underestimating the rebels. He was probably overestimating their ability to make trouble, but she supposed he stayed alive by being cautious. She found she rather liked that quality, even if he'd learned it by making his way up the ladder in a criminal organization.

She didn't mind helping him prepare for trouble she hoped wouldn't happen. "I don't completely disagree with Beltrano and the other separatists," she told Rafe. "Then again, this really isn't my country or my culture, no matter how much time I've spent here. Beltrano could be dead wrong about what the Maya of Quintana Roo need and want. Still, the economy's a mess and the indigenous culture is ignored by government policy. There's a lot wrong, and he's right that your people don't help."

"I asked about Beltrano," Rafe reminded her, "not his politics."

"It's his politics that make trouble for me."

"I noticed. Why?"

The road was growing particularly rough and rutted, with standing water making it hard to tell how deep the brimming potholes were. Up ahead, the Hummer obliviously barreled on through the pond-size puddles. She didn't have an overpriced luxury land yacht. All she had was an old Ford truck loaded with valuable cargo. Carrie downshifted and slowed the truck to a crawl.

"Want me to drive?"

She flashed Rafe a withering look. "No."

"Beltrano?"

She sighed and got back to the subject. "Mayan artifacts are very big business on the black market. Lots of things are very big business on the black market down here—artifacts, endangered tropical birds. Lots of things that are supposedly protected by the government, but have a way of disappearing anyway. The government does the best it can and it's rightly touchy about the subject of archaeological finds being taken out of the country for study. Things that used to be taken to universities and museums in other parts of the world had this unfortunate tendency to stay with the people who 'borrowed' them. Many a fine museum collection has been built that way."

"Sounds like out-and-out theft."

She laughed. "Sounds like it to me, too. It hasn't just happened in Mexico. You should hear the Egyptians on the subject of trying to get their stuff back from the people who 'found' and 'protected' it. First Napoleon ripped them off, then the English and the Germans and—"

"What about Beltrano?"

She gave him an annoyed look. "Hey, I'm an archaeologist. It's my absentminded scholarly prerogative to go off on boring tangents about my profession. Don't you drug dealers sit around having absolutely *fascinating*—at least to each other—conversations about whatever it is you do?"

For all her sarcasm, Rafe had to nod in agreement. He was half-tempted to tell her that he'd recently taped quite a few of those detailed conversations. "I've seen stuff on TV about ancient Egypt," he told her.

She looked surprised. "A thug who watches PBS?"

He folded his arms across his chest. "I may be a thug, but I'm not a *mindless* killer. I went to college. And I send the L.A. PBS station a check every year during the pledge drive."

Carrie didn't know how to react to this. She stared at the road ahead for a few moments, then asked, "Are we doomed to have surrealistic conversations from here to Mérida?"

He put a hand on her shoulder. "I can't help it if I'm a person, Carrie, one who has things in common with you, and not some stereotypical movie bad guy."

She wanted to tell him to get his hands off her, but the gesture was too comforting for such a knee-jerk reaction. She sighed. "But you are a bad guy."

Rafe sighed, as well. "I'm here to protect you. You may find that hard to believe, but it's true."

As he spoke, the rain began to pour down. She switched the wipers on as high as they would go, but that didn't help visibility much. The Hummer was barely visible up ahead. She slowed the already crawling vehicle even more. There was silence between them for quite a while. When he took his hand away, she was as aware of the absence of his touch as she'd been of its presence.

To tell him that she didn't want his "protection" would be banal and repetitive. Why bother stating a truth they were both well aware of? Why bother with whining and protests and accusations? Because it made her feel better? she asked herself, then smiled with rueful acknowledgment that she could be so petulant and childish.

Rafe liked her smile. He knew it wasn't for him. She wasn't looking at him; her gaze was fixed on what little could be seen of the road through the rain. He liked watching her smile, though he had no idea what it meant. He wanted to ask. He wanted to know everything there was to know about her. It was a long way to Mérida. Chances were there was a lot they could talk about. Then there was the awareness that hummed between them, the unasked-for need that sizzled in the blood and deep in every look and gesture that passed between them. Temptation beckoned, and they each had to fight their own battle with it.

Chances were it was going to be a very long ride for both of them.

Chapter 4

The daily rain had been particularly wretched. So had the roads. It took hours longer than it should have for the vehicles to make their way to a slightly larger road and turn north. Carrie's hopes of spending the night in Carillo or Felipe Puerto faded along with her energy as the drive dragged on. Every time Rafe offered to take the wheel, she steadfastly turned him down. She didn't know why she was playing this control game. After all, the times she'd made this trip in past years, she'd had at least two other people with her who'd shared the driving. She guessed she was just playing it because it was the only kind of control she had. Even knowing why she was being so stubborn, Carrie didn't give in.

It didn't help her mood that the first town of any substantial size they came to was Ciudad Alguna.

She speeded up when they reached the edge of town, hoping to get past the place as quickly as possible. It shouldn't take long. The place wasn't so much a town as a patch of land that had been slashed and burned out of the rain forest. Ciudad Alguna hadn't existed five years ago, at least not in its present prosperous form as a haven for drug smugglers. Where a rundown village had once stood, Ciudad Alguna had sprung up. It existed for a single purpose—to cater to entrepreneurs in only one trade.

The place was thriving even though the population was maybe a few hundred at any given time. People came, did their deals, went, and the tiny permanent population just took their money and looked the other way. It wasn't the sort of place that had a police station. Tourists were not encouraged to come here. Carrie had driven through Ciudad Alguna before on her way to Mérida. She'd gone as fast as she could, without looking around any more than her driving required and with never any intention of stopping. The place had a Wild West feel to it. It had a three-story hotel, more bars than houses and an airstrip. There was a cemetery. Probably a gun shop, Carrie surmised. Brothels, too.

"We'll stop here for the night."

She cast a disgusted look at Rafe. "Why am I not surprised?"

He grinned cheerfully. "Because you mistake me for the sort of man who hangs out in places like this."

"You're not?"

He put his hand on his chest and made an effort to look sincere. "I'm a choirboy, *querida*. Just ask anybody."

"Uh-huh." She almost preferred him calling her Carolina to the endearment. No. He could make anything he called her sound soft, sexy, possessive. His voice just *did* things to her nerve endings, and it was completely unfair. She considered calling him a few choice names, maybe even an endearment or two herself. How about "Bubba"?

But she decided acknowledging him like that would give him too much evidence of how he affected her. Yeah, right. Like he couldn't tell that she responded to him without her having to say a word. Her body, which ought to be ashamed of itself, was doing far too much talking already.

"I suppose you have lots of friends in Ciudad Alguna."

"I know a few people," he admitted.

Manolo had already pulled the Hummer into what passed for a parking lot beside the coral pink plastered walls of the hotel. Carrie sighed in disgust, but pulled up beside him. Rafe jumped out of the truck, then came quickly around to open the driver's-side door for her.

"Ever the gentleman," she grumbled, then slid out of the truck. She landed in churned-up mud, on legs that had been sitting for too long. She stumbled, and Rafe put his hands on her waist to steady her, then slipped them slowly higher as though he had no control over their movement. She felt the tips of her breasts stir as their gazes locked. Electricity sparked between them, and they both quickly stepped back as Manolo approached. Carrie's back bumped into the door of the truck, so she leaned back against it while she caught her breath and her mental balance. The men started talking to each other. She found herself looking at the building and couldn't help but be impressed that something so pretty had sprung up so quickly in such an evil place.

Little balconies with white painted wrought-iron railings jutted out from the rooms on the upper stories. The front of the building was covered with a pink-and-white striped awning, and there looked to be a walled garden in back, beyond the muddy parking lot. A black cat jumped down off the pink wall while she watched. She couldn't help but smile at the lean, graceful animal and compare its lithe movements with Rafael Castillo's.

Carrie shook her head in disgust and looked at Rafe just as he said, "I'll be right back."

While he went inside the hotel, Carrie drafted Manolo to help her check the boxes and crates carefully stored in the back of the truck. They made sure that the rough terrain they'd traveled over during the day hadn't caused any shifting or breakage of the crates. They'd just gotten out of the truck when Rafe came out of the hotel.

"I got us a couple of rooms," Rafe told them as he approached. He tossed a key to Manolo and pocketed the other one himself.

Carrie considered this development for a moment and couldn't keep from questioning, "Two rooms? One for you and Manolo and the other one for me?" Rafe lifted an eyebrow in response. Manolo chuckled. Carrie sighed. "Just as I suspected. No way am I sharing sleeping quarters with you for another night, Castillo."

Rafe ignored her protest as he grabbed their bags out of the truck cab. "Meet you in the lobby?" he called out to Manolo. After the other man nodded, he said, "Come along," to Carrie.

When he walked into the building, Carrie didn't have much choice but to follow. She wasn't going to stand alone out on the main street of Ciudad Alguna.

The three-story building didn't have an elevator, but it did have a wide carpeted staircase in the center of the lobby. On one side of the stairs was the entrance to the bar; the front desk was on the other side. Carrie only took the briefest look around the crowded lobby. The people she saw looked unsavory enough that she didn't hesitate about hurrying to follow Rafael up the stairs.

She caught up to him on the landing. "Talk about your hive of scum and villainy," she grumbled as she followed him down a long hallway and around a corner. "Obi-wan Kenobi wouldn't bring Luke Skywalker into a place like this—and the Force is hardly with us, Bubba."

He stopped at a door and dropped their bags. Before putting the key in the lock, he glanced over his shoulder at her. "Bubba?"

She gave him a toothy smile. "Just trying out a few choice nicknames for you for a change."

"I see." He opened the door, then gestured for her to enter before him. When she hesitated and backed up toward the opposite wall, he sighed. "What?"

After a long, tense moment, she said, "I don't want to spend the night with you." After the words were out, Carrie wished fervently that she hadn't put them quite that way. "I mean—"

"I know what you mean." He snagged her by the wrist and pushed her ahead of him into the room. "You hear that noise?" he asked when he'd closed the door behind them.

Carrie was all too aware of him standing at her back. She was all too aware of the big bed that took up a good part of the room in front of them. She was all too aware of the heavy thudding of her heart. In fact, she was so aware of her body's reactions, it took her a few moments to react to his question, to listen. When she did, her knees went weak.

"Is that gunfire?"

The sound wasn't faint; it wasn't distant. She didn't really need him to identify it for her.

"You're safe with me," was his answer to her question. He stepped away from her. "Wash off some of the mud, and then we'll get something to eat."

With the sound of people shooting at each other in her ears, Carrie was almost scared enough to ask Rafe to accompany her to the bathroom to help her wash off the dirt. She certainly didn't feel like arguing anymore about not wanting to share sleeping quarters with him. Maybe being with him wasn't safe in a very profoundly sexual way, but he was her only guarantee of physical safety in this lawless place.

She almost thanked him. She almost said she was grateful. She managed to catch the reaction in time, then marched into the bathroom for a very quick wash accompanied by a stern talking to herself instead. By the time she'd splashed on water and reminded herself just who the good guys and the bad guys were, she was ready to face Rafael Castillo again.

That he'd changed into a tight black T-shirt that showed off his muscular chest and arms didn't help her resolve any. The sight of him just set the blood racing in her veins again. It reminded her that he was dangerous and that he was her sole protection. He was also wearing very tight black jeans.

She sighed, then looked him up and down. "Dressing formally for dinner, I see." She was glad when he slipped on a denim jacket to cover the gun worn in a shoulder holster that was his major accessory.

"It's the custom here in Ciudad Alguna. Let's go." He held out his hand.

For some reason she didn't want to explore, she took it.

Carrie let Rafe hold her hand as they walked down the staircase. People watched them, with both shadowed glances and blatant stares. Carrie did her best not to make eye contact with anyone they passed. She knew that some of those looks were not meant to assess Rafael Castillo's potential as a threat, but her potential as a bed partner. As much as she hated to admit it, she took a great deal of comfort from his presence and the gently firm clasp that linked them together. For all the insanity of it, being physically, emotionally, linked to this bad man felt all too right. She was a fool, and he was her anchor in this dangerous, evil world of cold-eyed stares and barely concealed weapons.

"Hungry?" he asked.

Oddly enough, even though it meant eating in a cantina full of unsavory characters, she was very hungry. "Starving," she answered, and was afraid, from the hint of desire in the quick look he gave her, that the word had come out full of unintended innuendo. "Not like that," she grumbled.

He chuckled. "Yes, you are. So am I."

"Drop dead."

"Very likely, *querida*," he promised. "And soon."

He was joking, but the words twisted in Carrie's gut. The fear wasn't for herself, but for him. She knew she shouldn't be feeling anything for him, especially not worry. He was a criminal who knew exactly what he was doing. He'd made the choice to live this life in this dangerous world. Still, the brightly lit hotel lobby took on ominous shadows for her. She became far too aware that every man in the place could be an enemy of Rafael Castillo's. Suddenly, she wasn't quite so hungry anymore. Worse, the urge to somehow protect him jolted through her.

Rafe looked around carefully as they went downstairs, spotting several people he recognized. He made a mental note of each of them, their positions in the room and whether or not any of them posed a threat. Ciudad Alguna was a violent place for dealers who crossed each other, but it was also a sort of neutral ground. He figured that if they didn't bother anyone tonight, they were safe enough. He did have some business here, but nothing that either Carrie or Manolo need be involved with. In fact, the last thing he wanted tonight was any witnesses. He needed to get them through dinner, get them to their rooms and then get on with his meeting as quickly as possible.

Unfortunately, from the look on Manolo's face when Rafe spotted the other man, Rafe saw that peace might not be as easy to maintain as he hoped.

"What's he glaring at?" Carrie asked, putting Rafe's own question into words.

Rafe took another quick look around and made a disgusted noise. "Him."

Carrie looked across the lobby until she saw the man

Manolo must be looking at. He was the sort who stood out
in a crowd, even a crowd such as this. Actually, he stood
a bit apart, his back to the brightly painted wall. He was
broad shouldered, with short dark hair. She suspected he
was taller than he looked because he had a decidedly
hunched stance. Carrie wondered why Manolo was giving
the stranger such a deadly glare.

"Who is he?" she asked.

It was Rafe who answered. "Estaban Quarrels."

Which answered her question, but gave her no information other than a name. Maybe she didn't want to know
any more. The one thing she was sure she was safe assuming was that Estaban Quarrels was another drug dealer.

Rafe didn't bother with a second glance toward Quarrels.
He put himself in front of Manolo, blocking the man's
view. He put a hand on Manolo's shoulder. "Not here."

"I say we kill him. Here."

Rafe shook his head. He kept his voice low. "When
Torres tells me to kill him, I'll kill him. Not before."

"Why not? We'd be doing the boss a favor."

"It's not our decision," Rafe insisted. "We have our
orders. One job at a time, my friend. That's all we have to
do."

Manolo looked anything but convinced. "What if Quarrels tries to kill us first?"

Rafe shrugged, smirking. "Then I'd be happy to kill him.
But we're not starting anything, not in Ciudad Alguna. We
don't know how many men he has with him. I want to get
out of here alive. More importantly, I want to get Carrie
out of here alive."

"Thank you *so* much," his ostensible prisoner muttered
from her spot beside him. He ignored her sarcasm to continue concentrating on Manolo. She'd tried to escape his
grip, and he'd felt her hand go cold in his, but he kept his
tight grasp on her. He didn't want her wandering off and

drawing the attention of Steve Quarrels any more than he wanted Manolo drawing a gun on the man in the middle of the hotel lobby.

"Calm down," he said to Manolo. "Let's get something to eat. Quarrels doesn't know who we are or why we're here. Let's let it go."

"He knows us," Manolo reminded him. "We were at the meeting Torres had with him. You arranged the meeting."

Rafe frowned. "So? I never actually talked to Quarrels when I set up the meeting. When he talked to Torres, we were just in the room. No reason he would remember us any more than the furniture that was there."

Manolo reached slowly into his pocket. Rafe let him, knowing that what the other man carried there was a small cellular phone.

Rafe put his hand out as Manolo brought the phone up to his ear. "I don't think so."

After a few tense moments of both men glaring at each other, Manolo finally nodded. "We'll let it go. For now." He put the phone back in his pocket and rubbed his hands briskly together. "I'll kill him after dinner. Let's eat."

Rafe laughed with more enthusiasm than he felt. "After dinner and a few drinks, *compadre*." When Rafe turned toward the entrance to the bar, Quarrels was nowhere in sight. That eliminated the problem, if only for the moment. "Let's eat," he said, and ushered Manolo ahead of him toward the bar.

He noticed speculative looks being directed at Carrie—more than speculative. A great deal of bold interest was shown to any beautiful woman who walked into a place like this. Everyone in the lobby was wondering if the lady was for sale, or at least for rent. He put a possessive arm around her shoulders and arrogantly returned a few of those looks. The glance and gesture made it quite plain that the lady was not only with him, but that she was his.

It wasn't even partially an act.

He leaned forward to brush his lips across Carrie's cheek and whispered, "Look at me, *querida*, like you love me."

"Not on an empty stomach, Castillo," she whispered back.

His chuckle this time was genuine. He slipped his hand down her arm, twined his fingers through hers, and they accompanied Manolo into the dim, noisy interior of the hotel's cantina.

The bar wasn't crowded, but it was full of smoke and noise. Rafe remembered from other trips that the food was good. It was the sort of place where nobody sat with his back to the door. He and Manolo automatically sought out a table near the wall where they could sit facing the room. Rafe made sure Carrie's back wasn't to the door, even if she wasn't quite facing the wall. When the voluptuous waitress slunk her way over, Rafe ordered beers, with tequila chasers for himself and Manolo, and dinner for all of them.

Carrie was not impressed with the beer when it came. She didn't complain, however. She just slowly sipped the warm liquid and listened in silence as the men talked. Talked and drank. Rafael ordered another round before the food came, one with dinner and more afterward. She ate slowly and drank only the one beer. So did Rafael. Manolo didn't notice that he was the only one downing all the alcohol, but Carrie did.

Manolo was in a very relaxed state by the time the dishes and glasses were cleared away. He leaned back in his chair, loose limbed and smiling benignly. She was afraid he was just going to slip under the table and start snoring.

When Rafael stood, he gave Carrie a pleading look. "Help me get him to his room?"

She frowned, but didn't balk at helping him get the other

man on his feet and moving. Fortunately, Manolo didn't pass out completely until he was safely tucked in bed. He did sing on the trip up the stairs and down the hall, however. He insisted that Rafael and Carrie sing Tejano love songs along with him.

Carrie looked from the sleeping man sprawled across the bed to Rafael. In the semidarkness, Rafael Castillo's large form gave the appearance of being made out of the dark shadows that surrounded them. "You did that deliberately," she said to the shadow man. "Got him drunk enough to pass out. Why?"

Rafe took her arm and drew her to the door. "Manolo is a very cheerful drunk."

"I noticed. But why did you deliberately get him drunk?"

"I didn't want anyone to die tonight."

Her annoyance at what she'd thought was some sort of practical joke or worse on Rafael's part disappeared. She realized that what had just transpired was a judicious act of diplomacy. "You thought he'd go after this Quarrels person on his own, didn't you?"

He nodded. "I don't want anyone to die, *querida.* Not my friend, not my enemy." He shrugged. "Not tonight, at least. Come on."

Carrie didn't know what to think, what to believe about this man. He seemed to have this gentle side to him, a compassion that existed along with a killer's cold instincts. She didn't get it. She didn't understand at all. She did know that the man who spoke of having friends and not wanting to see anyone die tonight was far more dangerous to her than the man she'd first seen using a gun in Maquiero's. One thing she was sure of, though. She just knew that she didn't want to spend the night alone with him.

He felt her hesitation in the way her steps dragged as he put his hand under her elbow and escorted her down the hall. A man passed them as they reached the door to their room. A hard-eyed man with pockmarked cheeks and extravagant tattoos showing on his bare arms. He exchanged a flick of a glance with Rafe, but the man's gaze lingered hungrily on Carrie as he went by. She gave no indication of noticing the stranger, but Rafe was very aware of him. Very aware of his interest in Carrie. Very aware of the man's footsteps as he turned a corner and stopped.

Rafe unlocked the door to the room and pushed Carrie inside. He closed it behind them and leaned his weight against it. Carrie stood stiffly in the middle of the room. She looked from him to the bed, back again, then at the floor.

He made an elaborate show of looking at his watch. "I don't have time to ravish you tonight, either, Carolina."

He was rewarded with an indignant look. "And why not? I mean—"

Her blush was deep red, and he couldn't keep from smiling as her dark eyes lit with anger. He almost stepped forward and took her in his arms. He very much wanted to kiss away her outrage, feel it being slowly replaced by desire.

"I do have it on my calendar for later, though," he promised.

She tossed her hair. "Don't tease." Then she shook her head as if to clear it. The dismay on her face made him smile, but he sympathized completely. "I'm crazy," she murmured. "I don't know what I'm saying." She sat on the bed and put her hands over her face for a moment. "My mouth has become totally detached from my brain."

"I'm going out for a while," Rafe told her, drawing them both back to reality. "Don't open the door to anybody."

Carrie's gaze met his. "I don't want to open it to you, Castillo," she retorted defiantly.

"Yes, you do."

He was gone before she could answer. The man who'd passed them earlier was not gone, as Rafe knew he wouldn't be. He found the stranger smoking a cigarette and leaning against the wall just around the corner from their room.

Rafe stepped up very close to him, using his size to intimidate the smaller man. Small but dangerous, Rafe was certain. The man looked to have the speed and wiry strength of a ferret. He certainly had an ugly sneer. "Isn't it about your bedtime?" Rafe asked him. The man said nothing while they made eye contact and glared at each other, a pair of narrow-eyed, dangerous men. "She's mine," Rafe went on, his voice low, soft and deadly. "I want you and everyone else in town to know it, *amigo*. No one comes near her. No one speaks to her. So there's no need for you to stand here and consider the possibility of trying to get into her room. This is a no-smoking floor," Rafe went on. "And you should leave."

The man said nothing, and the hostile silence dragged on just long enough for Rafe to consider drawing a weapon. Carrie Robinson was worth fighting for, and not just because it was his duty to protect her as a DEA agent. He didn't have to fight this time. The man must have seen in Rafe's eyes the willingness to enforce his words with violence. The stranger's response was to drop his cigarette to the floor, crush it under his foot and walk away.

Rafe watched until the man was out of sight. He felt relief, but with none of the tension draining from him. In Ciudad Alguna it was best to remain alert and tense. And he was more alert and tense than he'd ever been in his life when he walked down the staircase at the back of the building, but more because of the woman waiting in his bedroom than the man he was going to meet.

* * *

The night was dark, starless. Rafe stepped off the terrace and into the walled garden. The area was fragrant with night-blooming flowers, and soaking wet from the latest rain shower. He didn't turn when he heard someone come up behind him.

"Hello, Steve."

Though they had exchanged only the briefest glances in the lobby, he had expected to find Quarrels waiting outside for him.

As Rafe turned, Steve grumbled, "It took you long enough. I've been waiting for three hours. Girlfriend didn't want to let you out of the bedroom?"

Rafe ignored the comment—for the moment. "Manolo saw you."

Steve swore. "The last thing I want is to run into anyone that loyal to Torres. I don't want to run into any of his men until we take them down. We're close." Steve gave a tired laugh. "Close enough for me to dream of going home to my kids and stop playing badass rival to the local drug lord for a while."

Steve was a widower and deeply devoted to his young children. Rafe wondered why the man kept taking dangerous assignments, but it was something they never discussed. He knew that if he had something to come home to, there was no way he'd do fieldwork like this anymore.

Rafe nodded at the other man's assessment of the situation. "Close. Just one more piece of evidence to collect and we move in on him. However, Manolo would happily have shot you on sight today. I told him I'd take care of it. But I had to put a lot of beer and tequila down him to keep him from calling Torres. That's where I've been."

Steve rubbed the back of his hand across his unshaved jaw. It made a scratching sound, like a match being struck. He gave Rafe a thoughtful look. "Where's Manolo now?"

"Passed out in his room."

"Want me to make sure he stays that way?"

Rafe didn't like the dangerous tone of his fellow agent's voice. "You are referring to having him arrested, right?"

Steve shrugged. "Whatever's most convenient at the moment. I'll enjoy confiscating the Hummer. I can really use a set of wheels like that."

Fortunately, Rafe knew his fellow agent wasn't as gun happy and amoral as he projected. It was just the same sort of veneer Rafe used to cover his own emotions and reactions to the moral ambiguities of the job.

"Getting Manolo out of the way before we reach Mérida would be convenient," Rafe acknowledged. He fished Manolo's room key out of his pocket and handed it over.

"Consider it done." Steve leered. "You and the girlfriend need more privacy?"

"She's not my girlfriend," Rafe answered, annoyed at Steve's suggestion.

"Who is she, then? Torres's girlfriend?"

"No." He must have sounded a little too adamant because Steve didn't bother to hide his grin. Rafe scowled at the other agent. "She's part of the case. Innocent bystander that got pulled in to act as a mule. She's scared to death and afraid I'm going to kill her," he added, aware that his voice betrayed his sadness and bitterness at the situation.

He was used to the bitterness; it ate at him more and more lately. The sadness came from hurting Carrie Robinson, and it was tearing him apart. He didn't know where his objectivity had gone, where he'd lost his ability to simply focus on the case no matter what. Having discovered that he had feelings again, he wasn't sure he wanted them. A sense of justice was important to the job, though ethics had long ago proved to be optional. Any other emotions were damned inconvenient.

Steve was a good friend, a trusted friend. They'd worked together off and on for years and saved each other's life more than once. Steve was about the only one who would understand Rafe's conflict. "I hate myself."

Steve put a hand on his arm. "You want to hate somebody, hate Torres."

"Him, too."

"A few more days and Torres is history. You cut off the source of his money, and my squad goes in to take out him and his men."

Steve sounded as if he was prepared for a full military assault on Torres's compound. Rafe didn't doubt that that was exactly what was going to happen, but it was important to him to keep casualties to a minimum. "You don't go in until I get back," he reminded the other man. "We have an agreement with the government about the use of violence. I can get to Torres without anybody getting hurt."

Steve took out a cigarette and lit it. "If you say so."

"Those things are going to kill you."

Steve looked at him through a puff of smoke. "Something's bound to kill me sooner than later. Might as well be my choice."

Rafe shook his head, but didn't bother to argue. He wanted to get an early start in the morning. He needed to get some rest. He was also both anxious and dreading returning to the room—the rather comfortable bedroom—where Carrie Robinson waited. There was no way he could chance leaving her alone in a place like Ciudad Alguna. Probably no way he could get any sleep sharing a bed with her, either. He'd left her on her own longer than he should have. He nodded a farewell to his friend and walked away.

Chapter 5

Carrie sat on the edge of the bed and picked up her hairbrush. Her hair was wet and blessedly clean. Now it was time to work the snarls and tangles out. It was a pity a bit of thorough brushing couldn't do the same for her emotions. A hot shower had been wonderful, but it hadn't helped ease the tension any. There was only one thing, she thought, that could help that. "'My thoughts this morning,'" she quoted an ancient Japanese poem, "'are as tangled as my hair.'" Carrie wondered if the court lady who'd set down those words hundreds of years ago had known Rafael Castillo, too.

She thought about just getting up and walking out. She thought about it, but not very hard. Rafael was right. Ciudad Alguna was no place for anyone, man or woman, who wasn't armed and dangerous, to be wandering around alone. Not at night. Not anytime. One didn't call the police from a location in Ciudad Alguna. They wouldn't come. She was trapped here, in this room, with Rafael Castillo—whenever he chose to come in from wandering the streets like a big old dangerous black tomcat.

It annoyed her that she wondered if he was all right. It annoyed her that she wanted him to come back. Mind you, that was due in large part because she didn't like being left alone, even with the door securely locked. She wasn't a wimp, but she knew when she was out of her depth.

She was out of her depth in a lot of ways, and the thought of having Rafael spend the night in the same room with her was almost more frightening than being alone. No, not almost, she admitted grimly. It *was* more frightening. She wasn't afraid of what *he'd* do. It was what *she* was tempted to do that really scared her. She wanted to touch him all over. She wanted his hands on her. She wanted to taste him, to feel those extraordinary full lips against hers. She'd never been hungry for a kiss before. She'd never even believed such a thing was possible, and she'd been kissed quite pleasantly many times. But she knew kissing Rafael Castillo wouldn't be a pleasant experience. Nothing so tame as pleasant.

This was wrong. Ridiculous. Her attraction to Rafael was something she had to stop thinking about. Something she had to deny. Something that had nothing to do with the real Caroline Robinson. She had to force her body to stop wanting something her heart and head knew she could not have.

"Then again," she said to the image in the mirror hanging across from the end of the bed, "maybe he's a lousy kisser. Men that good-looking aren't necessarily great lovers." She made herself shrug nonchalantly. "It's probably no big deal. I've just been out in the jungle too long. Need to go home and get myself a boyfriend." Yeah, her thoughts mocked her. You need somebody safe and pallid and predictable. Need. But that isn't what you want.

She wanted all right. She wanted Rafael's touch as she'd never wanted anything in her life before. Heat flared deep inside her as images of what she wanted rose unbidden to tease her senses.

"Maybe I should just jump his bones," she muttered. Then she shuddered and almost doubled over with revulsion. She shook her head wildly, tangling the damp hair she'd been working to unsnarl. You're sick, Robinson, she accused herself. Really sick. You're dying to make love to the man, and dying's the operative word, she reminded herself sternly. He talks to you, he smiles and he teases, he even has serious conversations—nothing he says or does means a thing to him. He's a cold-blooded killer who works for a cold-blooded killer. Torres will have Castillo shoot you the moment you're no longer useful to him, or if something goes wrong with the pickup. Do you think the man will hesitate for a moment just because you've shared a few interesting conversations?

When the cold-blooded killer walked in just then, locked the door, flopped wearily down on the bed and said, "Honey, I'm home," it did nothing to help her ambivalent, overstressed mood. It was a queen-size bed, but it looked smaller with him on it.

As he stretched out, Carrie jumped up and dropped the brush. It landed on his chest. He grabbed it and sat up. He studied it for a moment while Carrie hovered skittishly by the dresser. He could feel her eyes on him, but he didn't look at her just yet. He'd seen the look of wild fear she flashed toward him as he entered the room. He wanted to give her time to calm down a little, to find the well of strength that let her face him with humor and bravado. Besides, he was too weary, too ashamed of what he was doing to her, to face her hatred.

He ran his thumb over the thick bristles; they were both soft and stiff. He turned the brush over and over in his hands. He frowned, then looked disapprovingly at Carrie. "Is this real tortoiseshell?"

"Yes."

He wagged a finger at her. "You should be ashamed of yourself."

"That brush is a family heirloom," Carrie defended herself indignantly. "It belonged to my great-grandmother. Possibly my great-great-grandmother. It's not my fault nobody worried about the environment back then," she added, and tried to take the brush from him.

He held it out of her reach. "Sit down." He tugged on her hand to get her to comply. When she sat, she huffily turned her back to him. That was fine with him; it gave him a better view of her long, thick hair. He moved closer. He couldn't keep from getting closer. Rafe rested one hand gently on Carrie's shoulder.

He didn't mean to start brushing her hair. He was sure she didn't mean to let him. It was a far too intimate contact for what they were to each other—guard and prisoner. Once started, he didn't stop, though. She tensed, but she didn't pull away.

Carrie knew he shouldn't be doing this, that she shouldn't be letting him, but it felt so good. The dueling impulses to both fear and trust this man were driving her crazy. Even crazier, and she must be imagining this, she believed his emotions were just as ambivalent as hers. When he was out of her sight and she was out of the range of his charisma, of his overwhelmingly masculine presence, she could almost objectively think of him as the scumbag he really was. When he was near her—well, thought was hard enough. Feelings were worse. When she was with him, it wasn't just sexual attraction that clouded her reason. She liked being with him.

She liked the soothing, sensual, animal pleasure of feeling his hands on her as he patiently stroked the brush through her hair. Only, after a while it stopped being soothing. It became foreplay. His hands never reached for her.

She didn't turn into his embrace. They were passionately connected just the same.

At some point, Carrie managed to drag her eyes open just a little. It took them a long time to focus. She moistened her dry lips with her tongue. She was all too aware of the heaviness in her breasts, the tenderness of the peaks straining against the soft fabric of her cotton knit T-shirt. Her hair was long dried, but she could feel the faint sheen of sweat on her heated flesh.

Carrie took a long, deep breath. She forced herself to regain the control that was desperately necessary, but very hard to hold on to. "This is a bad idea."

His reply came in a strained whisper. "I know. I should stop."

"Yes."

"Do you want me to?"

"Yes."

"Liar."

"It feels good."

His laugh was low, sensual. His lips were very close to her ear. "Like your mother used to do it?"

The warmth of his breath against her throat sent molten butterflies through her stomach. "No. Nothing like when my mother used to do it."

"You have beautiful hair."

"You have gentle hands."

"We better stop."

"We?"

"You know what I mean." He sighed. It sounded closer to a frustrated groan. "If I stop, then what?"

Carrie hesitated almost a risky moment too long before she managed to say, "Then we go to bed. To sleep. Just sleep."

"Right. Sure. I'm going to put down the brush now." He made it sound about as dangerous as offering to throw down his weapon in some kind of outlaw standoff. "I am not going to make love to you." He said the words through gritted teeth, and she didn't think he was talking to her. "It's the last thing either of us needs." A hand skimmed her shoulder and slid through her hair. He tossed the brush aside.

The next thing she knew he was kissing the back of her neck. A tingling heat spread down her spine and deep inside her. It was the merest contact of lips to flesh, enough to make her want more. She wanted to turn into his embrace, to feel his mouth covering hers.

This was ridiculous. Insane. She should be screaming, fighting, pushing him away, denying the need that raced through her veins.

Instead, it was Rafael who backed off, who stood. Who said, "Let's go to bed. To sleep."

"Fine," she agreed. She stretched, trying her best to make the movement nonchalant. She tried to forget the insistent craving inside her. "We could both use some sleep."

"Think we'll get any?"

"No."

"Me neither."

Once she was lying down on the soft mattress with a fluffy pillow under her head in a dark room, all the tension that had built up between herself and Rafael Castillo didn't seem to matter quite so much. He'd promised not to "ravish" her. They'd managed to survive the "Hairbrush Incident" as she dubbed the past few minutes. She hadn't promised not to do the same to him, but she supposed that was an implied contract between them. She was tired. She was comfortable. She'd never had trouble sleeping.

It took a while for the bed and the darkness to lull her, for her thoughts and pulse to stop racing, but she did slowly relax, her mind and body growing heavy and drowsy, and begin to forget the day's fear, the adrenaline rushes. The seduction of sleep blunted even the keen edge of desire for the man beside her. Eventually, Carrie sighed, turned over and snuggled close to the large, warm form resting beside her. Her body and his fitted perfectly together in the shared bed, nestled, nested. She sighed again and, without knowing it, put her hand over his heart.

Rafe tensed when Carrie turned to him. It wasn't that he was afraid of rolling over and forcing himself on her; he had more self-control than that. The truth was, he was terrified of Carrie Robinson. He wanted her. Any man in his right mind who wasn't completely blind, or actually dead, would want her. He wouldn't even bet on a blind man not noticing. She had a sensual aura about her that was heart stopping, traffic stopping, and that she was barely aware of. It wasn't her beauty that disturbed him, stirred him. He'd had beautiful women before. Not one of them had made him feel the way she did.

And how was it she made him feel?

Real. It was an odd way of describing the sensation, but the best he could define his reaction to her was that when he was with her he was himself. He had no masks, no defenses. Despite the fact that he still lived under a false identity in her presence, every word, act and gesture he made with her was spontaneous, honest, sincere. In fact, it felt so right being with her, that holding her close as he fell asleep was the most natural thing in the world, even if it wasn't the easiest.

It was the deep mournful moan that woke Carrie more than the heavy weight pushing her down into the mattress. She could hear the thrum of the air conditioner, but she was nearly stifled with the heat, covered by a hot, hard-muscled body. Rafael, restless and suffering from one very bad dream if the sounds he made were any clue, had rolled over on top of her. Only half-awake, lying flat on her back, Carrie took a few moments to react.

"Rafe, wake up. Move over."

When she tried pushing against him, she found that she had very little leverage. He was lying flat on top of her, burying her. Rafe groaned again, a sound like the wail of a lost soul. Carrie struggled harder to get out from under him, growing alarmed enough to dig her nails into his bare flesh, raking along his arms and shoulders.

His reaction was instant—and terrifying. The next thing Carrie knew, his mouth was covering hers and she felt him pressing hard against her thigh. His hand was on her breast.

She couldn't scream, and kneeing him in the groin was out of the question. Any attempt to raise her leg would just make her more vulnerable. She couldn't risk it. She couldn't afford to fall into the deep well of panic that threatened her. She also couldn't afford the other headier, wilder emotions that teased at her control as his tongue probed hungrily into her mouth, and her body heedlessly began to mold itself against his.

There was nothing worse than being helpless, but she didn't know what to do. She might not be able to heave Castillo off her, but she could fight her own reactions. They weren't as strong as her fear anyway, and her annoyance at a situation that he wasn't consciously to blame for outweighed the fear. Still, she had no intention of being raped by a sleeping man. And no intention of trying to deal with the ambiguity of it maybe not being quite rape, or him not even being aware of what he was doing. Fighting her own confused emotions, she began to struggle harder.

The dream had no business being this real.

The lips beneath his were soft, warm, pliant. The skin was firm to his touch, satin smooth and female, smelling of almond-scented soap. She'd never felt, tasted, been this real before, no matter how vivid the dream.

She was better than any dream.

In the dream, he wasn't afraid to love her. The love was intensely, passionately real.

It was the reality that woke him. The reality of her nails digging into the flesh of his upper arms and back. The reality of the cries smothered by his mouth over hers. The reality of the body frantically writhing and squirming beneath his. The reality of suddenly realizing that he was forcing himself on a frightened, struggling woman.

Dream turned to waking nightmare in the flash of an agonizing, awful instant.

Rafe was up and off the bed the second the dream vanished. Desire died even before he opened his eyes. The dregs of it curdled instantly in his gut. The shock of what he'd been doing—and not even being aware of it—sent a wave of nausea through him.

"Carolina, I'm sorry. I am so sorry." The words came out of him in a breathless rasp just as she switched on a bedside lamp. The sudden light blinded him. The last thing he wanted was for her to see him. The last thing he wanted to see was the revulsion and contempt on her face. Even as his eyes adjusted to the light, he couldn't bear to look at her. "I was asleep. I didn't know—I was dreaming about…"

He hated the rush of words, the disorientation, the raw vulnerability he couldn't hide. He was a man of masks, but without the resources now to call up a single one of his disguises. It even took Rafe a few moments to realize where he was standing; for the world to stop whirling around him. Eventually, within a few heartbeats, he became awake enough to discover that he was standing by the door.

He forced himself to look at Carrie. He was fully prepared to see anger, fear, hatred, any number of negative emotions. The concern in her dark eyes was almost worse than the loathing he expected. It melted his heart.

"Look at it this way," she said calmly, reasonably, her voice only shaking a little. "At least you didn't pull a gun in your sleep."

Her attempt to make light of the past few minutes only made him feel worse, but by now he was in enough control of his emotions not to flinch visibly. She couldn't know that the particular dream he'd been having frequently had an ending where he didn't end up making love to the beautiful woman from the bar. He'd woken up in a cold sweat a few times from the dream where he pulled the trigger. He went cold now at the memory, at the reminder of what a son of a bitch he really was.

Carrie was surprised by the appalled look on Rafe's face. "It was a lame joke," she admitted. She patted the mattress beside her. "Come back to bed. Just keep your hands to yourself," she added, since the guilt he radiated seemed to require some sort of reprimand. She supposed she should be appalled at his behavior, that she should put on some sort of show of sullied, outraged maidenhood. But since she felt none of that, she'd rather just forget it and go back to sleep. "Do you know what time it is?" she demanded when he didn't budge from his spot by the door.

In a way, it was ridiculous that the man she'd first met in a bar fight could be so upset over unconsciously letting his hands rove a little. It was so incongruous, so…endearing. It was enough to make her want to get up and hug him. It made her want to smile fondly and say reassuring things while she ran her fingers soothingly through his hair. Almost. She did manage to recall that she was his captive before she gave in to this ridiculous impulse. Even recalling that she wasn't sharing the room or bed with him of her own volition, she couldn't manage to churn up much sense of outrage. She'd known he hadn't meant her any harm even while she was fighting to get him off her.

She said sarcastically, "You haven't got ravishing me penciled in on your schedule, remember?"

He couldn't help but smile. Her humor, her attempt to defuse the situation, touched him deeply. It helped steady him enough to get some perspective. It had only been a dream. Nothing terrible had happened; his sense of reality was just too skewed by living under cover.

He took a few deep breaths, then ran his hands through the hair that had fallen across his face. The desire that had raged inside him was under control. Rafe did his best to look relaxed. He gave her the most reassuring smile he could summon. He took a step away from the door before the impulse to flee got the better of him.

"If I was a gentleman," he said, "I'd spend the night out in the hall."

"If you were a gentleman—" Carrie cut short the comment. This was not the time or place for sarcasm. Rafael Castillo needed a light, gentle touch right now. Though why she was concerned about his tender feelings, she refused to consider. She patted the mattress again. "Never mind. I'll verbally abuse you in the morning. It's late. We both need to get some sleep."

Rafe didn't know the time, but it must be well into the night. It would be emotionally safer for him to spend the rest of the hours before dawn restlessly roaming the streets of Ciudad Alguna. But it wouldn't be physically safer—not for him; certainly not for Carrie. His number-one job was to protect her. He owed it to her to get her out of this situation safe and sound. It wasn't just a sense of duty or professionalism that made him vow to keep her safe. In a few intense hours, Carrie Robinson had come to mean more to him than anyone else in the world.

He wouldn't tell her. His caring was his painful secret to keep. He'd already intruded enough on her life. Whatever he felt for Carrie couldn't possibly be returned and he was just going to have to go on wanting what he couldn't have. Somehow, he'd have to live with it, and fight the physical attraction that drew them together.

At this moment, he was halfway to telling her that he'd die for her. Instead, he said, "You want me to sleep on the floor?"

Carrie considered telling Rafe that what she really wanted was to take him into her embrace and cuddle him into a peaceful sleep. Fortunately, she was well aware that this was a ridiculous, self-destructive impulse and she curbed it, though with difficulty. *The deal with Torres does not require my baby-sitting the bodyguard,* she reminded herself sternly. *It certainly doesn't require my getting emotionally involved with him. I am a hostage. My job is to stay alive, not to develop Stockholm Syndrome.*

Not to fall in love.

No, she wasn't going to let herself even think that word again. *That is a road you are not going down, Robinson. You hear, me? You are not even going to look in that direction.*

After giving herself this firm lecture, she managed to turn a bland expression on him. "Suit yourself." She shrugged, then wrapped herself in the sheet and settled down on the bed. She refused to hope that he'd get back into bed beside her.

Rafe told himself he was glad she'd remembered that he was the bad guy. He fought the impulse to tell her differently. Ciudad Alguna was no place for the truth. He grabbed a pillow off the bed and lay down in front of the door. Sleeping on the hard wooden floor would serve as partial penance for sins of omission, commission, thought, word and deed. Not that he was likely to get much sleep.

He slept so well after the nightmare incident that he was almost embarrassed to wake up. All Rafe could figure was that there was something about Carrie Robinson that calmed as well as stimulated him. It was a rare combination. A charming one. Endearing.

He had it bad, and that was not good. He had no business having it—good, bad or indifferent. He did not let himself indulge in watching her sleep when he got up and went over to the bed. Today, he vowed, he was going to get her to Mérida, get her onto a plane and safely out of the country. Once on the plane, he could explain just who he was and what was going on and they could take it from there. Only "it" had nothing to do with their personal relationship. They did not, would not, and could not have a personal relationship. She was part of his assignment. The DEA needed her to help lead them to Torres's money-laundering contacts in Washington. She was going to be needed as a witness against Torres. Special Agent Castillo couldn't afford any personal interest in Dr. Robinson. The fact that he already had a deeply personal interest in her was something he was just going to have to ignore. Maybe after the assignment was over with…

No, he wasn't going to try to think beyond the assignment. To do anything but focus on the sordid, vicious world he inhabited at this moment, or on the job he had to do in it, could make him sloppy, reckless. It could be fatal, not just for himself but for the woman he was sworn to protect.

He finally noticed that while he was giving himself this talking-to, he had been standing by the bed, watching Carrie Robinson sleep.

Damn.

He shook her shoulder. "Wake up. It's time to leave."

Chapter 6

He didn't give her much time to get ready, though he insisted on taking a shower before hustling her out the door. She resented that. It was a minor annoyance, but she nursed it, using every scrap she could to build some sort of emotional wall around herself. She knew she should hate and fear the man, but liking and attraction kept getting in the way of her sense of self-preservation. Little things he did kept getting to her, kept making her believe he wasn't so bad.

Maybe that was how gangsters managed to reproduce, she thought as they walked down the stairs to the lobby. In gangster movies, bad characters played by famous actors were always having romances with adoring women—women who knew exactly how bad they were and loved them anyway. What was worse, it didn't just happen in the movies. Many a criminal was a happily married grandfather. It surprised her that bad men could have normal relationships, that they could love and be loved. It didn't seem to be right, but she was beginning to understand how it could happen.

Not that she was going to fall in love with Rafael Castillo. It was just an unwanted sexual attraction—the primitive allure of the dark and dangerous. Or her biological clock turning into a time bomb—or something.

Maybe there was something wrong with her. She'd been berated once long ago for having a recklessly sexual nature, accused of things she'd never even thought of. Maybe... No. She wasn't going to let that memory surface.

She stuffed her hands into the pockets of her shorts and tried not to watch the play of muscles in Rafe's broad back as he moved ahead of her. Her fingers found and fiddled with the small plastic case full of credit cards and IDs in her pocket rather than succumb to the temptation to reach out and straighten Rafe's mussed hair. She wasn't going to touch him.

Not talking to him was not an option. Once they reached the lobby, she looked around and asked, "Where's Manolo?"

"Suffering from a very bad hangover, I should imagine."

"No doubt, but where is he?"

Rafe took Carrie's arm and steered her through the deserted lobby. There was a certain tentativeness about his touch, as though he was still silently apologizing for last night. His voice was expressionless when he answered blandly, "He won't be joining us today."

Carrie was curious, but she kept any more questions to herself. Knowing the whereabouts and activities of a drug dealer was not information she needed.

She wanted breakfast, but, more importantly, she wanted to get out of Ciudad Alguna. She wanted to get to Mérida. She wanted to get on a plane and see the last of Rafael Castillo. Not that getting on a plane to Washington would end her troubles. She still had her errand for Torres, but as awful and illegal as it was, playing Torres's mule would at least get her away from Rafael.

But she'd only have to come back, and he would be waiting for her.

She sighed.

"What's the matter?"

"Nothing. Let's get this show on the road."

When they reached the truck, he said, "I'll drive."

Carrie was surprised at herself when she didn't protest. For the moment, she was too dispirited to care. Maybe she'd feel better after she'd had some coffee, but she didn't feel any urge to linger in this outlaw haven for breakfast. From the high-speed way Rafe drove along the deserted road out of town, it was obvious he didn't want to linger, either.

The day was dark, even more overcast than usual. It wasn't long before a crack of lightning split the sky, thunder rumbled in accompaniment and the daily deluge began. Headlights and windshield wipers did only so much good in the heavy downpour. Rafe was forced to slow his driving to the same snail's pace Carrie had driven the day before.

When he snarled and said a few choice words, she raised an eyebrow and questioned, "You always this nasty before you've had coffee?"

Rafe couldn't keep from turning a wry smile on her. "Always, *querida*." She tsked and gave the briefest shake of her head.

He firmly turned his attention back to the road. Concentrating on driving forced him to focus his attention on something besides her. The narrow road was slippery with water and mud, more of a stream, really, than a road. They were going uphill along one of the few hilly stretches in the area. It felt like he was driving up a waterfall. The road was winding, with the forest canopy closing in over it in many places.

"This is not the sort of spot even an ecotourist would want to visit," he commented as the truck crested a ridge and began to head downhill around a long, looping curve.

Maybe this was no place for tourists, but Rafe saw a group of people and a trio of parked vehicles blocking the road up ahead as he drove ever so slowly around the curve. About a dozen men were standing out in the rain. Even through the patchy visibility, he could tell that every one of them was holding a weapon of some sort.

"Waiting for us," he said as he slowed the crawling pace of the truck even more.

Carrie leaned forward until her nose was almost touching the windshield. "What's going on?"

"Ambush."

She twisted toward him on the seat, radiating outrage. "What? Us?" He nodded. She turned back to stare outside. "Who?"

Even through the dim light and pouring rain, he recognized some of the men. "Munoz."

At the same time, Carrie said, "Beltrano."

They darted quick sideways glances at each other.

"Those are the other drug dealers he said he'd go to?" she asked.

"This is an ambush," he repeated.

"For my artifacts?"

He almost laughed at her outraged fury. "Munoz has probably been told we're carrying drugs in the truck."

"So you think Beltrano did make a deal with the drug runners? To get the artifacts?"

"You heard him threaten to do just that. If they get the drugs, he gets the Mayan artifacts."

"But we aren't carrying drugs!"

Munoz was going to be disappointed when nothing he

considered valuable was found in the truck. Munoz shot
people when he was disappointed. Sometimes he shot people just because he liked to.

They were now only a few hundred feet from the cars
and crowd. A truck was parked across the road. Men were
cautiously walking forward, guns not yet aimed at the truck
cab, but held at the ready. Rafe wasn't going to let Carrie
be one of the people who got shot.

"Beltrano's not getting my stuff."

He didn't know what Carrie thought she was going to
do to prevent it, but for a mad moment he couldn't help
but admire her ferocious, protective stubbornness. "You're
one hell of a woman, Carolina," he said. Then he leaned
across the truck cab, opened the passenger door and pushed
her out of the slow-moving vehicle.

He heard her cry out as she landed. It was a sound of
outrage rather than pain. He smiled grimly as he slid across
to the passenger seat, keeping his foot pressed hard on the
gas pedal. With one hand on the wheel, he aimed the truck
straight at the vehicle blocking the road ahead. Then, under
cover of the open door and the pouring rain, Rafe jumped
into the ditch after Carrie.

He heard shouts as men jumped out of the way of the
driverless truck. He heard it crash into the one blocking the
road. Rafe didn't see any of it. He was too busy getting the
clawing hellcat who'd jumped on him from behind off his
back.

"You bastard!" Carrie hissed in his ear—just before she
bit it. "You're letting them have my stuff!"

Rafe managed to get enough leverage to flip her over his
head. She landed with a shriek and a loud splash.

Rafe dived after her to keep her out of sight as much as
possible, but she slipped out of his wet hands. She kicked
back at him as he tried again.

"I should never have let you drive!" She tried to scramble up the side of the ditch, only to slide back down the muddy bank. Rafe grabbed the back of her shirt, pulled her out of the water, then into the cover of the forest. She struggled the whole way. "Where do you think you're going?" she demanded. "I have to get to my stuff!"

There was gunfire behind them. Munoz didn't like leaving witnesses. This was no time to politely explain that her life was more important to him than some very heavy carved stones. He pushed her behind a tree, then shoved her against the trunk and held her there. "People are shooting at us!"

"People are shooting," she countered to the background accompaniment of distant gunfire. "They aren't necessarily shooting at us."

"Do the bullets know this? Come on."

The gunfire continued over Beltrano's shouts of protest. It seemed the separatist didn't want the archaeologist murdered, just robbed. Rafe knew very well that nobody was going to listen to him.

"Never lie down with dogs, *amigo*," he murmured as he hurried Carrie along ahead of him, then stepped a little farther into the forest. "You get up with fleas." He rubbed his ear. "Though I'm the one who's gotten bitten."

Carrie shook wet hair out of her face. Rafe held her arms at her sides, leaning most of his weight against her. Since she couldn't wipe either the mud or the tears of frustration off her face, she wiped her cheeks on the soaked shirt plastered to Rafe's wide shoulder. Caught in his unyielding embrace, she had no choice but to calm down and to listen. The forest was dense here, and distance of sound hard to measure. It seemed like they were a long way from the road. She could barely make out the voices of the men shouting at each other, but she heard enough.

The person Beltrano was arguing with was adamant about not leaving any witnesses. She didn't have any trouble hearing people searching the edges of the forest for them. Or the occasional shot.

They were lost—and in deep trouble. This was no time for her to be freaking out over the loss of something she and her team had worked years to excavate. This was also no time to howl in frustration because she strongly suspected that Beltrano was about to sell the Mayan people's treasures on the black market to finance his revolution despite his protestations that she was the real thief. She *did* think it might be a good time to start screaming in terror because people really were shooting at her, but she didn't suppose that response would help get them out of this mess.

The sensible thing was to escape from the men who were shooting at them and then worry about rescuing the artifacts from Beltrano. Just take things one at a time.

She found herself looking trustingly at Rafael Castillo. Carrie took a deep breath. When she spoke, it was in a careful whisper. "You can let me go. We have to get out of here."

Rafe was so relieved that Carrie was being reasonable that he almost kissed her. Instead, he met her gaze and studied her closely for a moment. He didn't see any hint that she might be lying or on the verge of hysteria. While the woman who looked back at him wasn't exactly calm, she was very much in control. He gave a brief nod, then stepped back.

Carrie moved away from the tree as Rafe bent over for a moment. When he stood, he tossed something toward her.

"Here."

She found herself holding a gun. He was holding one, too. Despite the situation, she couldn't contain an amused outburst. "How many of these things do you have?"

He flashed a quick, fierce grin. "You can pat me down and find out."

"Maybe later." Her gun was smaller than the big 9 mm

in Rafe's hand. Her emotions were definitely mixed about holding a weapon. She didn't know whether she was more frightened at the idea of using the gun, or pleased that the man who was her captor trusted her not to turn the thing on him. The fact that he trusted her was *not* something she should be pleased about—but she was.

Fortunately, she didn't have time to meditate on the ambivalence of the situation. They were still hidden by the thick surrounding foliage, but she could hear people still hunting for them. A burst of gunfire from an invisible hunter strafing the nearby undergrowth was their cue to move. She looked at Rafe—trusting him—for guidance.

He pointed. She nodded, then followed as he moved rapidly off. Focusing her attention on Rafe helped keep her from thinking about the men on their trail. She was amazed at how silently he moved, the cautious, alert way he studied the terrain. She got the impression that the man must have had commando training. It made her wonder about his past and how he'd gotten involved with Torres's organization. This was hardly the time for curious questions. She could only keep quiet and try to emulate him.

The rain helped hide them. It made Rafe miserable, but he was grateful for it. Grateful for the fact that the men looking for them weren't used to tramping around in soaking wet, overgrown jungles. He knew very well the sort of men he was dealing with. They might be dangerous, but they were also lazy, miserable and annoyed with Munoz's paranoia. Some of them were Beltrano's men, who thought of themselves as freedom fighters. Beltrano probably hadn't given them orders to kill. They might not mind killing him, but he hoped they'd balk at murdering an innocent woman.

He also had the advantage of having thoroughly studied the terrain around Ciudad Alguna when he and Steve Quarrels had mapped out a plan to assault the whole town in one massive raid. Though the raid hadn't gotten past the planning stage, at least Rafe knew how to get through this forest and to a well-traveled road. He figured they had a good chance of getting out of this alive if the weather stayed rotten and they were lucky.

It took several hours of traveling very, very cautiously, with frequent stops to hide in the thick, bug-laden undergrowth, before Rafe was certain they'd escaped their pursuers. He gestured for a halt in a tiny clearing above a narrow ravine. A small river rushed through the bottom of the gap, about twenty feet below.

Rafe stood on the edge of the clearing and looked down at the rain-swollen current. "There's a road on the other side," he told Carrie when she stepped up beside him. He gestured at the water. "We just have to get across that. In the dry season, the river's just a trickle."

"This isn't the dry season."

"I've noticed." There wasn't a part of him that wasn't soaked, mud splattered or dripping. He raked his hands through his hair, pulling it back off his face. Looking at Carrie, he decided that the one good thing about the time they'd spent out in the rain was that her wet clothes clung to every soft, feminine curve of her body. There was something very alluring about the way she seemed nearly naked while being completely clothed.

"What are you staring at, Castillo?"

She looked all ripe and sensual and female. She sounded tired and irritable. She looked tired, as well. She was also still holding his .22 caliber backup gun. He'd tucked the 9 mm into its shoulder holster hidden beneath his jacket quite a while ago. To be fair, she didn't exactly have anywhere she could stash it in the shorts or blouse she was wearing. It was the thoughtful way she was holding it up and looking at it, then at him, that made Rafe nervous.

"I don't think the water's all that deep now," he said,

pretending that most of his attention wasn't on the weapon in her hand. He edged closer to her.

She edged closer to the edge of the ravine. He followed, then found himself perched on a tangled patch of ferns and vines with a far too clear view of the space below for comfort's sake.

"You want something, Castillo?" she asked, holding the gun toward him.

He wasn't sure whether she was aiming it at him or not. He held out his hand and very nearly overbalanced. "You want to give me that?"

Carrie took a step backward. Her eyes sparked with wicked amusement. "I'm not quite sure I take your meaning."

Carrie knew she was not acting in a reasonable, mature manner. She had no interest in guns; she had never even held one before having the pistol tossed to her this morning. It was lighter than she thought it would be and fitted her grip in a way that seemed natural. She had to admit it gave her a certain giddy sense of power. She wasn't actually aiming the gun at Rafe when she held it up. She intended to give it back to him. It wasn't as if shooting him was going to help her situation with Torres. Threatening her captor, however, did have a certain vengeful allure. An allure that only lasted a few moments. In fact, even the idea of his being threatened made her queasy. When he held his hand out, she sighed guiltily and handed it over.

The last thing she expected was for the gun to go off.

She screamed and dropped the gun. It fired again as it hit the ground.

Rafe ducked as the first bullet whizzed past his ear. It was the second bullet that hit him. The impact against his upper arm was just enough to turn his body and send him plunging over the side of the ravine.

"Oh, my God!" Carrie heard his body crashing down

through the trees and underbrush. She heard the splash as he hit the water even over the roar of the swift current. She looked around for a way down, but realized swiftly that there was no easy descent. She'd just have to cling and slither, making her way as fast as she could.

First she snatched the gun up off the ground. This time, she found what must be the safety, made sure it was in the right position, tucked the little gun into her bra and started to climb down the wet slope. She didn't know if Rafe was dead or alive, but she had to find him.

"Don't let him be dead," she prayed as she hurriedly scrambled and slid toward the bottom of the ravine. "Don't let me have killed him. Don't let the fall have killed him. Don't let him have drowned." The thought of losing Rafe not only filled her with guilt, it broke her heart.

She was scratched and bruised when she made it to the water's edge, but she got there swiftly. She saw Rafe in the water on the other side of the rushing stream, his body wedged against a fallen tree trunk, his head resting on a twisted limb. If not for the downed tree, the swift current would have dragged him under and away. The fall might have killed him, the bullet might have killed him, but she had the faint consolation as she searched for the best way to get to him that at least he hadn't been drowned. Finally, with no other choice, she decided to test his theory that the current was swift but the water not all that deep. He needed her. She didn't have any option but to plunge into the racing water.

He was right. It wasn't that deep, just up to her shoulders in places, waist-deep most of the way. The stones beneath her feet were slippery, the current bruising, but she kept her eyes on the sprawled body of the man caught against the tree trunk and didn't let anything so inconvenient as a minor flood stop her. She eventually reached the tree and swung herself up onto the trunk. She had to crawl along its length to reach the spot near the shore where Rafe's body had lodged.

His skin was so cold when she finally touched him that she almost screamed. The spasm of grief that shot through her was a heart-stopping, physical pain. Tears blinded her for a moment. Alternately praying and swearing in every language she knew, she perched precariously on the fallen tree and felt for a pulse on the side of Rafe's throat.

"Don't you dare die on me," she ordered. "Don't you dare." When she found a strong, steady pulse beneath her fingers, she laughed with joy and came to her senses. Carrie looked around at the steep sides of the ravine and wondered how she'd made it down to the water so quickly without breaking her own neck. More importantly, she wondered how she was going to get Rafe's unconscious body up the other side.

Her first job was to get him out of the water and check his wounds. He might be alive, but she had no way of knowing how much longer he might stay that way.

"I will not have you dying on me," she told him as she waded in beside him. She worked his arms free of the tree branches and got a good grip on his shoulders. "You're heavy, you know that?" She tried to ignore the blood that soaked his wet jacket sleeve.

He groaned and opened his eyes just as she managed to get all of his long form up on the bank.

"Now you wake up," she complained with equal amounts of sarcasm and relief as she knelt beside him. He sat up just as she knelt, and they very nearly bumped heads. She had to grab his shoulders to keep him from tipping back over. She told herself that what she did next was not really a hug, that she didn't clasp him tight for a long moment for any other reason than to check to see if he had any broken bones. For whatever reason, she embraced him, but quickly released her hold. Then she really did check to see if anything was broken.

Rafe sat slumped forward, forehead touching his drawn-up knees, and let her run her hands over him without any complaint. Well, he did groan loudly when she touched the lump at the back of his head. When she pushed aside his hair, she didn't see any blood, but the swelling was big and could easily be a sign of something more serious.

"Does this hurt?" She pressed down. He groaned and flinched. "Guess so."

She moved to check his arm. Getting the jacket off wasn't easy. Fortunately, the bullet had just grazed the skin on his upper arm below the edge of his short-sleeved shirt. It took her a while to tear off the hem of her shirt to use as a bandage.

"This is always much easier to do in the movies," she muttered as she tied the makeshift bandage around Rafe's biceps. He lifted his head when she spoke, but his eyes weren't focusing when he looked her way. She couldn't help but touch his cheek in a brief, reassuring caress. "Well, at least you're awake." *But not by much,* she added to herself.

Coaxing him to his feet took even more effort than tearing the bottom off her shirt. Getting him walking, with his arm around her shoulders as she grasped him tightly around the waist, was no picnic, either. It had to be done, they had to get moving, so Carrie gritted her teeth and got the show, and them, on the road.

Fortunately, she found a worn path on this side of the ravine. Even helping and half supporting the semiconscious man, she found the climb wasn't too difficult, just slow going. Rafe was right about there being a road on this side of the river. They reached it eventually. Carrie decided she couldn't get Rafe any farther on her own. She helped him to sit and hoped that he would either come around or that someone who wasn't trying to kill them would come driving along the road. Actually, she hoped that both would happen—and quickly. All she could do was wait.

The rain stopped at some point. Carrie didn't notice when. They waited on the side of the road for quite a while. Rafe sat, groggy, eyes closed, propped up against the trunk of a tree. Carrie paced restlessly in the rutted track while the day grew hotter and hotter. Her rain-soaked clothes dried as she paced, robbing her of any cooling relief. She occasionally made quick, worried checks of Rafe's injuries. She was glad when his arm stopped bleeding completely. She began to worry that the real problem was the blow to the head Rafe had taken when he fell.

Actually, not too much time passed before an old pickup truck came wallowing along the waterlogged track. Maybe an hour. Carrie stood squarely in the middle of the road and flagged the vehicle down. She was more than a little relieved when a grizzled old farmer emerged from the cab rather than a gun-toting drug dealer.

When she explained that she and Rafe had been in an accident and desperately needed a ride, the farmer looked skeptical but didn't ask any questions.

They needed to get to Mérida. The truck she waved down was going to Tulum. The driver was willing to let them ride in the back, but he wasn't willing to change his route. Carrie only hesitated a moment before nodding her reluctant agreement and steering Rafe around to the back of the vehicle. Getting him up into the partially loaded cargo bay was not the easiest task in the world. Neither Rafe nor the truck driver offered her any help. Fortunately, years of hauling around dirt and stone at archaeological digs stood her in good stead as she maneuvered the half-conscious Rafe into the truck. The driver stood at the side of the road with his arms crossed, frowning at her, the whole time. Carrie tried to be grateful that the man was giving them a ride and ignored his amused snicker at her efforts.

Once she and Rafe were in the truck, the driver got in and drove on. Now that they were actually moving, Carrie almost didn't care where they were headed. What was important was that they were alive. That Rafe was alive. She was too relieved and too exhausted to worry about any other complication until they reached somewhere at least vaguely civilized. She had no idea how far it was to Tulum. It could be minutes or hours away. There was nothing she could do until they got there anyway, so she wasn't even going to let herself think about anything. She was too tired to think.

She put her arm around Rafe, steadying them both as the truck bounced around on the rutted road. He rested his head on her shoulder. "You stay awake," she told him. "You may have a concussion."

Unfortunately, she was too emotionally and physically drained to listen to her own words. She was asleep within minutes.

Chapter 7

She knew the area around Tulum very well, so it didn't take her very long to realize that they were close to the seaside town when she woke up. She had no idea how long she'd slept. When she looked worriedly at Rafe, he raised his head briefly to look back. Relief flooded her to see much of the look of disorientation gone from his eyes. But he didn't look good and he didn't say anything, though he definitely seemed in better condition than when she'd passed out on him.

Rafe was even more alert by the time they reached Tulum. He hardly needed any help getting out of the truck when the farmer stopped at a stand of trees above the beach on the edge of the town. The driver pulled away before Carrie had a chance to thank him.

Carrie put her hand underneath Rafe's elbow. "Come on." She helped him to sit under the shade of a tree. "Stay here."

Rafe grunted as he tilted his aching head tiredly back

against the tree and closed his eyes. She studied the hint of gray underlying his bronze complexion and shook her head worriedly. He probably needed a doctor for the bump on his head if not the bullet wound. She'd made the decision as they reached the outskirts of Tulum that he wasn't going to get one. It was a ruthless decision; and one she wasn't proud of, but it was a necessary one.

The wound wasn't all that serious, she assured herself. A graze. Still, it was a bullet wound. The bump was probably just a minor concussion—maybe not even a concussion at all. He was suffering from a tiny amount of shock from plunging down a ravine into a raging river.

No big deal, right?

She tried not to feel guilty over her decision. "There's nothing wrong with you that a little R and R in a seaside town won't fix," she said. "We're in Tulum," she added.

If they went to a clinic, there would be questions. Questions that might lead to the doctor reporting treating a gunshot wound to the police. This wasn't Oro Blanco, where Torres owned the police. If the local authorities were called in, there would be more questions. They might be detained. If the subject of the local rebels came up, then the military would be called in. There would be an official investigation. An official investigation might lead to the military finding her stolen truck of artifacts, which might very well lead to some untrustworthy members of the military "losing" her shipment. Losing would be a euphemism for their being sold on the black market. Maybe the authorities they'd encounter would be honest, but right now she wasn't willing to take the chance that anybody was honest.

Besides, there was a far more important reason she needed to get her truck back and get out of the country as quickly as possible without any questions or red tape. If that meant that a murderous drug dealer didn't get official medical treatment for a more or less minor injury, then that was the price he was going to have to pay for being a drug dealer in the first place. This is all his fault, she told herself. Though it was no comfort for the ache in her conscience or the pangs of worry when she looked at him.

She leaned over him. She pushed a heavy lock of dark hair off his forehead and rested her palm against it. His skin was hot and sweaty, but she couldn't tell if it was from the heat and exhaustion or if he was feverish. He opened his eyes, and once again she was struck by their amazing tawny color. The fact that his gaze focused on her bosom made her glance down. She discovered that the top of her already tattered shirt was gaping open and that he had a good view of her breasts.

She straightened quickly. Rafe gave a weak chuckle. It was the first sign of sentience she'd had from him in hours. She couldn't help but be delighted. She ruffled his hair. "You'll be fine," she told him. "Just don't go anywhere."

He closed his eyes and waved her off.

Carrie left him under the tree and trudged wearily toward the road. To her left, sand stretched down to the aquamarine water like a soft golden beige carpet. She longed to take off her sandals and walk down to the sun-sparkled water. The sand would be warm and soft beneath her toes, restful for her tired feet. She'd always liked it here, but right now she didn't have time to linger and be nostalgic. She kept on walking. The upper reaches of the beach were dotted with tiny ramshackle buildings. The little buildings made their corner of the beach look like a miniature refugee camp, but in fact they were cabanas the locals rented to the more nature-loving poor student element of the tourist population. The cabanas offered no amenities; they were really no more than a roof over one's head, but they had charm if one didn't mind roughing it.

The ruins of a Mayan temple rose dramatically above the

tree line. Carrie gave it only a passing glance, then headed into town.

It wasn't until after Carrie left that Rafe became fully conscious. He remembered letting her leave, but after she was gone it occurred to him that he shouldn't have let her go. He had no guarantee that Carrie Robinson was going to come back. She had no reason to. He wouldn't blame her if she ran from the whole harrowing situation. She owed him nothing. His was not a trusting nature. He couldn't afford to be trusting, but he didn't get up and go after her. He briefly considered it, but decided to wait instead.

It had nothing to do with his physical state. Now that he was completely awake, he could function well enough despite exhaustion and physical discomfort. He stayed where he was and rested simply because he trusted her to come back to him. His tough-minded, practical thought processes were not involved in this decision. This was something his heart told him. He knew listening to his heart was a pure, unaffordable, weakness, but he gave in to it just the same. He even dozed off and dreamed.

Despite the heartfelt trust, he was still surprised when a foot nudged his thigh, and she said, "That's enough beauty sleep for you."

Carrie sensibly jumped sideways after she nudged Rafe because she was pretty sure how he would wake up. The fact that his hand reached automatically for the gun that was no longer tucked beneath his jacket proved her assumption to be correct. She might have given a smug nod if the move she correctly anticipated hadn't been the survival instinct of a dangerous animal.

"I took your big gun away before helping you up the side of the ravine."

Through the rush of adrenaline, through the jolt of pain set off by his quick movement, through the instant, jarring transition from sleep to wakefulness, underlying all that was the nearly overwhelming burst of joy—at hearing her voice though the tone was sarcastic, at seeing her though her look was critical, at her touch even if it was a sharp prod from her toe.

"What ravine?"

"You don't remember?"

"No."

"Good."

He was aware of talking to her, but the words were just cover while he tried to get himself under control. His reactions to her were too swift, too strong, too charged with longing and need and emotions he couldn't afford. There ought to be some way he could control it. He wasn't some teenage boy with no power over the surging hormones racing hotly through his blood. He was a grown man, used to being in complete command—of his emotions, his reactions, of any situation. But here he was, sprawled at her feet and looking up longingly despite a wicked headache and the sharp pain in his arm. He didn't even remember how he'd gotten hurt. And there she was, looking down at him with an expression full of concern that he didn't deserve, with fear deep in her eyes and body language that acknowledged the same unwanted desire.

Need pulsed between them for what seemed a long, intense time. Then Carrie blinked a moment later. She shivered in the heat of the day, but told herself it was from some errant breeze blowing in off the surf. Her focus, which had narrowed down to one specific point containing only herself and Rafe Castillo, widened out to take in the sights and sounds of the world around them. She took a deep breath and remembered who they were and what they were doing on a beach in Tulum.

"You all right?" she asked Rafe, hoping the huskiness of her voice didn't betray anything more than her very real tiredness. She didn't offer him a hand as he got to his feet. Something had changed so swiftly she had no way to comprehend it. All of her concern for an injured man fled. She'd been holding on to him, touching him, prodding, probing and manhandling him for hours. All that unthinking intimacy shifted to memories of her flesh against his, even though there had been nothing sensual in the contact at the time. She knew she didn't dare touch him now. She feared that the merest brush of his bare skin against hers would do her in. It was a foolish notion, and she forced it away. She made herself concentrate.

He stretched, rolled his shoulders, touched the makeshift bandage on his arm. "I'm okay." He blinked, looked puzzled, then grim. He lowered his eyebrows as he looked at her. "I remember most of what happened now."

She shrugged. "You bleeding?"

"No." He pointed at the bag. "What's that?"

"Supplies. Supper."

"Supplies? What kind of supplies?"

"Bandages. Peroxide. That sort of thing."

He made a face. "Peroxide hurts."

"It stings. You'll live through the experience."

He grimaced. "You aren't the one who's been shot."

"No. I'm the one who shot you."

"You don't have to sound so pleased about it."

Carrie felt the blush spread slowly through her, but she refused to look away or apologize no matter how guilty she suddenly felt. Feeling guilty about shooting him was a much easier emotion to handle than the constant, unreasonable compulsion to knock the man to the ground and have her way with him. "Come on." She walked onto the beach, not looking to see if he followed.

He caught up to her before she'd gone more than a few feet. He put his hand on her arm. "Where are we going?"

"I rented a cabana for the night." To her it sounded like

an invitation. She just hoped it didn't sound that way to him. Because it wasn't. Really. And to think a couple of hours ago he'd barely been awake. It looked like the shock of the fall had more than worn off.

Rafe tried not to sigh. It looked like another night spent out in the wet heat of the Quintana Roo spring. This time with sand and pounding surf as an added bonus, along with a headache, the pain from a wounded arm and the sarcasm of a justifiably resentful woman. Another night of temptation. If he was lucky, the pain would be enough to keep the longing at bay. He doubted it. It had been a hell of a day, but time and rest had helped him recover.

He tried not to complain as Carrie turned and walked away through the shimmer of heat undulating up off the sand. If truth be told, he hated the local climate. He wanted to get back to Los Angeles, or at least some place where the heat was dry, the beer cold, the population center densely high-tech urban. Instead, he was stuck in the out-of-the-way tourist destination of Tulum. Anyone else might have found the setting, and the company, romantic.

He watched Carrie's gently swaying movement as she walked across the sand. Maybe he wasn't here for romance, but he had to admit that there was one bit of scenery he appreciated. The thought of another night alone with her held as much anticipation as it did frustration. Even though he couldn't succumb to the desire to touch her, he couldn't get enough of looking at her, of being with her. She'd be gone from his life soon enough, he thought as she paused to take off her sandals and bury her toes in the golden sand. He might as well soak in as many memories of being with Carrie Robinson as he could. When she tossed her hair and turned her head to look at him, he knew that he couldn't possibly be seeing enticement in her glance, but his heart wanted to see it. He hurried to catch up with her.

"We could go to a hotel," he suggested as he followed

her down the beach. He felt the heat of the sand through the soles of his shoes. This place was very different from the inland rain forest, and he was grateful for the change. If he had to be hot, he might as well be dry. The sunlight burned down on his head and shoulders. He brushed hair out of his face and breathed in the salty air. He supposed the place was picture-postcard gorgeous, but the beauty was lost on him.

She gave him a caustic look over her shoulder. If there had been a hint of sultry invitation there a moment ago, it was gone now. "The hotels are all booked. This was the best I could do."

He caught up and put a hand on her shoulder. "I know you did. I'm sorry."

Her expression softened. "Does it hurt much? Because if you're being petulant because you're in pain, that's okay. But if you're just being a jerk—"

"It's because I'm in terrible pain," he broke in, though he couldn't keep from smiling as he said it. He stroked her cheek and brushed his hand across the side of her neck.

"You're definitely feeling better." When his fingers would have lingered, she moved away. Rafe sighed, then followed where she led.

The cabana she'd rented was on the very edge of the high-tide line, a stick structure more suitable to the second of the three little pigs than human habitation. "I've had bigger doghouses," Rafe remarked as Carrie opened the flimsy door.

"Then you must have had some pretty big dogs. This place isn't so bad." She ducked inside. "I can almost stand up in here."

Rafe followed her in, then sat down quickly on the sand floor rather than try to straighten his hunched posture. He crossed his legs, thought better of leaning against the fragile wall and asked, "What do we sleep on?"

Carrie rummaged around in her bag and brought out a bundle of blue-and-pink mesh. "Ever sleep in a hammock?"

He groaned. "Say it isn't so, Dr. Robinson." He looked critically at the walls. "No way you can hang a hammock in here. The place will fall down on our heads."

"These cabanas are a lot more sturdy than they look," Carrie assured him. "I worked on a dig near here when I was a grad student. I've spent a lot of weekends holed up in a cabana on this beach. Once during a tropical storm, I was scared to death I was going to get blown away, but the cabana didn't budge." She felt around the walls until she found hooks for the hammock and quickly strung it up. "I've had plenty of practice with these," she replied to Rafe's curious look.

"Just one?" he asked.

"It's big enough for both of us," she promised him. "But don't get any ideas."

He chuckled. "I've got plenty of ideas, Carrie." Despite his laugh, his words were serious.

She sat down beside him and sighed. "Me, too."

Rafe rubbed his jaw thoughtfully, then asked, "Should we talk about this?"

"No."

He echoed her sigh. "Okay."

"There's nothing to talk about."

"True."

"And guys would rather do it than talk about it, right?"

"I know I certainly would."

"Then it's settled."

"Definitely." Rafe's brows lowered in confusion. "What is?"

"Our talking about not talking about it."

He put his good arm around her shoulders. She leaned against him, but only for a moment. She pulled her bag to her, leaving a trail in the sand floor. She opened it and began to unpack it.

"Candles and matches. T-shirts. Toothpaste and brushes. Soap. Large, ugly gun. Small, ugly gun. At least we'll be well armed if there's an amphibious invasion." She glanced at him. "It's a good thing I keep my credit cards in my pockets or we'd be starving in the dark and sleeping on the beach."

"We are sleeping on the beach."

"Yes, but with a roof over our heads."

He glanced up. "More or less."

"Humph. If I was with anyone but you, I'd call this a romantic adventure."

"Romantic adventures," he pointed out, "are the memory's way of recalling misery in a more pleasant light."

"Very philosophical."

"I think I heard it on a sitcom."

"You watch too much television."

"You'll have to improve my education, Dr. Robinson."

"I could lecture you on the Mayan blood rituals, but it'd just give you nightmares."

"I have enough of those already, thank you." The words were out before he could even think about them, and the honesty of what he'd said left Rafe appalled. But, why should he try to hide that truth from her? She'd been all too involved in the reactions from one of his nightmares last night.

Carrie chose to ignore Rafe's words, to stop herself from asking any questions. The temptation to get personal with this man was too strong. Better to let it go before she found herself entangled in a conversation that was best avoided. Emotional involvement was not an option, she reminded herself yet again. She continued unpacking their supplies.

She handed him a container of bottled water. Then she opened a pill bottle. "It's amazing what you can get over the counter in some places." She spilled three capsules into her palm and held them out to Rafe. "Take these."

He looked at her suspiciously. "What are they?"

"Perfectly legal painkillers."

"I don't like drugs."

"You're a drug dealer."

"That's why I don't like drugs."

"Don't be a baby, take the pills!" Carrie shouted. She was well aware of sounding like an exasperated mother. It didn't help that Rafe laughed at her attitude. She dumped them into his palm. "Do it, Castillo!"

"I'll take the pills, Carolina." He downed them on a long gulp of water. Then sighed. "Maybe they'll make me less grumpy."

"Maybe you should take the bottle, then."

He quirked an eyebrow at her. "You trying to poison me?"

"I've considered it."

Neither of them spoke for a while. Carrie placed candles around the little room, standing them up in the sand. With plenty of light still coming in through the open door, she didn't bother lighting any just yet. She left a pack of matches next to the candle nearest the door, then looked at Rafe. He leaned back tentatively. When the building didn't fall down, he rested his broad shoulders against the wall. The cabana was small; Rafe's large presence made it seem even smaller. He looked tired, but not quite so drained and wasted as he had a few hours ago.

"Painkillers must be working," she observed.

"They're working."

He opened his eyes. Their amber gold hue caught the fading glow of the sunlight. They seemed to gleam out of the dark at her. The intensity of his expression made it impossible for her to look away.

After a tense and heated silence, she managed to croak out, "What?"

"Why didn't you just leave me? Why don't you leave me?" He pointed toward the cabana door. "Run for you life, Carolina. I won't try to stop you."

It was a generous impulse, but momentary, she was certain. He had to do what Torres wanted if *he* wanted to stay alive. He'd recall that soon enough. She did look toward the doorway. For a moment, she did toy with the temptation to run toward some illusion of safety. Some *other* illusion of safety that didn't have Rafe Castillo in it. Then responsibility and duty reared their ugly heads and she said, "If it was just my life on the line, I'd be long gone, Castillo."

One moment he was leaning against the wall, obviously tired, looking relaxed. The next moment he was looming before her, grasping her arm tightly to pull her close, his size and strength overwhelming. The sheer fury he radiated overwhelmed her. The heat of it robbed her of air. "What are you talking about? What is that bastard holding over your head?"

The anger wasn't at her. It was for her. This realization sent such a strong wave of emotion through her that it made her dizzy. She thought for a moment that she was going to faint, but her luck wasn't that good. She wasn't able to just pass out and escape having to deal with her own feelings—or him.

Rafe shook her, just a little. "Tell me how Torres forced you into this?"

His concern touched her—then it rubbed against all the wounds inflicted on her in the past several days. She pushed at him, but wounded or not, he was as immovable as a rock. "Why should it matter to you?"

"It matters." His voice was low, intense and full of pain. Pain that was for her, she thought, though that made no sense. For all the madness of it, she didn't balk when his good arm came around her and he drew her against his chest.

"Tell me," he urged.

She sighed. It was a deep, bone-rattling sigh, and Rafe felt it as much as she did. For a moment it was as if they were one body, one soul. It affected him as nothing ever had before. It was as if from this moment on she would never stop being a part of him.

She said, "Torres told me he'd kill everyone who works for me." She looked up at him, dark eyes bleak. "I have to go through with it. Good people will die if I don't."

Rafe went very still, his face losing all expression. He nodded. "Torres is desperate enough, cruel enough, to do it." His voice held no emotion. *This is my fault,* he thought. He'd slowly, carefully, insidiously destroyed Torres's organization. He'd made an already dangerous man a desperate one, as well.

He hated the reminder when Carrie said, "Torres wouldn't do it. You would." Despite the edge of contempt in her voice, she didn't try to move out of his comforting embrace.

"No, *querida,*" he answered. "Not me. That's one order I wouldn't obey. I didn't come home to Oro Blanco to help kill the people there." That was the exact opposite of why he'd taken the assignment. "It won't happen," he promised her. "I won't let it happen."

This time she did pull away from him. "As long as I do what I'm told."

"As long as you do as I tell you," he replied. "I'll keep you safe."

She knelt back on the sand. "Right. Sit down, shut up and let me look at your arm."

Her tone brooked no argument, so Rafe took a seat beside her on the soft floor. "This is going to hurt, isn't it?"

he asked as she took out bandages and a small bottle of peroxide.

"If I can help it."

"You're so *mean* to me."

"Don't tease, Castillo. I can't deal with it right now. Take off your shirt."

He didn't make even one single, solitary suggestive remark, tempting though it was. He did manage to struggle out of his shirt without asking for help. "Arm's bleeding again," he pointed out when he was done.

"Good."

"Mean. Evil. Wicked. That's what you are."

"Takes one to know one." He didn't dare argue with that as she moved forward to look at his arm. "You call that blood? Ha." She wiped off the smear of red on his skin, then pressed a pad soaked in peroxide to the small wound. He winced.

Carrie very firmly concentrated on what she was doing. She was supposed to be tending to the man's arm. So she looked at his arm and not the beautifully muscled expanse of his bare chest.

It was unfair, a bad guy having a chest like that. And that throat. His strong neck drove her crazy. His jawline was equally annoying in its firm, stubborn perfection. And those eyes. Those full, sensual lips. He had no business or right being so gorgeous. He had great thighs...and the way he moved. No man that big should be so graceful. Not that he was graceful at the moment. At the moment, she reminded herself, he was a tired, injured man slumped against a stick wall.

"How's your head feel?" She was aware of how tight her voice sounded, of the ache of longing deep inside her. As unwanted as it was, that ache was not going to go away. Not only wasn't it going to go away, the need for this man had become an essential part of her. A part that needed to be excised, cauterized, but there was nothing she could do about it right now.

"Better." The blow to his head when he'd fallen had done more damage than the minor graze from Carrie's accidental shot. Rest and the painkillers she'd given him were doing a good job of fixing the problem. "No concussion."

"And how would you know?"

"Had one before. This feels better. Just got a little disoriented there for a while." He smiled at her. "I'm not disoriented now, but I am hungry." He was lying about the disorientation, but it didn't come from a blow on the head. He'd been knocked completely out of orbit from the first moment he saw Carrie Robinson.

"Hold on. I'll feed you as soon as I can see what's in the bag." Carrie lit a match and moved around the shack, lighting the candles she'd placed in the sand earlier. The place took on a magical look as the golden light began to dance and flicker. Rafe couldn't help but smile at the change in the place. It was impossible to think of this atmosphere as anything but romantic.

Once she'd lit all the candles, Carrie reached into her seemingly bottomless bag and brought out their food supply. Then she retreated to a candlelit corner and ate her meal in silence. She looked sad, Rafe thought, tired, and far too thoughtful. He wanted to ask her what was on her mind, but felt that she didn't want to break the silence.

He wondered if she realized how beautiful she looked in the ethereal light. Her hair hung in dark, tangled curls around her luminous face. Rafe found himself wishing she'd pull her grandmother's hairbrush out of the big bag. Pity it had been lost along with all her precious artifacts. He ate the food she gave him without tasting it.

All he could think of was that the day had been hell, but he was happy because she'd been with him. He glanced around the tiny shack, made into a magical place by the fire of a few cheap candles. He sifted golden sand through his fingers and wished it was her golden skin he caressed. He watched her. He couldn't help but watch her as the heavy rhythm of the surf washed the beach just beyond the flimsy walls. Carrie Robinson, scientist, independent modern woman, gun-toting adventuress, his nemesis and rescuer. She was strong, stubborn, determined, compassionate and funny—and as tough as she had to be. In the candlelight, she was soft skinned, darkly mysterious, utterly female. Every shadow and flicker of light across her skin, every slight movement, held out a sensuous promise.

The peaceful, exotic setting alone after a day so rife with danger should have made this seem like a time apart to Rafe, like some sort of fantasy too good to be true. It didn't. He felt like he'd come home.

That was the true fantasy, of course. This sense of utter rightness and contentment couldn't possibly be real. For now, for just this one night, he let himself believe that something so wonderful, something as completely right as the way he felt with this woman, could happen to him.

Carrie pretended that she didn't notice him staring at her. She pretended that she couldn't *feel* his gaze on her, as real, as intimate as any physical caress. It wasn't the candle flames that caused the temperature to rise in the cabana. The heat was inside her, the fierce desire growing constantly. Time ceased for her. Even though she didn't look at him, awareness of Rafe Castillo became her whole world. She had no idea how long she'd been sitting with her knees drawn up on the sand floor, staring at nothing, when Rafe spoke.

"You're not hungry?"

She was hungry all right. She realized she still held an unopened package of coriander cookies in her hands. She tossed them back into her bag, then moved past Rafe to the door.

"Where are you going?" he asked.

"Swimming," she answered, though her throat was so tight with the strain of wanting him that she could barely get the words out. He started to follow her. "Stay here!" she ordered, then managed to add more calmly, "you're tired. Rest. You've done enough swimming already today."

She was gone before he could answer, but at least he didn't follow her. When she came back, totally exhausted, her skin still damp with salty water, she found Rafe curled up in the sand, sleeping on the lightweight throw that had been one of the many purchases in the voluminous bag. His head rested on his outstretched arm, dark hair shadowing much of his face. He looked peaceful in sleep, fallen-angel beautiful. She was more than half-tempted to trace her fingers around the sensuous curve of his lips, to run her hands along the muscles of his bare arms and thighs. She fought the urge and stepped over him to climb into the hammock instead, taking off her shorts and top and arranging herself carefully in the airy, woven bed swinging gently above the floor.

She lay on her side, wearing only her underwear, unable to sleep for a while despite having deliberately tried to exhaust herself to the point of oblivion. She found that she missed the comfort of sleeping in his arms, even if she knew that comfort was false. She'd never actually enjoyed sharing her space with anyone before meeting Rafe Castillo. It was ridiculous, really. She should not enjoy sharing space with him. The man was big. He suffered from nightmares. He kept guns concealed in undisclosed areas of his person. He was a criminal.

She slept like a baby when she was near him—when she wasn't fighting the urge to have her way with him. It made no sense. Staying awake, staring at him like a besotted fool in the light from the candles, made no sense, either, not when she'd worked so hard to get her body past the sheer physical craving and into a state where she could rest. Eventually, she went to sleep, but she was unaware where consciously watching him left off and dreaming of him began.

Rafe had awakened when she came into the cabana, but made no sound or movement as she sidled past. He listened to the creak and soft swoosh of the string hammock as she got into it, and then came the soft breathing of sleep after a longer while. He enjoyed those ordinary, domestic noises, the peacefulness of sharing a room—a bed—with someone else. He hadn't been aware of the extent of his loneliness until circumstances forced them to be together. Now that they were together...well, being apart from Carrie Robinson was not something he even wanted to think about. He didn't want to think at all. He was comfortable lying on his bed of sand. Having Carrie nearby made it easy for him to drift back to sleep.

Chapter 8

Rafe had no idea how much later it was when her muffled groan woke him. He was on his feet by the time the sound came again, hunched over to keep his head from hitting the low ceiling. Carrie cried out, and he was by her side.

"Bad dream, *querida?*"

His answer came as a small, shuddering sigh and a wild shake of her head. She sat up in the swinging hammock just as he reached out to touch her cheek. He didn't mean to, but his fingertips brushed across her breast as she moved. The accidental contact sent desire flaring through him. It was Carrie who grabbed his wrist and pulled him closer, her nipple hard and hot against his palm. He couldn't help but gently stroke the hard, sensitive nub he felt beneath the thin cloth of her bra. The sound she made in response was one of pure animal pleasure.

It was Carrie's other hand that came around his neck and pulled him down on top of her. He reeled forward, out of balance and out of control. He heard the threatening creak of the flimsy walls as he came down hard on the hammock. He felt as though he were floating on air with only Carrie's warm, soft body between himself and the ground.

Rafe was falling. Not to the ground, but into the passion he'd denied since the day he'd first seen her. Hunger overtook reason. The fresh, female scent of her skin drove him to distraction. Last night he'd been able to pull back from the brink. Tonight he was lost from the moment her needy cry woke him from his own fevered dreaming. All he wanted was to taste her, to bury his face in the soft swell of her breasts and breathe her in.

As if in response to his wishes, she pulled his head closer. Her other hand traced fire down his chest, to his belly and lower. Her hips lifted against his as he hungered to bury himself deep within her.

He didn't know whether she was awake or asleep, but he was powerless to resist the urgent demand of his own need to press his hardness against her. Her skin was hot beneath his, satin smooth and pliant. She tasted of salt when his lips touched the base of her throat. She cried out again at the kiss, but the sound was full of hunger that shook him to the core.

Carrie came awake to find her fingers curled in Rafe's hair. To find her other hand hovering at the elastic band of his briefs. Her pulse raced madly. She could barely breathe. What had been an erotic dream meshed seamlessly into erotic reality, but she didn't have even a moment of confusion. She only knew that the reality of his touch was far better than the images that aroused her as she slept.

"Rafael." She breathed his name, fervent as a prayer. When he raised his head from her breast, she kissed the warm spot where the pulse beat in his neck, and her lips moved on to brush his cheeks, his chin, his wide, welcoming mouth. They clung to each other, tongues exploring. His fingers stroked the hard peaks of her breasts while her hands grasped his narrow hips, pulling him closer, the heat deep inside her craving, begging, for release. She could feel his hardness pressing against her thigh, and her hand sought and circled the heavy shaft as he trailed kisses across her neck and breast. He gasped at her touch, back arching.

He said something, voice thick with passion, question, request, demand. She answered, the words a wild mix of Spanish, English and Mayan, acquiescence, plea, entreaty.

They understood each other perfectly. They didn't require words. The touch and taste of each other were all they needed. Desire made perfect communication.

A hammock was no place to make love. They tumbled onto the sand instead.

Carrie landed on top and stayed there as she kissed him from neck to navel. He'd stripped down to his underwear to sleep. So had she. That made for very little between them and the places their hands and lips sought.

Last night he'd touched her while he dreamed. He'd touched her many nights in his dreams. Her dreams brought them together tonight.

"I'm not dreaming now."

Her lips brushed his cheek, her breath mingling with his. "No." Her mouth covered his.

His hands trailed over her hips, skimmed her breasts, undid the fastening of her bra. He stroked and teased her freed nipples while their tongues delved and feverishly explored each other's mouth.

Carrie trembled from his skilled touch, a touch that both satisfied and intensified the growing craving in her blood. Fire arced between them, brought them together. The fire concentrated itself deep inside her, growing stronger with every kiss, every flicker of his tongue over her heated flesh, with every arousing touch. She wasn't sure when they changed positions, how she ended up beneath him, her body cradled between the soft sand and his hard masculinity. She wasn't aware of how they'd both become completely naked, but only of the necessity of being naked. All she felt was complete and utter arousal. She was conscious of the small, needy sounds issuing from deep in her throat, the fire in her blood, of clinging to his hard-muscled, trembling flesh as he covered her, of lifting herself to eagerly accept the quick, deep thrust that bound them together.

She cried out as he entered her, then wrapped her legs around his narrow waist. He moved inside her and murmured a name.

"Carolina, *querida*."

In this time, this place, this wild moment, it was her name, who she was for him. Passion burned away all she had been. For him she was Carolina—wild, impassioned, wholly abandoned. Nothing mattered but the way he filled, and fulfilled, her.

His words drowned out the small internal voice that told her this was wrong and she moved to meet each deep, hard thrust. She soared, gloried, her senses shattered, and she begged for more. Her muscles clenched and tensed around him with exquisite abandon as each powerful stroke brought her closer to the edge. She soared again, joining him in explosive release as his body stiffened. He spoke her name once more as he collapsed on top of her, his face nestling in the sweat-damp cleft between her breasts.

His breath was warm against her skin, his weight welcome. She cradled his head, held him tight, then fell into a satiated, dreamless, marvelous sleep.

There was one candle still burning. It had tilted sideways from where it was stuck in the sand floor of the cabana. Having woken from a light sleep, Carrie watched the tiny golden flame as it sputtered and twisted in the faint breeze that sneaked in through cracks in the flimsy walls. She listened to the roar of the nearby surf and the soft breathing of the man who sheltered her in his arms.

Shelter.

It was false and foolish to think so, but it clearly felt like it. She'd acknowledged the physical attraction all along. She'd thought honesty about her base and basic reactions to the sheer masculinity of Rafael Castillo would save her from any sort of emotional reaction to the man. Now she wasn't so sure. Which was really stupid of her, all things considered.

She had just spent the most wonderful hours of her life making love—not having sex, but making love—to the man who could so easily kill her.

What kind of person would do a sick thing like that? She'd willingly, wantonly, thoughtlessly, had the most intense erotic experience possible with a man she'd seen kill another living being, a man who was part of a drug cartel, a man who held her prisoner.

She had never been so disgusted with anyone in her life, but it wasn't Rafael Castillo she was disgusted with.

Unbidden, horribly, the things the old lady had said to her before she died rose out of the place Carrie had buried them. "Hot-blooded little bitch. I remember how that woman seduced my grandson. She didn't think about consequences. Your kind never do. You look just like her with your big tits and hot eyes and sultry mouth. Whore. Mindless little animal."

She'd been an old woman on her deathbed—senile and raving. She hadn't known what she was saying. She'd been a great lady. A grande dame. A matriarch of one of the oldest families in North America. Even age and impending death couldn't destroy her arrogant, elegant beauty. It had taken only a few minutes alone with her in the private hospital room for the old woman to rip her twelve-year-old great-granddaughter to shreds. She'd said other things. Awful, ugly, crude words—at the time Carrie hadn't even known what most of them meant. She'd still never been able to forget them. Every time she'd encountered one of those words as an adult, the memory had surfaced. And with it, the denial.

Carrie had never in her life told anyone what the old woman had said. When she'd run out of the room, everyone had thought her tears were of inconsolable grief. Better to let them think that than to tell them the truth. Better to keep her great-grandmother's words hidden inside than to speak them out loud—and perhaps see the flickers of agreement deep in the eyes of other members of the oh so discreetly reticent and polite Robinson clan. Carrie had always believed herself loved, accepted. After that day, she never quite believed it anymore.

Right now, lying on the sand, after a totally thoughtless act of unprotected sex, it was easy for her to agree with every hateful word her great-grandmother had said. No thought of consequences had entered her head. That had never happened to her before. She'd always been careful—until her wanton nature had finally caught up with her. She'd always told herself that the old lady was wrong, but at the moment she felt too weak and tired, betrayed by her own visceral response to Rafael Castillo, to dispute the matriarch's assessment of her. Her heart ached, her head was full of confused thoughts, and her stomach curdled with the disgrace of what she'd done. She knew herself to be a strong, capable, intelligent woman, but she found herself sobbing with the shamed pain of that hurt little girl.

Rafe woke to the sound of Carrie crying. No, not the sound. He felt her crying, felt her desperation and pain seeping into him, covering them both like a heavy, stifling blanket. His head and arm hurt, but it was her crying that woke him. His pain was bearable. Hers was not.

Even before he asked her what was wrong, he knew it

was his fault. He didn't even have to ask. Carrie was a good woman, a brave, ethical person who felt as if she'd just made the biggest, most morally degenerate, mistake of her life. The worst part was that she'd done it of her own free will. There'd been no coercion, nothing even vaguely resembling rape. She'd made intensely passionate love to him and was now regretting it with every fiber of her being. He didn't blame her. He wouldn't think much of himself if he'd just made love to a murdering drug dealer, either.

He didn't think much of himself for letting her think he was a murdering drug dealer for as long as he had.

Damn.

"I'm a fool."

Carrie heard Rafe say something, but only the sound of his voice, not the words, penetrated her awareness. She *felt* his words, his presence, deep in her bones. It was a presence she needed and also one she needed to escape, but when she tried to move away, he pulled her closer.

"Look at me, *querida*."

Though he gently stroked her face, she couldn't bear to open her eyes. Though she tried to turn her head away, he kept her face between his big hands. When he sat up, she was forced to sit up, as well.

"Don't be afraid," he told her. She hated the concern in his voice. "Look at me."

She couldn't resist anything he urged for long. She looked at him, hating him, and herself. "What?" The word came out an angry, bitter snarl. "Why don't you just go to sleep and leave me alone?"

"Because I have to apologize to you." He stroked the tears on her cheeks away with his thumbs. "How can I sleep knowing you're hurting? How can I sleep when you're hurting and it's my fault?" He couldn't bring himself to believe, or say, that their making love shouldn't have happened.

His gaze caught hers. It was impossible to look away from those expressive amber eyes. Eyes that were full of remorse and an expression she could easily mistake for love. She swallowed hard, but couldn't help but answer honestly. "You didn't hurt me."

"I know." He gave the slightest of self-deprecating smiles. "I'm a gentle lover. I know that. That isn't how I've hurt you. You're angry at yourself. How could you make love to a drug-dealing, murdering scumbag? You're not that kind of woman."

The fact that he understood exactly what she felt struck her deeply, somewhere around the heart. She couldn't help but laugh. "Apparently I am."

He shook his head. "No, you're not. I'm not the man you think I am."

"But you're a hell of a man."

Rafe's hands slid to her shoulders. He shook them slightly, ignoring the sting of her caustic tone as he concentrated on getting her full attention. "You've got every right to be angry with me, but you don't have to be angry with yourself." He took a deep breath. He looked around, almost as if he expected someone to overhear. This was not the time or place to cling to furtive habits. "Darling, this isn't easy for me to say. I've been under cover so long I can barely get the words out."

"Under cover?" She tilted her head skeptically to one side. She knew what she'd heard, but didn't know what he meant. The sand was gritty beneath her knees, the heat of the room clung to her naked skin, and the surf roared and pounded outside as though it was trying to get in. All this added to her confusion. Maybe she hadn't heard him right. "Under cover?"

He took another swift breath. Though there was only a little light from the one burning candle and his skin was a warm, rich brown, she thought she saw him blush. His words came out in a rushed whisper. "Undercover DEA operative. I'm not a drug dealer. Bringing Torres down is my assignment. I never meant to drag you into this. I had no idea what he intended when he sent me to get you. I swear to God that I would never do anything to hurt you."

"DEA?" she asked, both confused and suspicious.

"Drug Enforcement Agency."

She drew back from him. "I know what the initials mean."

Rafe folded his arms over his chest and looked at her questioningly. "You sound more suspicious than pleased, *querida.*"

"Don't you *querida* me, Castillo," she responded sharply. She put her hands on her hips. "What are you talking about?"

"I'm talking about being an undercover cop," he answered just as sharply. He was very aware of the fact that the woman who confronted him so belligerently was quite naked and that he craved her body like a drug. She seemed unaware that neither of them was clothed. He tried to ignore it himself. Convincing her of who he was more important than looking at her. He still couldn't help saying, "An unclothed undercover cop."

Carrie gasped, blinked, then dived for her bag. She snatched up his underwear and tossed it to him before she pulled on her own panties and a T-shirt.

"Don't you believe me?" he asked as she dressed. He gestured toward the spot where they'd made love. "Do you think I'm trying to salve your conscience somehow by pretending to be a DEA operative? Would a real drug dealer bother to lie to a woman he'd just—pardon me for putting it this way, *querida*—but would a real drug dealer feel any obligation to a woman he'd just screwed? Which was not," he added hastily, "what we did."

Carrie ducked her head and mumbled, "Maybe."

"What?" His indignation reverberated around the small room.

"Maybe," she repeated. She looked at him. "The drug dealer might try to be nice if he was a vaguely ethical, kind of romantic, protective...sort of person."

Rafe's hands landed on Carrie's shoulders once more. "Carrie, please believe me," he said earnestly. "I live among them, I sometimes identify with them, but I'm not one of them." Carrie didn't respond for a while, but he felt the tension growing in her, the tightening of her muscles under his hands. He became afraid of what she was thinking, even more afraid of what she was feeling. "What's the matter?" he asked when the silence grew unbearable.

She lifted her head to glare at him. Dark eyes flashed. "You're a DEA undercover agent?" she demanded, more with fury than relief. "You're a good guy?"

He tightened his hands on her shoulders. When he would have drawn her into an embrace, she shook them off. "*Sí, querida.* Yes."

Her eyes blazed. "You let me think...you never said...how could...?" She held up hands that were balled into tense, tight fists. "You let me think I was falling in lo—attracted to—a bad guy?"

He shrugged. "I'm not a good man. I'm just not as bad as I let you believe." That she had almost admitted falling in love with him was not lost on Rafe. That she chose to deny it was bothersome, but not the issue that needed dealing with just now. Truth. Honesty. Reality. Those were the things that had to be settled first.

"I should have actually been aiming that gun when I shot you," she snarled.

Rafe sat back on his heels. He half expected her to strike out at him. Her reaction stunned him. "I thought you'd be pleased."

Carrie could practically feel her blood pressure rising

with her anger. "Pleased! Pleased? After all you've—we've... Why didn't you tell me this a week ago?"

He put his hands back on her shoulders—shoulders that were shaking with fury. This time he didn't let her go. He looked deep into her very angry eyes. He said softly, but very firmly, "Because we've only known each other a couple of days, *querida*."

"A couple of..." Carrie blinked. He could see the stunned confusion reeling in her eyes.

He nodded. "I don't know what time it is now, Carolina, but I know it's been less than seventy-two hours since Torres sent me to get you."

A couple of days.

Carrie couldn't believe that she'd known Rafael Castillo less than a lifetime. It was hard to think around her anger, hard to sort through the confusing revelations. She forced herself to do it anyway, though she had to close her eyes to keep from looking at Rafe to do it. Let's see, she'd been talking to Beltrano and... One by one, she ran through all the incidents that had totally changed her life and discovered that Rafe was right. It had only been two days, closer to three considering how late in the night it was, since she'd been drawn into Rafe's dark and dangerous world.

A world he told her he wasn't really a part of.

Maybe her instincts hadn't been wrong. Maybe her great-grandmother hadn't been right. Maybe he was someone she'd instinctively known she could trust.

And maybe he was lying. Why would he lie? She didn't know, but why did drug dealers do things? Out of greed, the quest for power. Maybe Rafe had his own scheme to take over from Torres. Maybe he wanted her to trust him so it would be easier for him to use her. She wanted to believe him. She was afraid her heart already believed him—no matter what he said. It was her head she had to keep clear, her scientist's objectivity that she had to use to guard her vulnerable heart.

Besides, he should have told her sooner. It hurt like hell that he hadn't trusted her with his secret identity before now.

"Why?" she asked though she knew she sounded like a hurt child when she said it. "Why didn't you tell me?" A sharp stab of anger jabbed through her distress. "I've been so frightened. So confused." She wasn't just angry at him while admitting this, but at herself. She told herself that she didn't want his comfort or reassurance. She told herself that she had every right to be angry and to stay angry.

When his arms came comfortingly around her, she couldn't deny that she was lying to herself about not wanting his consolation. It felt so good to be held by him. It felt just as good to slip her arms around him, to hug him tightly to her, to rest her head on his broad shoulder and breathe in the warm, masculine scent of him. Even if it was all false, she couldn't help but feel protected in his arms.

It didn't stop her from being angry, though. "Why didn't you tell me?" she demanded again.

"Maybe I should have." He kissed the top of her head, then the tip of her ear. "It never seemed necessary," he confided in a whisper. "If you'd known, you might have made a slip. A slip that could have gotten you killed. I'm responsible for your safety, *querida*. Even if it means your hating me, I have to keep you safe. I can't let you go," he added, because this was a time for complete honesty, "but I swear to keep you safe."

"You can't let me go?" Carrie drew her head back enough to look at Rafe's face. His hands moved over her, stroking her shoulders, her back, gentling her, but not enough to distract her from suspiciously asking, "Why not?"

"Because Torres is a threat to you, a threat to the people

you're protecting." He sighed. "And because you're the person he wants to pick up the suitcase in Washington. A suitcase that contains millions of dollars. I need that pickup to lead to the people who launder his drug money. I've made sure Torres has lost a lot of money in the past year, but I won't be able to completely destroy his operation until the American money people are arrested."

Millions of dollars, Carrie thought. Money laundering. Arrests. It all sounded very convincing. He looked and sounded so earnest. Maybe she just wanted to believe him too much. She believed the suitcase she was supposed to return to Torres contained millions of dollars. She just didn't know whether she could believe that Rafe didn't want to use her as a willing dupe to get the money for himself. It would be easier for him to have a comrade than a hostage. She hated being so cynical. It wasn't easy for her to feel that way, but recent events had left her with very few emotional defenses. If cynicism was the only weapon she had, it was up to her to use it.

It was hard to be anything but pliant and needy with him touching her the way he was. It was hard not to trust him when her arms were wrapped around his neck and her breasts were pressed against his broad chest. She became aware of the compact muscles of his bare thighs against hers, of his hand cupping her buttocks, of the fingers of his other hand tracing soft, slow circles down her spine.

Rafe found that at some point he'd lost track of what he was saying to Carrie as heat rose in his blood once more. They'd made love once, and once only made him hungry for more. Longing distracted him though he didn't mean for it to do so. The last candle had long gone out, but darkness only made touching her more intimate.

He wanted nothing more than to kiss her as he leaned her back onto the sand and make love to her one more time. He forced his hands to drop to his sides instead. He moved away from her, then became aware again of the aches in his arm and head as they separated. Somehow, he lost track of his injuries while there was the least contact between them. He was glad of the reminder now. It served as distraction and forced him to recall what they'd been through and why.

She was a witness. His job was to protect her. He was a professional, never mind that he'd forgotten that not so long ago. He wouldn't forget again. He wanted to be with her. In an unbelievably short time, she'd become desperately important to him, but now was not the time to give in to what he wanted. He sighed and clasped his hands behind his back to avoid any more temptation.

Carrie felt bereft and lost outside of the shelter of Rafe's embrace, though she refused to let herself feel that way for more than a moment. The fact was, she had let herself get lost in sensation and had no idea how long it had been since the two of them had said a word. If Rafe hadn't stopped, she probably wouldn't have, either.

She sank wearily onto the bed of sand. He hovered over her, barely visible in the almost complete darkness. She looked up and asked, "Why'd you stop?"

He settled down on the cover beside her, but not touching. He said only, "Go to sleep."

His tone brooked no argument, and she was physically and emotionally exhausted enough to do just that.

Rafe woke to the scents of salt air and melted wax, and to an empty spot beside him on the sand. It was his body that missed her before he was conscious of being alone. His hand reached out to touch her even before he opened his eyes. When he touched nothing but empty air and soft sand, a jolt of panic and disappointment brought him swiftly and completely awake. Sharing space with this woman, even when he wasn't holding her protectively in his arms, brought him more peace than he'd ever known. When she wasn't there, he missed her, even in his sleep. Awake, the need to be near her was even stronger. Sitting up, he instantly looked for her.

She wasn't in the cabana, and the door to the little shack was open. He felt a moment's fear that she might have fled, but when he went out into the bright glare of the morning sunlight, he found her sitting on the beach just a few feet from the tiny building, looking out at the peaceful aquamarine sea.

He paused before approaching her, taking a good, long look before disturbing her reverie. He loved the warm, coppery glow of her skin and the riot of dark curls she'd pulled away from her face and fastened at the back of her head with a rubber band. He loved the way she sat, posture very straight, looking very prim and proper despite the fact that she was wearing khaki shorts and a painfully bright green T-shirt. He loved the contrast of Dr. Robinson and the wild, wanton and adventurous Carolina. He loved her.

He just didn't know what he was going to do about it.

Just looking at her, not even touching her, made him as soft and tender and needy as a boy with his first love. He might as well have never been with another woman. He didn't care if he was ever with another one. He couldn't think why'd he'd want to be.

Rafe tried to hide all these emotions he shouldn't be feeling and couldn't express as he sat down in the sand beside her. He tried to cover his longing to take her in his arms and kiss the frown on her face away with humor. "You know who you remind me of?" he said. "Indiana Jones."

Carrie gave him a disgusted, sideways glance. "That's me, Rhode Island Robinson."

Rafe guessed she'd heard the comparison before and didn't like it. Then again, she probably hadn't had any ad-

ventures that warranted the comparison before she met him.
"Forgive me," he said, and meant it. He raked tousled hair
out of his face. "You're a serious scholar."

She drew her knees up and wrapped her arms around
them. "I'm an out-of-work one." She sighed and stared
out to sea again.

Rafe let the silence draw out between them while he took
inventory of his physical condition and tried not to feel
guilty about the loss of her precious cargo of artifacts. To
him, it was more important that he'd gotten her safely away
from the ambush. He touched his head and then his arm,
reminders of yesterday's violent encounter. He found that
he felt much better than a man who'd been shot and fallen
off a cliff had a right to. Maybe it was because the small
caliber bullet had barely grazed him, and the fall had really
been down the side of a ravine, not over a cliff. He chose
to think that Carrie's more or less tender ministrations made
all the difference in his quick recovery.

"You'll be happy to know I don't have a headache, *querida.*"

She continued looking at the waves. "I'm not."

"My arm barely hurts."

"That's too bad."

He wanted to get her full attention by taking her in his
arms and kissing her senseless. He settled for touching her
shoulder instead. She shrank away from even that light contact. "You mad at me?" he questioned.

Carrie almost smiled at the hurt-little-boy tone in his
voice. He was being cute, and it was driving her crazy. She
couldn't stop herself from turning her head to look at him.
He didn't look any different to her than he had yesterday—big, large-featured, boldly handsome, with a sinner's
mouth and a fallen angel's intense eyes. She wondered if
he should somehow look different, more heroic, more trustworthy. Problem was, he hadn't looked any less heroic or

trustworthy yesterday when she was convinced he was a different man entirely.

She still wasn't completely persuaded he wasn't who she thought he was yesterday. She hadn't loved him any less when she *knew* he was a drug dealer than she did now—when she wasn't sure whether he was or not. *It's still not love,* she told herself. *No matter who he is, it's still just lust, or some kind of hysterical reaction to the whole insane situation.*

Whatever her feelings really were, she shoved them to the back of her mind. She had a more immediate problem to deal with right now. There was something she'd woken up thinking about. Something she couldn't get out of her mind. Something she desperately needed.

She stood up and he followed suit. She looked him firmly in the eye though she had to look up several inches to do it. She put her hands on her hips. "I want my stuff back."

He put his hands on her shoulders. She tried unsuccessfully to shrug him off. "*Querida,* we don't have time for this."

Her expression was cold, completely intractable. She'd made up her mind what she was going to say while waiting for him to come out of the cabana. "This is the way it goes, Mr. DEA undercover cop. You figure out a way to get the Chalenque artifacts back from Munoz and Beltrano, or the deal is off."

"Your deal is with Torres," he reminded her bluntly. "Bring back his money or your crew dies. Remember?"

He felt her quiver with rage beneath his hands. Her eyes blazed. "And you're using me to catch him. Or is bringing his money back really what you're after? Or are you trying to steal it for yourself?" There was a note of hysteria beneath her accusing tone. "Are you just playing games to get me to trust you?"

He wanted to shake her, to kiss her—he didn't know

which. Her words tore at him. "Last night wasn't a game. I promise you that."

She didn't pay any attention to his sincerity. "Whom do you work for really? Torres or yourself? Are you really with the DEA?"

"Is this a test, then?" he demanded, his anger flaring to match hers. "You want me to prove myself to you by risking my assignment to get back a couple of tons of useless old stones?"

"They're not useless to me, Castillo."

He could have kicked himself. Talk about saying the wrong thing at the wrong time. He knew his thoughtless words were only going to serve to make her even more stubborn on the subject. Besides, getting the contents of the truck back wasn't totally about the pursuit of Mayan history, was it? This was mostly about them—about what was happening between her and him. It was a matter of trust. It was about truth. His word wasn't good enough. She was asking for some concrete evidence that he wasn't one of the bad guys. She didn't completely believe him. She was searching for a reason to trust him outside of what her own tangled emotions told her.

How could he blame her? He couldn't. Sometimes he couldn't be sure himself of who he was. How could he ask this woman who'd been threatened and terrorized and blackmailed to take him at just his word? He shouldn't take her lack of trust personally, but he did. It hurt that he had to prove himself to her. It stung his pride. Why should he have to justify himself to anyone?

When was the last time anyone had asked anything of him—other than to sell his soul for the sake of the assignment? It was a long time since he had been held accountable. It was an uncomfortable feeling.

It also sparked something else—something pleasurable deep inside him. He couldn't quite define it, but it was humbling, almost—holy. It was a longing to give this woman what she needed, to provide for her, to take care of her, to please her. To give her anything she asked for without wanting any reward other than to know it made her happy. Why shouldn't he give her the sun, the moon—or a truck full of Mayan artifacts—if it made her happy?

Maybe it *was* love.

Maybe he was crazy.

This did not bode well for the assignment. He risked blowing his cover. It slowed things down. He shouldn't give in to her unreasonable demand. He said, "I'll make a phone call."

She blinked. She expected more argument than this. "A phone call?"

He rubbed his jaw and became aware that he badly needed a shave. He smiled at Carrie. "A phone call. I'm going to need some help if I'm going to get your stuff back. I'm not a superman, you know." He gestured expansively. "Or would you rather have me face all those men in some macho action-movie gunfight all by myself? I will if you want me to," he added.

The fact that he gave her the most charming smile she'd ever seen after he said about the most stupid thing she'd ever heard made Carrie want to kick him. It also reminded her that she was demanding he do something dangerous. It didn't change her mind.

"You know people who'll help you?" Visions of an army of desperadoes rose in her mind.

He nodded. "*Sí.* I have a friend."

Even though her image of an army dwindled considerably at his comment, Carrie refused to give in to her nagging conscience. She hardened her heart and said, "Then I think you'd better make that phone call."

Chapter 9

She was a selfish fool. A complete idiot. What had she been thinking? How could she have let him go? Why had she made him go? Why hadn't she gone with him?

"Because he wouldn't let me go," she reminded herself as she paced restlessly once more between the road and the door of their cabana. She had no idea how many times she'd made the trip, but she was wearing a trail in the thick sand. "I should have gone with him."

They'd had quite a fight about her going with him. He'd turned out to be more stubborn and adamant about her staying and had used the threat of not getting the artifacts back at all if she didn't agree to stay out of harm's way. She'd had to give in. The fact that she'd sent him into harm's way didn't register until he'd disappeared down the road into town to make his phone call and do whatever he was going to do. As the hours dragged by, Carrie's obsession with recovering the stolen artifacts faded while her fear of Rafe getting hurt or killed grew. Maybe he really was a bad guy. Maybe he was just using her. Those maybes didn't matter. He mattered. So much that it frightened her. She shouldn't let him matter to her. He was using her. Even if he was exactly who he claimed to be, he was still using her.

Still, she was terrified of his being hurt. She hated having him out of her sight.

"I've just gotten used to him," she grumbled as she stopped by the side of the road and stared into the distance down its heat-haze-obscured length. She ignored the heat that radiated up from the sun-baked paving as she held her hand up to shade her eyes. *I was a reasonable, sane human being before I met him,* she reproached herself. *Now, here I am, forcing people into danger—when I'm not acting like a lust-crazed madwoman.* "What has that man done to me?"

Whatever it was, it had to stop. She had to get out of this insane situation and get her calm, conservative self back. She had her work to think of, her family and what they thought of her to consider. She had no room in her life for crazed behavior, lust or otherwise. She needed Rafael Castillo out of her life.

And why did that thought, sane and reasonable as it was, send an aching stab of pain through her?

"Stockholm Syndrome," she said decisively, then concentrated on watching the road instead of adding to her own confusion.

Several more hours passed. The day slowly inched toward sunset while she kept her eye on the road. Finally, she thought she saw a truck approaching. Though her heart raced at the sight, she knew that it didn't necessarily mean anything. Plenty of trucks used this road. Still, she waited, holding her breath, her stomach knotting, as the vehicle drew gradually closer.

It was a beautiful day in Tulum, hot and sunny after a

brief rain late in the morning. Carrie had paced even in the rain. She paid no attention to the tourists who flocked to the beach after the sun came out. She could hear people laughing and talking behind her, down near the water's edge. The carefree sounds only added to her nervousness. A car, going way too fast, passed the truck and threw up a spray of muddy water from a pothole in the road as it sped by the spot where she stood. She jumped back, but still got soaked. She sputtered with shocked anger and scrubbed at her face with the hem of her T-shirt.

By the time she'd wiped the dirty water out of her eyes, the truck was pulling to a halt on the side of the road nearby. From this distance, it looked more than familiar. It was indeed her truck, though it looked considerably the worse for wear. The front bumper was missing and the grill was smashed in. Was that a bullet hole in the passenger-side door?

She didn't want to think about it. She didn't care. When Rafe opened the door and hopped to the ground, all that mattered was the sight of him. She ran toward him, arms outstretched, but he was the one who snatched her up in a fierce embrace. They would have shared an equally fierce and passionate kiss if the sound of a deep chuckle from the man who came around from the driver's side of the cab had not made them both sharply turn their heads. Rafe's arms dropped to his sides while Carrie took a step back.

She stared at the dark-haired Anglo who approached them. He was handsome, lean, broad shouldered, with eyes as brown as dark chocolate. He looked familiar, and she wanted to tell him that he should stand up straighter. "Estaban Quarrels," she said. She looked from the other man to Rafe. "That's Estaban Quarrels." She pointed. "That's the drug dealer Manolo wanted to kill."

"He's my friend," Rafe told her. "Steve Quarrels."

"You called another rival drug dealer for help?" Her

reaction went beyond indignant and skipped straight to flabbergasted. "I thought you said you were..." She stopped herself from revealing that Rafe *might* be an undercover cop just short of blurting it out in front of Quarrels. Maybe Quarrels was Rafe's friend, but he wouldn't be a friend for long if he suspected Rafe was on the side of the angels. *If* Rafe was on anyone's side but his own, that is. All she knew was that whatever kind of man Rafael Castillo really was, she couldn't bear the idea of putting him in any more danger.

Quarrels smirked and brushed a thumb across his cheek. "Manolo and I had a talk," he told her. He had a deep, rumbling voice and he sounded cynically amused. "We're best friends now. In fact, he's decided to testify against Torres."

Rafe put his arm around her shoulders. While she stared in confusion at what the other man had just said, Rafe turned them to face Quarrels. "You didn't mention that before."

Quarrels shrugged. He patted the truck door. "You were too intent on getting this back to the girlfriend here to talk about other business."

Carrie waited for Rafe to deny any charge that she was his girlfriend, but he didn't contradict Quarrels. She didn't contradict him, either. She looked at her truck and spotted what were definitely bullet holes marring the already battered paint job, then she looked from one man to the other. They looked a bit battered, as well, she had to admit, though neither seemed to be wounded.

"How did you get my truck back?"

"Negotiation," Rafe answered.

"Liar. Fire power," Quarrels said. "By the time we tracked down the dealer and the rebels, they were having a little falling-out. My men just happened to outnumber everybody who was left. Wasn't too hard to scare the rest off and drive away with the prize while my men took the survivors to the *federales*." He patted the truck. "Your artifacts are all still neatly packed and ready for transport."

"They better be," Carrie grumbled, then slipped away from Rafe's embrace. She forgot the men as she climbed into the rear of the truck to check for herself. She heard them talking quietly while she did a quick inventory, but wouldn't have paid any attention even if she could make out what they said.

By the time she got out of the back of the truck, a realization had sunk into her head. Rafe and Quarrels had retreated to the shade of the trees near the road. Quarrels was seated on the ground; Rafe leaned casually against a tree trunk. She couldn't help but notice how graceful he looked, as still as a lounging panther.

She approached them and pointed at Quarrels. "You're with the DEA, too, right?"

He sprang to his feet, smirking. "Not so loud, sweetheart."

She was not deterred by any warning. "You're a cop?"

He waved a hand. "Shh. Yes," he stage-whispered, "I'm a cop."

"Really?"

Rafe looked disgusted. "You still don't believe me, do you?" He waved at the truck. "After all I went through to prove myself to you?"

Carrie cringed at the hurt in his voice and expression. She looked at the truck. She recalled the worry and guilt that she'd been feeling only a few minutes ago at forcing him into rescuing her artifacts. She didn't blame him for being annoyed. She found herself digging her toes into the dirt like a chagrined little kid. She cringed and couldn't bring herself to look at him. Something inside her—hurt that he hadn't trusted her enough to tell her who he was sooner, residue of all the recent terror she'd experienced, stung pride—kept her from apologizing though she knew he deserved it.

Carrie made herself meet his gaze. "I believe you. Thank you for bringing back the artifacts," she added. Then, to distract herself from staring longingly as Rafe came toward her, she said to Quarrels, "Do you ever have this fantasy that you're in a room full of a hundred drug dealers and suddenly everybody in the room pulls out a badge and yells 'Police, you're under arrest'?" Rafe frowned at her joke, but Quarrels laughed.

"I can see that happening," Quarrels answered.

"Not a fantasy," Rafe said. He came up to her now, and his fingers reached out to stroke her hair. "More like a nightmare."

Carrie stood very still. She was very aware of his touch, but she pretended not to notice and deliberately overlooked his serious tone. "Sounds like a scene from one of Bobby's films," she mused.

Rafe's frown deepened. His hand circled the back of her head. He drew her closer. "Who's Bobby?"

Quarrels laughed again. "You jealous, *compadre?*"

Rafe ignored the other agent. His breath brushed across Carrie's cheek as he leaned close to repeat, "Who's Bobby?"

"My brother," Carrie answered, all too aware of his imposing male presence. Her voice caught for a moment before she could manage to go on. "One of them. The one who went to film school."

He heard the pride in her voice and noted the easing of the jealous tension that had filled him at her mention of another man. He let the subject drop and refused to even look at Steve Quarrels. He could tell that the man was smirking even without looking at him. If Carrie had noticed his reaction, she studiously ignored it. He forced himself to move away from her. He had barely realized that he'd been

touching her, it had been such a natural, necessary thing to
do.

He forced himself to regain at least a veneer of professionalism. They didn't have the time, and this wasn't the
place, for anything personal. "We're leaving," he told her
as Quarrels went back to the truck.

Carrie turned her head to watch as Steve Quarrels disappeared around the other side of the truck. There was a
disturbing finality in the way he slammed the driver's-side
door. There was something ominous about the heavy sound
of the engine turning over against the background of laughter from down on the beach.

When Carrie would have followed Quarrels to the truck,
Rafe stopped her. Though she struggled, there was no
breaking his tight grip. "We're taking a plane out of Cancún."

"No, we're not. Mérida," Carrie said stubbornly. "My
cargo plane leaves from Mérida."

"Your cargo plane leaves from Mérida," he agreed.
"You aren't going to be on it."

She shook her head. "That consignment of artifacts—"

"Will get to Jefferson University without you."

"I'm going with my stuff."

"I've chartered a plane."

"I don't care." She barely noticed when Quarrels tossed
her and Rafe's luggage out the window. She barely noticed
the jaunty wave he gave her before driving off. What she
did notice was his driving off. Despite Rafe's grip, she
managed to jump up and down on the road. "Come back
here!" When she started to run after the truck, Rafe was
impossible to escape. "Let go of me, you big bully!"

"No."

"I'll scream."

"Go ahead. You're making my arm hurt, *querida.*"

"Good." Despite what she said, the reminder that he was injured persuaded her to stop struggling.

"Look at me, Carrie."

She reluctantly turned her gaze from the road. She wanted to scream with frustration. She'd barely gotten the artifacts back, and they were already out of her grasp again. "That shipment is my responsibility," she reminded Rafe.

He nodded. "I know. Don't worry. They're in good hands. Bringing Torres down is more important."

"Oh, *really?*"

"Yes."

"I don't agree. There's life beyond Torres. At least for *me.*" She had trouble believing it. That was why she was so adamant in saying it was the truth—to attempt to make herself believe it. She was terrified her life would never return to any semblance of normalcy.

Her words stung. He found himself goading her in response. "There's no life in those old stones, Carrie, other than what you bring to them. Those inscriptions have waited for hundreds of years for somebody to read them. They can wait a while longer. I want to get you safely away from Torres."

"You mean you want to get on with your investigation, don't you, Agent Castillo?"

"That, too," he admitted. "My 'stuff' is as important to me as your 'stuff' is to you." When all he got from her was an even angrier glare, he added, "I'm trying to save lives, Carrie. Your life, *querida.*"

"Don't call me that."

He smiled. "Carolina, then?"

"No."

Rafe put his arm around her waist and pulled her closer. He lowered his voice. "Admit it, you're just being stubborn because you're mad at me—and yourself."

Carrie couldn't stop herself from leaning into his embrace. Angry as she was, she couldn't resist the contact of her body against his. Despite the warmth that shot through her as she looked into his intense gaze, she couldn't stop her angry words. "Are you saying that I'm sulking because I discovered that you're a complete and utter jerk?"

He nodded. "Yes."

"You're absolutely right."

He ran his fingers through her tangled curls. "What about the people you're protecting? Are you going to let your hurt feelings get in the way of your responsibility to them?"

"We can't fly out of Cancún together," she told him.

"And why not?"

"I thought you were supposed to stay in Mérida, wait for me there while I got Torres's suitcase. You said you'd be recognized in Washington."

He pulled strands of hair back off her face and began to massage her temples with his thumbs. She found this very relaxing, very distracting. But not enough to keep her from listening carefully to his explanation. "I don't think you quite understand the nature of undercover work, *querida*. I've always had every intention of being the person who intercepts the laundered money in Washington. I'd been working very hard to get Torres to send me when he got the bright idea that using a mule would be safer. *He* told me to wait in Mérida. I never planned to."

"Oh. I sort of got in your way, I guess."

"*Sí.* But since the money man is now waiting to contact you, my job is to keep you safe until we can arrest him."

Her stomach knotted with tension, but she said, "I know there's no way I can get out of this."

"I wish there was. Believe me, I truly wish there was."

When he gently kissed her forehead, she sighed and tilted her face up. She discovered that her hands had somehow crept to his shoulders. The possibility of being kissed by him almost overshadowed the knowledge that her truck was on its way to Mérida without her. His lips brushed against hers, a brief touch full of infinite promise. She almost didn't want to get out of it. Because that would mean never seeing Rafael Castillo again. She wasn't ready for that just yet. "You're not playing fair," she told him when he drew away.

"I don't have that luxury. I never have that luxury." He stepped away from her and left her feeling very alone as the afternoon sun poured down onto the dusty roadside where she stood.

She hated to admit it, but he was right. She was sulking. She did want to do everything her way. While the shipment of artifacts was important to her, it really wasn't life and death for her to be with those crates once she knew they were safely on their way. There would be a team of skilled conservators and technicians waiting at the airport in Washington to transfer the shipment safely to Jefferson University.

The truth was, she was terrified of returning to the States and fulfilling her role as Torres's mule. And she was angry with Rafe for being a knight in dented and tarnished armor when she should be thankful that he'd turned out to be a knight all along. Just because he wasn't completely blameless and perfect was no reason for her to take her disappointment out on him. At least not much, or for too long.

She shrugged. "All right. I'm acting like a spoiled kid. I'm grateful you got my stuff back. I'll attempt to believe that the artifacts will get to Jefferson University without me. They're the lab's and cataloguing department's responsibilities for the next few weeks anyway." She crossed to the spot where their luggage had landed and picked up her bag. She glanced over her shoulder at Rafe. "So, how do we get to Cancún?"

"A car should be arriving any minute."

"Fine." She sat down amid the luggage on the roadside.

Rafe hated the way her shoulders slumped dejectedly as she leaned forward to rest her arms on her upraised knees. He hated himself for putting her through any of this. He hated having to use her. He wondered if she'd ever be able to forgive him. He reminded himself that this was an assignment, that how she felt about him wasn't important. He didn't believe it, though.

Needing to flee from the way his emotions tangled when he was near her, he said, "I'll go get our things from the cabana."

"Fine," she said without looking at him.

When he came back, the car was waiting, with one of the agents that worked with Quarrels driving. Rafe climbed in the front and Carrie got in the back. No one spoke a word all the way to Cancún.

They didn't talk much on the flight to Miami, either. In fact, Carrie curled up in the seat beside him and slept with her head on his shoulder for most of the trip. Rafe used the modem and fax capabilities of the laptop he'd been given by a fellow agent who'd met them at the Cancún airport to catch up on a lot of paperwork, reports and the strategy for wrapping up the Torres operation.

Details still weren't finalized by the time the plane landed, but at least a plan for protecting a civilian inadvertently involved in the operation was in the works. They changed to a commercial flight in Miami, and neither of them risked conversation while crowded on board an airplane full of strangers. Rafe stared out the window for the length of the flight. Carrie thumbed through a magazine for a while, but eventually her head landed on his shoulder as she went to sleep once more. Rafe didn't wake her until the other passengers had exited the plane.

"A car's supposed to pick us up," he told Carrie when

he woke her up. "But it's caught in rush-hour traffic. We'll have to wait."

Carrie stretched and yawned, barely aware that the plane had landed. "Are we there?"

Rafe couldn't stop the affectionate smile. He couldn't stop the warm feelings, either. She sounded like a five-year-old, but looked like a sultry-eyed vixen just coming awake after a night of lovemaking. It had been a hard fight to concentrate on work and cloud patterns with her warm weight pressed against him during the flights. He was very tempted to lean across the seat and kiss her fully awake now.

Instead, he stood up and held out his hand. "We're there. Welcome home, Dr. Robinson. Do you always sleep on planes?"

She stretched again and shook her head. "Always. Saves being nervous and bored. We're really in Washington? Shouldn't we have gone through Customs in Miami?"

"We are. Did you hear me tell you that a car's going to pick us up?"

"Yeah. Sort of. Why a car? Customs? Can't we get a taxi?"

"We don't have to go through Customs."

She let him help her to her feet. "I guess that's one perk of traveling with a DEA agent," she commented as she followed him to the exit. She checked her watch, surprised at the amount of time that had passed since she'd been standing worriedly on the beach in Tulum. She barely remembered changing planes. She always reacted badly to flying, but she put this dazed reaction down to shock, nerves and exhaustion.

Well, buck up, she lectured herself, forcing some of the cobwebs from her head. *You're home now. Pull yourself together.* Another part of her mind replied to this stern lecture that she'd be happy to pull herself together, but she wanted to brush her teeth first. With these thoughts upper-most in her mind, Carrie straightened her spine and walked purposefully off the plane.

Rafe knew he should be acting the complete, competent, uninvolved professional now that they were back on American soil. He should have been acting that way the whole time. His only excuse was that he'd slipped too deeply into his undercover role and that had clouded his emotions. The truth was, Carrie Robinson had clouded his emotions and was going to continue to cloud them as long as they were together, and maybe forever after.

Maybe he should be acting professionally aloof, but he would have taken her hand as they walked through the busy airport corridors if she'd let him. She was the one who proved to be reticent. It wasn't that she shook him off, but she suddenly took on a reserved aura that made him hesitate about touching her without even being conscious of it.

In fact, something changed decisively in Carrie Robinson even before they stepped off the plane. It was subtle, but she somehow was no longer a wild adventuress, but very much someone who was clearly identifiable as a sophisti-cated woman. One who was high-powered, extremely in-telligent and used to getting a great deal of respect. It was something in her straight posture and carriage, the proud tilt of her head, a slight thinning of her lush mouth. The best way he could define it was that she went from being Salma Hayek to Katharine Hepburn in the blink of an eye. He wasn't sure how she did it, but he had no doubts about her being from New England, especially after she stopped in a ladies' room and came out with her hair up and wear-ing a demure black dress and beige linen jacket. Her clothes were only slightly rumpled from being tossed around inside her suitcase through all the adventures since leaving Oro Blanco.

"You certainly know how to pack," he told her when she joined him in the corridor. "I barely recognize you."

"I feel much better now," she answered. "I'm really not the T-shirt-and-shorts type. That's just field wear." She checked her watch. "How long do we have to wait?"

Rafe patted the cellular phone in his pocket, another high-tech addition to his working equipment that he'd been given in Cancún. "I'll get a call when the car arrives out front."

"Oh." Carrie looked around the concourse. "You hungry? I'm starving." She pointed. "There's a restaurant over there."

"I'm starving, too," he agreed, but he was looking her over when he said it.

She gave a caustic laugh. "I think what you really need's a steak." She headed for the restaurant without waiting to see if he'd follow.

He quickly caught up with her. "You're right." He almost said he'd save her for dessert, but that wouldn't be professional. And it didn't seem quite the right thing to say to the woman in the severe hairdo and business outfit. She seemed more like a stranger than his Carolina.

The place was busy, but not so busy that they weren't seated right away. A waiter appeared, asking about drink orders before they had a chance to look at the menus.

"We'll have two Robin Reds," Carrie said to the waiter, then opened her menu. After a moment, she noticed the silence and glanced up over the tall menu to look at a frowning Rafe. "Yes?"

"I like to pick my own beer."

"You'll like this," she assured him. "Trust me."

"With my life," he answered. "But I'm not sure about my beer." The waiter returned with two tall glasses of a garnet red liquid. "Beer should be brown."

"Or as amber as your eyes." He lifted an eyebrow at her comment. "Just take a drink, Castillo."

Rafe took a cautious sip. "You're right," he agreed. "I like it."

"Good." She grinned. "I'll be sure to let my dad know he's got a new fan."

He raised his eyebrow again. "Your dad?"

She closed her menu. "I think I want a hamburger. Or the fish and chips. How about you?"

"Your dad?" he repeated. He drank some more beer. It was really good, a rich, dark brew. "Your father's a beer maker?"

"Brewer. Actually, he started out owning a bar, then he started a chain of fern bars. Never mind the M.B.A. from Wharton, his hobby was brewing beer. First he started selling Robin Red as the house microbrew. Eventually he cut a licensing deal with a big brewery and now it's becoming popular all over the country."

"You sound very proud of him."

She nodded. Then she found herself admitting, "It's not just about bartender makes good, either. It's kind of a revenge thing. At least for me. Dad doesn't think that way. He's never cared what his family thinks. Says I shouldn't, either. Mostly I don't." The look of intense interest on Rafe's face kept her talking, pouring out things she normally kept to herself.

"And what is it his family thinks?" he asked softly. Rafe would have liked to reach across the table to take her hand, but he kept the width deliberately between them. She was being a bit standoffish, and that was good. He had to remember to keep their relationship professional now that they were back in the States, but he didn't try to turn the conversation away from the personal. He didn't think Carrie realized how sad she looked as she discussed her family. She was a very different person since their departure from Mexico. The sharply intelligent, confident, adventurous woman he'd lost his heart to had disappeared under a reserved facade so fast he found it quite disturbing. Carrie probably didn't even notice that her body language had changed. So had her voice.

"Some of the Robinsons thought Dad would never make anything of himself," she answered. "That he'd made a big, ugly mistake when he married his mom's housekeeper and quit working on Wall Street to do what he wanted. God forbid a man should be happy doing something the Robinsons 'just don't do.'" She sighed. "They're good people, my dad's family, but 'conservative' and 'snobbish' are words that come readily to mind when describing them.

"Not all of them, of course," she added. "My grandfather's okay, so's my cousin Jeremy. Jeremy's a banker," she explained about her favorite cousin. "But he's interested in the sort of thing I do. He helped me get funding for the dig. He even visited Oro Blanco a few times. Says he's proud of the Mexican connection. But Grandmama can drive me a little crazy. And only Great-Grandmother Robinson...well, Great-Grandmother's been dead for a long time. I'm almost recovered from her attitude."

"Your great-grandmother's dead? The one who gave you the hairbrush?"

She was touched that Rafe recalled their conversation about the brush. "She left it to me in her will."

The diamonds, emeralds, pearls, antique cameos and trust fund had been left to Cousin Alicia, the only other great-granddaughter. Carrie tried to tell herself that the old woman's leaving her a tortoiseshell comb, brush and mirror set was a much more personal token, as steeped in family history as a bunch of old jewelry, but she didn't really believe it. To be fair, Alicia had sold everything but the cameos to help fund a women's shelter.

"Great-Grandmother was my grandfather's mother. My

grandmama was born a Barett, related to the Adamses and Van Houtens, don't you know? Old money.'' Carrie chuckled and shook her head. "What a woman. Starchy and distant are good ways to describe her.'' She took another drink of beer and looked up as the waiter came for their orders. "Actually, we love each other dearly despite our differences. The same couldn't be said for my relationship with Great-Grandmother Robinson," she couldn't help but add.

She was shocked at herself. She didn't know what had gotten into her. She'd never said an unkind word about her great-grandmother before. Thought them, yes, but the galling, snobbish, wounding unkindness from the old woman was something she'd never admitted to anyone before. There was something in the interested, sympathetic way Rafe looked at her that made him easy to confide in. Even confidences she didn't particularly want to reveal. He'd worn down barriers she hadn't realized she'd erected.

Rafe was surprised at how pleased he was to finally learn something about Carrie, especially without any prompting. She'd been avoiding his prying questions since they met. He realized he had no business wanting to know more about her, but he did. He wanted to know what made her who she was. He had from the moment he first saw her. She was the most beautiful woman in the world to him, and not just on the outside. In the past few days, she'd come to mean everything to him. His complete concentration on her was going to have to end soon, but he was reluctant to let their time together draw to a close.

He leaned forward and put his elbows on the table after the waiter had gone. He sensed that she was very uncomfortable with what she'd just said, so he switched the conversation elsewhere. "Your mother's from Oro Blanco?"

"No. Near there. A crummy little village that got washed away in a flood a few years back. The government relocated the few people that still lived there after everything they had was destroyed. Most of the young people, like my mom, had long gone off elsewhere to try to make a living." Carrie sipped her beer. "That's how she got to the United States."

"Where she met your father whose family disowned him for marrying a Mexican, so he moved to Rhode Island, bought a bar, had a beautiful daughter and made beer."

Carrie smiled at his summary of her family history. "Not quite. Robinsons don't disown their own—that would be way too obvious for them. Let's just say that there's been some disapproval at Dad's less than conventional behavior, but no outright acrimony. Outright acrimony would be better," she observed. "And Dad and Mom didn't just have a daughter. I've got two brothers."

"You mentioned someone named Bobby."

She nodded. "Yep. Robert's younger than me by two years, and Michael is older by six. Bobby and Mike are as unconventional as Dad. Comes from their growing up over the original Robinson's Roost, Dad says. Bobby makes independent films. Mike writes a syndicated humor column. I'm the staid one who followed Granddad into academia. My parents and my grandfather and my cousin Jeremy all encouraged me to explore the Mayan side of my heritage."

"Which is how you came to be working at Chalenque and inadvertently got involved with Torres."

"Torres is *not* part of my Mayan heritage. He's from El Paso. Most of his people are from Texas, Panama or Los Angeles."

"Like me. How do you know so much about Torres?"

"I asked him. How long did you work for him anyway? I never saw you around Oro Blanco before the day you showed up in Maquiero's. Not that I got into Oro Blanco's thriving and thoroughly metropolitan city center all that often," she added dryly.

He finished his beer and ignored the urge to order another. He took coffee with his meal and waited until the food came and she was almost finished eating before he answered her question. "I kept a very low profile with Torres's organization. I wasn't part of the more publicly presentable part of his image. I knew about the man's church work and his support of charities, but my job was accompanying him on drug deals and to business meetings. I learned quite a bit. I gathered a lot of evidence about his and other drug lords' organizations. I fed that information to other agents who raided his operations. He's lost a lot of money in the past year.

"And I shouldn't be telling you any of this," he admitted, "especially not in public." He ran his hands through his shoulder-length hair. "What are you doing to me, woman?" Before she could respond, his phone rang. After a brief conversation, he stood, then left money on the table for the bill. "Car's here. Time to get you to a safe house."

Carrie gave him a hard look. She didn't stand up. "I'm not going to a safe house. I'm going to my own house."

He came around the table and took her by the arm. "Oh, no, you're not."

He led her out of the restaurant and to the curb where the car was waiting. Carrie refused to budge as he tried to urge her into the car. "I haven't been home in five months," she told him. "I want my own house, to sleep in my own bed, to use my own shower and phone. I want to cook in my own kitchen."

Rafe couldn't help but smile. "In short, you want your stuff."

She smiled back while the driver looked on with an air of disgust. "I think we understand each other."

"Has anyone ever told you that you're a very stubborn woman?"

"You have."

"You are."

"Besides," she reminded him, "Torres said the instructions for the pickup will be sent to my house...though I don't want to think how he got my home address."

"Money makes it easy to find out about people," Rafe replied. "Your phone's listed, right?" She nodded. "And you're on the Internet and you've written books, yes?" Another nod. "Not to mention all the paperwork that you must do for the college and government. It's easy to find out about people."

"I guess so."

"And there must have been plenty of mail with your address forwarded to you at the dig or to my aunt's house," he added. "Aunt Juana wouldn't even tell me your name after the bar fight, but that doesn't mean Torres didn't bribe someone else to find out about you. Besides, I recall that you know a lot about him."

She ignored the curiosity that tinged on jealousy in Rafe's voice. "We met in church," she reminded him. "That doesn't mean I told him anything about me."

"But he found out anyway."

"That's disgusting." She refused to shudder with dread at knowing that the drug lord knew where she lived. "But disgusting or not, don't I have to be at my house to get the instructions?"

"Someone has to be at your house to get the instructions. It doesn't have to be you."

"But it might as well be."

Rafe sighed. He gave in. "All right. We'll go to your house. But I'm staying with you."

"But—"

"I can be stubborn, too, Carrie," he reminded her.

She drew herself up stiffly. "Fine. Be stubborn." She got in the car. "See if I care."

It wasn't until they were halfway to her town house in Brook Run, a small college town that was one of Washington's Virginia suburbs, that some of the possible ramifications of Rafe Castillo's staying with her struck Carrie. Of course, by then it was too late to change her mind about going home.

Beside, she wasn't sure she wanted to change her mind, either.

Chapter 10

"I think I've gotten used to having you around, Castillo."

"Why do you say that?" he questioned as she unlocked the door. "Perdóneme." Rafe shouldered past her, cautiously entering the house first. Except for a rectangle of light coming in the open door from a nearby streetlamp, there was no other light. The place was very quiet. His senses told him the house was empty, that everything was as it should be. He gestured Carrie inside. "Not that I expect trouble," he said as she followed him into the dark entryway, "but it's best I keep in practice."

"I see. You're trying to protect me? From what?"

"Your unopened mail, maybe. Now, why do you say you're used to me?"

"Because..." Carrie stopped herself just short of blurting out how empty a place seemed to her when he wasn't there. It was something she wouldn't have let herself say to him when she thought he was a drug dealer. Somehow it seemed even more appropriate to keep it to herself now that she knew who he really was. She felt she owed him—what? More professional courtesy, more deference, she supposed. Never mind that they'd been lovers last night—or had that been the night before?—she should try to be impersonal and let him get on with his job. She couldn't forget what it had been like to make love to him, but she should consign all those thoughts to the back of her mind for the time being at least.

Right now, she owed him her help though what she wanted to do was show him to her bedroom. Any personal involvement with an agent on an assignment could hinder his mission and put him in serious danger. And she didn't want to see him in danger again. She wanted to be out of danger herself, no matter how protected she felt when she was with him. The sooner the money launderer was arrested, the sooner this whole nightmare would be over.

She did want it to be over, didn't she? Even if it meant never seeing Rafe again? What would it mean to have this finished with? Would Rafe walk away once his job was done? Was it for the best if he did? They had a mutual sexual attraction. They had been forced to spend time together in threatening situations. Did he feel anything for her other than a desire fueled by an adrenaline rush?

What about her feelings for him? Did she want him to make some sort of commitment to her? Did she want to make one to him? Could she sort reality from that same adrenaline rush any more than he could?

"I am *so* confused," she muttered. Actually, when she just went with her emotions, she was fine. It was at moments like this, when she tried to think clearly, that the world spun and fractured. She was terrified of where she'd be when the kaleidoscope effect wore off. Would she be in Rafe's arms? Or on her own once more?

Rafe's hand landing on her shoulder brought an end to her agonized musings. "You're confused? Sweetheart, this is your house. I don't even know where the light switch is."

She couldn't help but laugh as she realized they were standing in the dark entry hall. She quickly flipped the switch next to the door. "There," she said as light filled the hall.

The entrance contained two doorways and a staircase. The walls were painted a teal green, the stair banisters and trim around the doorways were highly polished dark wood. The hall contained a brass coat tree, a mirror with a beaten-silver frame hung on one wall and a colorful, handwoven Peruvian area rug covering a large square of floor. A delicate-looking table underneath the mirror held a Mayan pot and a blown-glass paperweight.

"*Mi casa es su casa,* and all that."

He grinned as he put down his bag. "I hope you mean that."

All her good intentions about keeping to a professional relationship melted away with the warmth that spread through her at his look. She sighed. "You are a very bad influence, Castillo."

"I'm a very bad man," he agreed, stepping closer.

Carrie just barely managed to shake off the urge to step into his embrace. She took a step back, then gestured. "Want a tour?"

Rafe wanted to ask where the bedroom was. He put his hands in his pockets. "Sure. A tour would be great."

"Upstairs first."

She shouldered her bag and headed up the long staircase ahead of him. The thick carpet runner muffled the sound of his steps behind her, but didn't lessen her awareness of his presence any. She didn't understand how anyone so large could move as quietly as he did.

"The place is long and narrow, and the ceilings are too low," she said as they reached the upstairs hallway. "It's been renovated a couple of times, but still has all the disadvantages of its era. When I bought it, I thought it was charming. Figured it would be great to live in a town house built in the nineteenth century—and within walking distance of the campus, too.'' Her expression rueful, she added, ''That was before I started getting the repair bills.''

Rafe listened with an eagerness to know about her everyday life that surprised him. It was nice to learn that Caroline Robinson was firmly grounded in a mundane life far removed from the dangerous, outlaw environment where they'd met. As they walked down the narrow hall, the world of secrets and shadows, greed and swift death they'd escaped only a few hours before fell even farther behind him.

When she turned to him with a smile, he felt reborn. Stunned and joyous, he found himself standing next to a white-painted door.

''That's the spare bedroom,'' she told him. She opened the door and switched on the ceiling light. ''You can leave your bag in here,'' she told him as they entered the room.

It held a large, wrought-iron bed as well as a dresser and chest of drawers. Rafe thought it had a very lived-in look for a spare room. He tossed his bag down on the quilted bedspread. ''I'm supposed to have some fresh clothes delivered tomorrow,'' he said, and opened the closet door. ''Okay if I hang them in here?''

''You're my guest,'' she answered. ''Go ahead.''

He saw that there were already quite a few men's clothes in the closet. A dark rush of jealousy shot through him just at the sight of a stranger's tailored jacket hanging innocuously inside. Rafe told himself that it wasn't important, that her private life—a life he really knew very little about—was none of his business. He still turned an annoyed look on her.

His tone was harsh when he asked, "You sure the room isn't already in use?"

For a moment Carrie didn't know what he was upset about. Then it occurred to her that this undercover cop who was using her to bring drug dealers to justice might have his mind on something besides business. In general, she disliked the idea of confronting a jealous male. Specifically however, this evidence of possessiveness warmed and reassured her.

She also set him straight quickly—not that having other men's clothes in her house was any of his business. "My brothers use this room when they're in town. So they keep some clothes here. Well, it's mostly Bobby's stuff."

"Brothers." Rafe cleared his throat and pretended not to be embarrassed at the suspicions that had instantly taken hold of him. He didn't understand it—he wasn't normally the jealous type. To ease the tension that suddenly arced between them, he asked, "You're close to your brothers?"

She nodded. "Oh, yeah. They're great." She sighed, looking wistful as she spoke.

"That's how I feel about my brothers, too. And my sister." He was used to keeping his private life very, very private, so private that he rarely even let himself think about his family. He'd been thinking about family far too much since meeting Carrie. "You make me crazy, Carolina," he told her.

She tilted her head sideways and gave him a concerned look. "Why?"

"Never mind," he snapped. "Show me the rest of your house."

They went back into the hall. One by one, she opened and closed two doors on the other side of the hallway. "Bathroom. My room." Then she marched stiffly back downstairs.

Rafe followed guiltily after her. In the front hall again,

he stopped her with a touch on her shoulder. "I'm not usually so moody," he explained when she turned to look at him.

Carrie's hands went to her hips. "Is that an apology for being jealous and cryptic?"

"I would never admit to being jealous or cryptic," he answered, ducking his head and peering at her through the thick fringe of his eyelashes. He tried his best boyish smile.

"Oh, stop it."

He moved closer to her. He couldn't stop himself. He continued to smile as his gaze raked over her. He hated her simple dress, the concealing jacket, the way her curls were held prisoner by the tightly coiled hairstyle. He longed to run his fingers through the heavy silk of her hair, to see it framing the high cheekbones of her oval face. He wanted to trace the proud arch of her nose, to hold her close and trace his fingers all over the rest of her, as well. Every good intention he had about remaining professional and impersonal fled before the desire brought on just by looking at her.

She was, indeed, making him crazy.

"I don't think I want to finish the tour," he said as he put his hands around her waist.

His voice sent a shiver through her, his touch a jolt of electricity through her blood. Carrie succumbed to the fact that they could not keep their hands off one another. "We shouldn't," she said. She lifted her face for his kiss as she spoke.

"I know," he said, and kissed her.

It was fierce and tender at the same time. She barely noticed his hands, though she let them roam at will, leaving a trail of fiery sensation wherever he touched her. She tangled her fingers in his hair, drinking in his kiss, wanting more.

She wanted to fall on the floor and make love to him on

the rug. She almost let herself give in to the hunger that drove her to act so impulsively. Almost. Carrie hated coming to her senses. She didn't even know how she managed to do it. All she knew was that one second she was reveling in the feel of his thumb stroking the aroused peak of her breast through her clothing, and the next she was acutely aware of where they were, who they were and what they were doing. Passion didn't die, not at all, but hunger receded enough for her to think.

If the ghost of her great-grandmother was laughing cruelly somewhere in the back of her mind, she ignored the hateful sound. She pulled herself out of the growing spiral of desire because it was the sensible thing to do. She noticed that her hair had somehow fallen down around her shoulders and that her jacket was puddled at her feet. Her skirt was hiked up around her thighs. This had definitely gone too far, too fast.

She didn't ever want to stop kissing him, but she did. "I think we better slow down, monkey boy," Carrie said, taking his hand away from her breast. "We're not supposed to be doing this." She broke out of the circle of his arms and pulled down her skirt while he looked at her, his amber eyes darkening with craving to old gold. She was almost frightened of the emotion in his eyes, not because of the raw need she saw there, but because of that craving. It was calling to her. "Cold shower," she muttered in a low groan, turning away. "Need a cold shower."

It took Rafe more than a moment to get his breath, and his body, under control. Even when he had enough air in his lungs to speak, he wasn't sure about controlling the rest of his body. He loved kissing her, touching her, and he wanted to keep doing it. "Slow down, *querida?*"

She gave a tight but firm nod. "Right now."

"Who says?"

"Don't you have some sort of rule about fraternizing with—whatever I am. A witness? Accomplice?"

"We've already broken that rule."

"I wouldn't want you to get into trouble."

"I take responsibility for my actions." When he would have kissed her again, she stepped farther away. He sighed, then gave her a narrow-eyed, puzzled look. "Monkey boy?"

She shook the hair out of her face. "What?"

"Did you call me monkey boy?"

She smiled. "Maybe."

"Huh?"

"You've never seen *Buckaroo Banzai?*" Carrie asked while she picked up her discarded jacket and hung it up.

"What's that?" He conceded that they shouldn't be making love, at least not at the moment. He began to straighten his disheveled clothing. "*Querida,* when did you undo my zipper?"

"I don't remember. It's a movie," she explained without meeting his gaze. "A very funny cult classic. The plot's totally impossible to explain, but let's just say that *Independence Day* wasn't the first time Jeff Goldblum got to help save the world from evil aliens."

"Monkey boy?" he repeated.

"It's something John Big Booty—that's Christopher Lloyd's evil alien character—calls humans." At his not unexpected, totally confused look, she laughed, then turned toward the living room. "Come on," she said, "I'll put on the tape."

He followed her. The room was long and narrow. On one side of the room was a desk holding a personal computer. It was flanked by tall bookcases. A couch and a pair of end tables with lamps, a television stand and a case of videotapes took up the center of the room. There was a fireplace on one wall. Lots of photos lined the mantel. A poster-size framed photo of the Chalenque temple and surrounding jungle hung over the fireplace.

"That's beautiful."

Carrie turned toward the picture Rafe was looking at. She smiled. "Isn't it? My cousin Jeremy took it when he visited last season. He's a great photographer. He took quite a few shots of Chalenque and had that one blown up and framed as a present for me."

"It's a wonderful photo. Gives a touch of wildness to the room."

"I don't need any wildness in this section of my life, thank you very much, monkey boy."

Rafe ignored the sudden sharpness of her tone and refrained from disagreeing with her. "Will I understand this 'monkey boy' after I see the movie?"

"Probably not. It's the sort of movie you have to watch two or three times before you really get it. That's why it's called a cult movie, darlin'."

"You called me darling," he said brightly as she opened a tape cabinet.

"Revenge for all those *queridas*. It was a slip of the tongue."

He settled onto the comfortable couch. "You were doing that earlier."

She stopped fiddling with her television and VCR controls long enough to glance provocatively over her shoulder at him. "Don't push it, Castillo, or I won't make you popcorn later."

"Oh, Lucy, you so *mean* to me." He did a passable imitation of Desi Arnaz.

Carrie laughed, comfortable with him now that the moment of passion-induced insanity had passed. "Okay, you can have popcorn."

Finished loading the tape, she settled on the couch beside him. His arm came around her shoulders. She rested her

head on his. He liked this. This was more the Carrie he
knew and not so much the woman who had emerged at the
airport. Or maybe there was a public and private Caroline
Robinson. He decided not to worry about any disparity in
her behavior and just enjoy being with her. Making love to
her was very much on his mind, but he pushed longing
aside for the simple pleasure of her company.

The operation for catching Torres's contact was well in
hand. All they could do was wait. Torres wouldn't expect
her to even be back in the country before tomorrow. He
half hoped the waiting would go on for days just so he
could spend the time with her. While waiting, they might
as well watch a movie. For now.

The truth was, *Buckaroo Banzai* made absolutely no
sense to him, though he took a great deal of pleasure in
seeing the enjoyment on Carrie's face as she watched. To
be fair to the film, he paid more attention to her laughter
and comments than he did to the dialogue. He was very
disappointed when the phone rang and her light mood instantly disappeared.

Carrie was reluctant to leave the comfortable circle of
Rafe's arm, but the persistent ring from the phone on her
desk drew her back into the real world. She paused the tape
and checked her watch. It was later than she thought, which
left her uneasily wondering who was calling as she reluctantly crossed the room to pick up the receiver.

She half expected—and was half-afraid—the caller
would be Torres's money contact. Rafe silently followed
her to the desk, looking very alert and businesslike. It occurred to her that her phone was probably tapped. Feeling
somewhat violated, she stared at the receiver as it continued
to ring. It was only the sudden fear that something might
have happened to her shipment of artifacts that overcame
her hesitation to share her private conversations with listening outsiders.

"Hello?"

"Caroline. Your voice mail isn't working."

"Grandmama?"

"Just when did you return from Mexico? I've been expecting you to call for several days."

Carrie winced at the lecturing tone. "I missed you, too," she answered as sweetly as she could.

"Are you being rude?"

"Of course not, Grandmama. I did miss you."

"I missed you very much. You should write more often."

"I E-mailed you."

"Dear girl, I am barely used to the twentieth century. Kindly stop attempting to drag me into your electronic age. It doesn't suit me at all."

Rafe stepped back, relaxing as he realized that the call was a personal one. Though Carrie looked less than comfortable talking to her grandmother, at least this wasn't someone she needed to be protected from. He went back to his seat on the couch, giving her a semblance of privacy, though he couldn't help but overhear Carrie's end of the conversation.

"No. I just got in a couple of hours ago. Yes. No. I'm fine. I do not sound tense, I'm tired. Jet lag. Jeremy's in town? Great. Oh. Sharon left him? He moved in with you? Yes, he always has too much luggage. You should have seen all the stuff he brought when he visited me last year. Then he lost half of it. Too bad he couldn't make it down this season. Yes, I'd love to see him, but I'm kind of busy this— Right. Of course. Look, isn't it kind of late for you to be calling? A party? What, to celebrate Jeremy breaking up with— Sorry. No, I don't think divorce is funny. I'm just a little tense and— The ambassador from where? Never heard of the place. And who? Nice guest list, Grandmama.

No, I don't think I can make it. I'm busy tomorrow night. Yes, I'll think about it. Goodbye."

Rafe sensed that Carrie's grandmother wasn't finished with her side of the conversation when Carrie hung up the phone. He sat forward as Carrie came back to the couch. She threw her head back on the cushion and closed her eyes. "You look wasted, *querida.*"

She gave him a wry look. "Have I ever mentioned that the women in my family are formidable?"

"I guessed that on my own."

"Don't ever get involved with a Robinson," she warned. "We don't age well. There's this matriarch syndrome we succumb to." She wasn't being fair to her grandmother, but her nerves were too strained to deal with the kind but authoritarian woman right now.

Rafe reached out and gathered her into a comforting embrace. He nuzzled her hair, then whispered in her ear, "I like being involved with a Robinson woman."

Carrie considered asking him to elaborate on the subject, but he released his hold on her before she quite worked herself up to it.

Rafe stood. "You're right about it being late. I think we ought to go to bed, *chica.*"

"Sounds good to me."

Carrie picked up the remote and switched off the television and VCR. She moved very carefully and thoughtfully as she put the device back on the end table, stood, stretched and looked at him. She could feel Rafe watching her, and she was hyperaware of his large, masculine presence.

Sensual current crackled between them when their gazes finally met. Carrie's breath caught, and her pulse picked up. Still, she managed to keep her voice steady, and her words as slow and deliberate as her movements, when she asked, "Your bed or mine?"

He reached out and took her hand. Their gazes stayed locked on each other as their fingers entwined. "Your bed, Carolina," he answered. "In your house, that's where I want to make my home."

She had told him that her house was his. She had never felt so much at home anywhere as when sharing her bed with Rafael Castillo. This time the lovemaking wasn't quite so frantic, even if it was as intense as the night spent on the sand in Tulum. Not only intense, but full of laughter and caring. Carrie was quite pleased to find several packets of condoms in the table by the bed in the spare room; even more pleased when Rafe enthusiastically thanked her for them and showed no hesitation in using the protection.

"For all your machismo, you're quite adorable," she told him, then proceeded to prove how adorable she found him with her mouth, her hands and her body.

After making love, they stretched out on the bed together. Rafe lay on his back, hands tucked behind his head, eyes hooded, a faint, satisfied smile curling up his full lips. Carrie rested with her head tucked on his chest for a while, but found she still couldn't keep her hands off him.

She followed her urge to explore by stroking her hands along his skin, kneading strong muscles while her gaze took in the sight of him, big and brown and masculine against the pale blue damask sheets. When she touched a small round scar on the side of his neck, she asked, "Bullet wound?"

Rafe put his hand over the spot. "Had a mole removed when I was a kid."

She gently touched the bandage on his arm. "How does this feel?"

Rafe thought it might make her guilty to let her know how sore it was, so he just shrugged. "I've had worse. It's healing fast."

She stretched out along his side and kept exploring. Much later, she stroked the length of a narrow ribbon of scar tissue. "Knife wound?"

"Appendectomy."

"You're no fun."

Rafe chuckled. "Bloodthirsty, aren't you?"

She lifted her head to give him a teasing look. "Must be my Mayan blood." She rested her chin on the ribbed muscles of his stomach. "Great abs. You work out a lot?"

"I worked out a lot with Torres. He's into bodybuilding." Rafe tucked his hands behind his head again. "I'm naturally lazy. I also avoid violence whenever I can, Carolina. Very low tolerance for pain," he explained.

She knew how dangerous Rafael Castillo was; she'd seen him in action. She also recalled how he'd complained when she'd treated the minor wound in his arm. Just because he was dangerous didn't mean the man went out of his way to get into situations where he could get hurt. But...she'd seen him kill a man. She'd been in the middle of the gunfight at Maquiero's.

Curiosity got the better of her. "Just what exactly happened in the bar in Oro Blanco?"

Rafe didn't particularly want to talk about it. Or he didn't think he did until she looked at him with an expression so earnest and sympathetic it made his heart melt with love for her. Love that helped ease the pain that had been eating into him more and more with every day he spent under cover.

"What happened?" He rolled his shoulders, half a shrug, half an effort to ease suddenly tense muscles. She reached up and ran a hand through his hair. He caught her wrist and planted a kiss on her upturned palm. "What happened? Something I always expected would happen, but prayed would not. I've done a lot of undercover work. I've seen people die, sometimes gunned down so quickly, so thoughtlessly. I've watched it happen, had guns pulled on me and pulled them on other people. Most of the time, just pointing a gun at someone, just being faster, looking more ruthless, is enough. I've been in some—battles is the only way to describe them—when maybe, probably, I was responsible for shooting someone. That day in Maquiero's was the first time I deliberately took a man's life. I pointed the gun and I shot.''

"It was life or death," she remembered. "He would have killed you."

"Yes. I know there was no choice." He sighed. "Still, it was—"

"It must have been awful."

Her sympathy both eased and stung his bruised conscience. Rafe shook his head. "No. Yes. Now it's awful. At that moment it was—liberating. Exhilarating. Something snapped in me. I was just like them, one of them. In that moment I could just as easily have killed you as walked away."

She nodded slowly. "I know. I saw it in your eyes."

He drew her up the bed and into his embrace. "But you still wanted me. I saw that in your eyes."

Carrie hid her face in the crook of his arm for a moment. He stroked her hair. When she looked at him again, it was to say, "That's your overactive imagination, Castillo. I was scared spitless."

"And turned on," he insisted. His hand moved down from her hair to caress her shoulder and then her back. She arched under his touch. "Admit it."

She splayed her palm across his chest. "Uh-uh. No way I'm going there, Castillo."

He cupped her buttocks. He felt himself going hard again. "After that day in the bar, you dreamed about me the way I dreamed about you."

Carrie blushed all over, her skin heated from internal fire, and she knew he felt it. She couldn't look away from his intense gaze or deny his words, even if she was ashamed of her reaction. She cleared her throat. "Maybe."

He shook his head, an amused glint in his eyes. "I think you like bad men." He pulled her on top of him. He lifted his hands to stroke her breasts.

Carrie hated to concede this point, but she sighed and nodded. She leaned into his expert touch. "Maybe."

He kissed her forehead. "I'm not such a bad man, just an actor who got a little too much into the role." His teasing expression faded. He looked suddenly weary. "Maybe."

His tone set off alarm bells in Carrie's head. Her relaxed, playful mood fled. She moved back, away from his caressing hands. She looked at him warily. "Rafe?"

He felt her body stiffen with tension, saw the flash of fear in her eyes. He fought through his own arousal and studied her worried face. He thought he knew what she was thinking, but he waited for her to ask. "Yes?"

Carrie remained silent for several long moments. How did you ask someone if you've been cavorting naked in bed with a complete stranger? Finally, she found the courage to lick her lips and say, "You really are Rafael Castillo, right? You're my friend Juana's nephew? You're from Los Angeles and have brothers and a sister? Everything you've told me isn't just a cover story, is it?"

"I'm Rafael Castillo." The relief that shone on her face both warmed him and amused him. He didn't blame her for her suspicions. There were so many things he should have explained to her sooner. "Rafe Castillo, idiot." He put his hands around her waist and eased her down beside him. He turned on his side to face her, his head propped up by the pillows. "At your service," he added.

"You went under cover as yourself?" He nodded. Her

big dark eyes widened. She looked appalled. "Isn't that dangerous? Excuse me for saying so, but isn't it stupid?"

"A bit difficult," he answered. He put his hand on her thigh; it was warm and soft as satin against his palm. "But not necessarily stupid. When Torres's operation was located working out of Oro Blanco, I mentioned to my boss that that's where my family came from, that I still had relatives there. My boss thought it was a good idea for me to cash in on the connection—an easy, fast way to insert myself into Torres's organization. There were plenty of people Torres knew who could vouch for my background, and my drug-dealer cover was set up very, very carefully. It didn't hurt that all of my relatives in Oro Blanco hated my guts when they thought I was working for Torres." He gave a dejected sigh.

She stroked a hand through his hair. "It hurt you, but it didn't hurt your cover. And the cover's always the most important thing, right?" She hated the hint of bitterness that crept into her voice, but she couldn't help it.

"My family came from Oro Blanco a long time ago," he reminded her. "Do you think I wanted to see the place where I came from used and corrupted by drug dealers? I had a chance to do something about it, maybe save a few lives. In the beginning, doing the job seemed worth giving up a little bit of my soul."

Carrie realized that they'd just reached territory where Rafe didn't want to go. Then again, she reasoned as she watched his expression become closed and tight, maybe, just maybe, he needed to explore that dark territory for his own good. Was it up to her to take him there? Did she have that right? That obligation?

If she loved him, she did.

Did she love him?

"Stupid question," she muttered to herself.

Rafe sat up higher on the pile of pillows. "What?"

"Nothing," Carrie answered. She held her lower lip between her teeth for a moment, then let her concern have its way. "Are you going to continue taking undercover assignments? Is that healthy? Pretending to be someone else all the time, I mean."

Rafe did not want to answer her. He closed his eyes and tried to not even think. "It's my job," he said at last.

"To put your sanity on the line all the time?"

He almost responded that he didn't have anything better to do with his life, but the words didn't come. He opened his eyes and looked into hers. Gently, with a growing sense of wonder, he touched her. In the past few days he'd found a lot to live for, to look forward to, even if he hadn't consciously realized it until this moment. No, he'd realized it all right, he admitted to himself. It was just so hard to come out and say it. Even harder to try to figure out what to do about it.

"You make me very happy," he told her. He kissed her before she could ask anything else. He made love to her again, living in the here and now as he was used to, before he could ask himself any questions about what happened after tomorrow.

Deep in the night, Carrie woke to find herself in Rafe's embrace with the memory of those words and what they'd shared fresh in her mind. She made him happy. She smiled into the darkness and reveled in the shared warmth and the texture of his hard-muscled body next to hers. She made him happy. Somehow those few words made up for every cruel thing her great-grandmother had said about her carnal nature. Making him happy was like a blessing, an affirmation that lovemaking wasn't some dark, wicked sin, but a gift, a sharing, a fulfillment that went beyond the physical act. Carrie had never been so content in her life.

She smiled, brushed the sleeping man's lips with her own, whispered, "You make me happy, too," and went back to sleep.

Chapter 11

"No."

Rafe moved to stand in front of the front door when she would have opened it.

Carrie glared. "What are you doing, Castillo?"

He leaned against the dark wood at his back and faced down her annoyance. "I'm keeping you safely at home."

She folded her arms under her bosom. "I have work to do. A job. A life. I haven't been in my office for months. I need to see if the shipment's arrived yet."

"My job is to keep you alive."

"You're just being difficult. Again."

"So are you."

"I made coffee," she told him, and gave a cajoling smile. It didn't appear to do any good. He didn't budge from blocking her exit.

He'd been sleeping soundly when she got up. He hadn't stirred when she'd kissed his forehead and brushed her hand through his hair before going to the bathroom. He was still sleeping when she got out of the shower and the entire time as she got dressed in a pair of black slacks and a gray sweater set before heading downstairs and puttering around in the kitchen. It annoyed her that the man seemed to materialize out of nowhere, barefoot, bare chested and wearing only jeans, the moment she decided to walk out the front door. All she wanted to do was stroll across campus to her office. It wasn't even so much the office she was interested in, but the getting there. She craved fresh air, the familiar, bland, peaceful scenery.

He did not look fully awake even as he glared adamantly at her. She tried another cajoling smile. She gestured toward the kitchen. "I figured you'd want some coffee when you woke up. Since you're up, why don't you have a cup? I'll be back in an hour, maybe less."

"You're not going anywhere."

"You could shave," she said. "Take a shower. Read a book. Relax. I won't be gone long. There's not a lot in the way of groceries. I thought I'd stop at the store on my way back and pick up a few things. I can't go very far," she told him. "I don't even own a car."

He leaned against the solid wood of the door and crossed his arms over his magnificent bare chest. "No."

"You're a pain, Castillo." She felt like stomping her foot in frustration, or kicking him. "I've been a prisoner for days," she blurted out. "I need some privacy!"

A flicker of pain crossed his face at her words. It disappeared, leaving him looking just as resolute as before, but with Carrie feeling like an insensitive fool. She had enjoyed his company. Even when she thought he was an outlaw, she had to admit that he'd been nothing but considerate. She really hadn't intended to vent her frustration quite so strongly. But she was dying to take a long walk all by herself to get her thoughts in some sort of order.

Right now, she was stuck in a veneer of calm over chaos

mode and she didn't like the feeling. It wasn't so much that she wanted to be alone—she was actually delighted with Rafe's company—but she did need some privacy. The hours spent frantically pacing the beach in Tulum didn't count. Worrying about the danger she'd recklessly sent Rafe into had dominated any coherent thought.

She sighed, then capitulated, because hurting him was the last thing she wanted to do. "Come on, I'll fix you breakfast." She turned and went through the doorway into the kitchen. He followed, but had only taken a step when someone knocked on the door. Carrie froze, the terror that had dominated her life rushing back in a stomach-twisting rush. Physical pain settled in her gut, while her heart lurched against her chest. She found herself staring at the blank face of the door and mouthing the name Torres without any sound issuing from her tight throat. It had to be someone bringing the instructions Torres had said would be sent to her at home. At home. Carrie shuddered.

Rafe saw the change that came over Carrie at the sound of the knock, and it nearly broke his heart. He'd never seen her look so afraid, not even the time he'd turned a gun on her in Maquiero's. She'd kept a brave face on through most of the dangerous days they'd spent together. He was shocked by this sudden fear, but not surprised. The woman who lived in this charming haven of a house on this peaceful street in this civilized college town never really expected to bring the jungle home with her. She wasn't mentally prepared to cope with the possibility of a message from a drug lord being delivered to her door. His Carolina, who seemed to be quite capable of coping with any situation, had been left behind in the Yucatán.

Or so it seemed for just a moment. The open terror disappeared from her face in no more than a second or two. He watched her push it back with an act of will, saw her momentarily hunched posture straighten, her chin lift proudly, her shoulders square. "I suppose I better get the door," she said as calm as you please.

Rafe was so stunned by the transformation that he barely heard the knock sound again. Then he shook his head, and his own tension eased. When she would have stepped around him, he still blocked the way. "I think it's for me," he told her, and opened the door.

Waiting outside was a young man he recognized from the team that had been assembled for this operation. He was carrying a large zippered garment bag. The man looked over Rafe's half-dressed, unshaven condition and shook his head. "Catch you at a bad time?" he asked, and just barely managed not to leer.

Rafe took the bag from him. "Thanks. You can go back to the surveillance van now." The young agent was still smiling at him when Rafe closed the door in his face. Rafe wasn't the slightest bit embarrassed about what anyone else on the DEA's strike team might be thinking about him right now. Maybe he should be. Maybe he'd be in trouble later. He didn't care. He was in charge of this operation. Once it was successfully completed, he'd face any consequences for being too involved with the woman he was protecting if he had to. He didn't much care about reprimands from his superiors. It was Carrie's opinion that mattered.

Sometime soon he was going to have to find the courage to talk about the consequences of what they'd been through in the past few days—and what it meant to them. Just now, after being told she wanted her privacy, after witnessing that flash of fear she'd covered up so well, he wasn't quite prepared to bring up the subject of their relationship or whether they had any hope of a future. He was too frightened of what her responses might be. Besides, asking the questions out loud would mean he'd have to think about the answers himself.

When he turned, Carrie was standing in the middle of

the hallway with her arms crossed. She had a puzzled look on her face. She didn't look relaxed, but both fear and the stern response to it had been wiped from her expression. "What's in the bag, Castillo?"

He held the garment bag by the hanger sticking out of the top. "The clothes I told you I'd asked to have brought to me. I told you about it yesterday, remember?"

She frowned. "Just how long are you planning to stay?"

It was on the tip of his tongue to tell her that he would stay as long as she wanted him. Instead, he said, "Until this part of the case is settled."

And after that? She wondered, but didn't say. *Where do we go from there?* She was going to have to bring the subject up sometime. After the scare she'd just had, she didn't think she was up to an emotional confrontation, though. "I need a cup of coffee. You need coffee, Castillo?"

"*Sí, querida.*" He hefted the bag in his hand. "Maybe I better put these away—and get a shower."

She nodded, but refrained from mentioning just how domestic that sounded. As he started up the stairs, she asked, "Did I hear you say something about a surveillance van?"

"I've got men at the front and back of your house," he told her as he continued up the stairs. "Inconspicuously. And with me inside, you're perfectly safe."

"You call that safe?" she called after him. His answering laugh drifted down from the top of the stairs. She looked after him for a moment. She was glad he'd made sure she was physically safe, though she wished he'd mentioned the surveillance sooner. Physically safe was nice. She didn't feel emotionally safe at all.

She wasn't sure what Rafael Castillo could do about protecting her emotions since he was responsible for a good deal of the danger that threatened her emotional well-being.

She turned toward the kitchen and dusted her hands together. "Might as well make breakfast while waiting for the apocalypse, I suppose."

"Great coffee."

"Thanks. More?" Carrie gave Rafe a refill without bothering to wait for an answer.

He nodded his thanks and sat back in the chair on the other side of the breakfast bar. She'd found freezer-burned frozen waffles and sausages in the freezer, and some solidified honey in the cabinet. She'd microwaved the honey to a gold liquid, toasted the waffles and fried the sausages by the time Rafe appeared in the kitchen doorway. They'd shared this bounty in a relatively comfortable silence, Rafe sitting on one side of the breakfast bar, Carrie standing on the other. She'd offered him more coffee after rinsing off their dishes and putting them in the dishwasher.

After pouring refills for them both, Carrie put the carafe back on the coffeemaker on the counter by the sink. Then she turned, mug cradled in her hands, and looked Rafe over. "You know, this is the first time I can say that you actually look like you might be a respectable, law-abiding citizen."

"Looks can be deceiving."

"I knew you'd say that." He was wearing a suit. She was used to him in tight jeans, a tight shirt and a jacket that was long enough to cover his arsenal of hand cannons, but not his very nice behind. "Nice suit." He was still wearing black and a collarless shirt that didn't need a tie. It wasn't exactly conservative, but the clothes suited him. His unruly hair was slicked back away from his face. As she continued looking at him, something occurred to her. "I'm used to having two brothers around," she told him. "I know good tailoring, and what you're wearing doesn't exactly look like something off the rack somebody at the office picked up on short notice."

He'd been staring rather pensively into his coffee mug. He looked up. "It's not. It's my stuff."

She was suddenly suspicious. "You live around here? Do you mean you could have gone home last night?"

"I work out of Los Angeles mostly, but I've been in and out of Washington a few times in the past year, making pickups and deliveries for Torres, getting briefed and filling out reports in between flights. Been here enough times that I've left some of my things at another agent's apartment. I need to go into the office today," he added.

She almost didn't hear his last comment. "You've been playing mule for Torres? Bringing drugs into the country?"

He nodded. "Drugs that never made it onto the street, *querida*. I had to seem to get my hands dirty. That was when I was new in his organization, before I worked my way up to bodyguard status."

Carrie banged her mug down on the counter. She was indignant as well as worried about the dangerous life Rafe had been living. He jumped as the cup thudded down next to his hand. "Rafael Castillo," she declared as she stabbed a finger under his nose, "you are giving up this undercover nonsense, aren't you?"

He stood and backed away gingerly. He was too used to secrecy about his job to tell her that one of the reasons he was going to the office in this lull while waiting for Torres to make a move was to discuss moving on to other types of assignments. He'd had enough. Everything that had happened with Carrie convinced him that it was time to get out. He'd lost his heart unknowingly; now he had to get his soul back before he could offer it to her freely.

He said only, "I'm thinking about it."

"Don't think about it. Do it."

"Don't give me orders, woman."

"Don't get all macho on me, man."

He smiled. "It's in the blood." He wanted to lean across

the counter and kiss her, but he backed toward the doorway instead. "I won't be long. You're not to leave the house. If you try, one of my people will escort you back inside." She stuck her tongue out at him in answer. He laughed. "Go hang out on the Internet, *querida,* and think warm thoughts of me while I'm gone."

She came around the counter. "Don't push it, Castillo."

He waved, then left hurriedly, just in case she was considering starting to throw things at him in a fit of Latin temper.

He'd pocketed a house key off a hook by the front door before leaving the house, so he didn't have to knock to get back in when he returned. The first sound he heard when he entered was the clacking of the computer keyboard. He followed the sound into the living room. Carrie only looked up briefly at his entrance, then concentrated her attention on the screen and what she was writing. He watched her fingers flying over the keys for a moment, fondly recalling the same intense look on her face the night he'd stood and watched her in the tent she used as an office at Chalenque.

He was glad she'd settled down to work. Her work was good for her, a necessary part of who she was.

"Anything interesting on-line?" he asked.

She barely glanced his way. She kept typing as she spoke. "Haven't been on-line. Been catching up on some correspondence. Also spent an hour on the phone with my grandmother. She still wants me to come to her party."

"Persistent woman."

"That's putting it mildly." She gave him a quick look over her shoulder. "I didn't tell her why I couldn't go tonight, despite some rather pointed questions and comments."

"That was wise."

"However, I will refer her to the Drug Enforcement Agency for an explanation when this is all over. Consider yourself warned.'' She turned back to the screen and concentrated on what she was writing. He watched her for a moment and thought how scholarly she looked in her subdued gray sweater, her posture erect, her hair pulled tightly back and fastened at her nape. Very little of his wild Carolina showed in the woman so diligently working at her desk even though what she was doing was no different from that night at Chalenque. It wasn't what she did, but the how that made him uncomfortable.

He worried that he wasn't wanted or welcome in this urban setting where she lived the other half of her life. He wasn't sure he belonged back in the civilized world, though he longed for it. He felt like a kid locked out in a storm, with his face pressed up against a glass door. He longed for the warmth and shelter indoors, but wasn't quite sure how to get inside. He thought Carrie was the one who'd open that door and let him in. He wanted her to invite him, because he was afraid to ask. Whatever either of them wanted, now was not the time to talk about whether they had a chance.

Not wanting to disturb her, he settled down on the couch and thought about his work while she got on with hers. His work was important to him, but frustrating for the present. The meeting with his superiors hadn't been long. He'd come away feeling that they were reluctant to let him change fieldwork for a desk job. It turned out he was reluctant to give up fieldwork himself. Some compromise that kept him from going under cover would have to be reached, but he'd need to have a long talk with his boss in L.A. before anything could be settled. He'd then held another consultation with his team, but other than staying alert, there wasn't anything they could do until Torres made a move. Carrie could keep busy, but he was in a waiting mode. He looked around for something to do, and his gaze was drawn to the large photo over the fireplace.

There was something familiar about it.

Rafe smiled to himself. Of course there was something familiar. It was a picture of the temple ruin of Chalenque. He'd spent the night there not that long ago. He leaned forward, hands on his knees and really *looked* at the picture. It was picture-postcard beautiful—a mysterious ruin seeming almost to float above the lush green forest. A sweep of wing from a brilliant red macaw showed in the forest canopy in the foreground. It was all so familiar.

Something so familiar that he never noticed it. Something that was part of the background of his daily life. He'd heard about the ruins in the rain forest, but he'd never been to Chalenque before going there to kidnap Carrie for Torres.

Maybe it wasn't Chalenque that was familiar. Maybe it was the photo. Maybe he was just reminded of something he'd seen on a television show about Mayan sites, but he didn't think so.

"Where have I seen a picture like that before?"

He spoke the words very softly to himself. Before he could find an answer, his cell phone rang. He stood, taking the phone from his jacket pocket. Carrie looked at him worriedly. He gestured for her to keep silent as one of his men outside reported.

"Good. Don't approach him. Follow him and pick him up when he's well away from the house—not that he's going to know anything. Talk to him anyway."

Carrie crossed the room to stand next to Rafe while he was on the phone. A cold line of dread trickled down her spine as he spoke. The moment he put the cell phone back in his pocket, she asked, "What's happening?"

Before he could answer, someone knocked on the door. She didn't need him to answer anyway. She'd known what was happening without having to ask the question. Maybe she'd been hoping that Rafe would have some other, easier, answer for her. Instead, he said nothing. He nodded, then gave her shoulder a reassuring squeeze before stepping back to let her go by.

Carrie answered his nod, took a deep breath and went to the door. The man outside was wearing a messenger-service uniform. The delivery van double-parked on the narrow street was the same color as his uniform and bore the same familiar insignia. He held a clipboard out to her. Carrie looked up and down the street before she stared hard at the deliveryman. This seemed far too mundane. She was expecting some sinister type to come skulking to the house at midnight. That the devil used Federal Express was downright offensive. She angrily scrawled her signature, grabbed the thin white envelope from the startled courier and slammed the door in his face.

Rafe tried to snatch the envelope from her the moment she turned from the door. She wasn't about to give it up. "That's addressed to me, Castillo."

After a brief tug-of-war, Rafe let her keep the envelope. "Fine. Open it." He put a call in to his people as she held the thing in her hands and studied the neatly typed address form on the front.

"It was mailed from Maryland." She looked sharply at Rafe. He was holding his phone up to his ear, but his attention was all on her. "Somehow I thought it would be sent from Oro Blanco."

"We'll trace the address," Rafe told her. He looked at her impatiently. "Will you open it?"

She shook it, and something rattled. She turned it over and over in her hands. Her stomach was in knots. She didn't want to read what was inside.

Rafe stepped close to her. His voice was soft, but very firm. "We don't have time for this, Carrie."

"All right!" She ripped the seal open, her hands shaking. She fumbled and nearly dropped the envelope. Another smaller, cream-coloured, square envelope fell out and landed on the brightly colored rug between them.

Carrie stared at it for a moment, then began to bend to pick it up. Rafe moved before her, and snatched up the small envelope before her hand reached it. He held it up. "Looks like an invitation." He held it out to her. "It's addressed to you."

Carrie's hands were still shaking when she took it from him. Somehow she knew what the invitation had to be. She made herself open it, take out the gold-embossed card and read it. She swallowed hard before she looked at Rafe. "It's an invitation to my grandmother's party."

He took the card from her numb fingers. "I suspected it might be." He read it aloud while Carrie looked at him, wide-eyed, hugging herself, her skin almost as gray as the turtlenecked sweater she wore. "Tonight," he concluded. "In Georgetown. In three hours. You have to show up at your grandparents' dinner for the Ambassador of Boravia at seven-thirty. That's where you'll meet Torres's contact."

Carrie heard his words and understood them, but she didn't believe them. Her brain was as numb as the rest of her. She wanted to shake her head to try to clear it, but couldn't find the strength. "But...why...how?"

Those were very good questions. Getting someone's address, phone number, almost any information, was easy enough. Getting something as specific as an invitation to what Rafe assumed was a very exclusive party was a more difficult matter. Not impossible. Money talked. Drugs talked. When he'd decided to use Carrie, Torres might have somehow planted, or bribed, someone close to Carrie's family to further ensure her compliance. There were millions of dollars at stake. Torres's survival hinged on this one pickup going smoothly. He might not trust that his promise to murder the people she worked with would be enough to secure her complete cooperation. Forcing her to make contact with the money man in the midst of her family would reinforce Torres's threat to destroy the people she cared for if that money didn't make its way back to him.

Or maybe the explanation was something far more simple.

Carrie had taken the invitation into the living room. Rafe followed, to find her standing by the French window, reading the invitation as though the words would be different if she read them in the clean afternoon sunlight.

He stood in front of the fireplace and looked up at the photo. "Can I ask you a question about Chalenque?"

Carrie whirled to face him. She wasn't up to talking about the dig just now. She wanted to snap at him that worrying about her family was more important than some old Mayan ruin, but he looked so serious, so professional, that she forced down the impulse. The man was working a case, she reminded herself, not being frivolous. She wanted very much to help him. "Yes."

"Is it a popular place? Well-known? Do tourists or photojournalists come there very often?"

"Are you kidding?" She couldn't help her incredulous, almost sarcastic response. "It's a minor site in the middle of a district with bad roads, which also happens to be infested with drug cartels. Nobody comes to Chalenque."

"You do."

"I was there before Torres moved in. I've been working the dig practically single-handed since I was a grad student. I only found the place because of some old legends my mother told me she heard when she was a kid. No one in Oro Blanco knew about the ruins in the forest only a few miles outside of town."

"It's a pretty place."

He was standing very still, all coiled grace and tension. She remembered how he'd reminded her of a panther the first time she'd seen him. He looked like one now, like a stalking panther following a fresh scent. His eyes blazed though his expression gave nothing away.

"What?"

"It's a pretty place," he repeated.

"The most beautiful place in the world to me."

"But no one has come to photograph it?" He pointed at the large photo of the temple on the wall. "No one professional?"

She shook her head. "Jeremy's not a pro, but he could be. He's never sold any of his work, but he likes to give copies of his pictures as gifts. He took hundreds of photos of the ruins when he visited last year."

"I see."

Carrie put her hands on her hips. The invitation crumpled in her hand. "What? What are you getting at? Do your questions have anything to do with Torres's contact inviting me to my own grandmother's dinner party?"

"Perhaps."

She waited, but he didn't seem inclined to explain any further. He turned back to study the photo while she worriedly watched him. A trail of impossible suspicions began to weave its way through her mind. She pushed the ridiculous notions aside. She also decided she didn't want to know what Rafe was thinking. Then again, maybe she needed to know.

Before she could work up the courage to ask, some of the coiled tension in him visibly eased. Still looking very serious, he said, "This will have to be planned very carefully."

"What will?"

He grinned, the hunting-cat gleam blazing in his amber eyes once more. "The takedown, *querida*. The thing we've been working for."

She gulped and tried not to show the fact that she'd just gone cold inside. "Right."

He took out his cell phone and held it in the palm of his hand. "Tell me," he asked, "just how formal is this formal affair?"

"There's the ambassador and other embassy people, I imagine," Carrie answered. "Some State Department officials. A smattering of think-tank types, a university president or two. And a freshman congressman Grandmama's been trying to set me up with." She gave a faint smile, some of her humor returning. "That's the real reason she's been so insistent I show up for this little black-tie get-together."

Rafe noted the reference to matchmaking, but let it go. He had to concentrate on business. Besides, he figured he was up to scaring off at least a first-term congressman from sniffing around his woman. In fact, he was probably up to warning off any male, up to and including Cabinet level, if he had to. Putting jealous thoughts aside, he considered all the other people she'd mentioned. "That's pretty formal."

"People in Washington like to have places to see and be seen. Grandmama's always been quite the political hostess. Her parties are A-list affairs. All sorts of power-suit types…" The smile faded slowly off her face to be replaced by alarm. "Do you think one of them is Torres's contact?" She put her hand to her mouth. "That one of the VIP guests is a drug dealer?"

Rafe wondered if he should tell her exactly what he thought, then decided against it. Tonight's operation was going to be a very delicate one. You didn't just march into a party full of VIPs, pull out your guns and make a noisy arrest. No, the bad guy was going to have to be taken down quietly, with subtlety. If Carrie acted suspicious at the wrong time, she could give the whole game away. Better not to risk telling her. Besides, she wouldn't want to believe him.

"It could be anyone in the house," he said, which was the truth. "Could be someone from the catering staff. Maybe a guest, maybe a party crasher. Anyone." He sighed. "And I have three hours to get my people inserted into and around the house in a way that won't cause a diplomatic incident."

"You could call my grandparents," Carrie suggested. "Warn them. I'm sure they'd be willing to let you—"

"No, *querida,*" he interrupted. "Letting them know might inadvertently tip off Torres's contact. I won't do that."

She looked at him, incredulous with shock and annoyance. "So you'll put the entire party—an ambassador, my grandparents and cousins, everybody—in danger? For the sake of making an arrest?"

"For the sake of stopping Torres. Do I have to tell you how many lives he and his dirty business have destroyed?" He didn't wait for her to answer. He flipped open the phone. "First I have to make some calls. Then I have to go outside and talk to my people."

"Fine." She turned away from him and returned to looking out the window. It was a French door that opened onto a minuscule brick patio and the town house's small backyard. There was an apple tree in the yard, old and squat, crowded up against the high back fence. Under normal circumstances, it was not the most beautiful tree in the world, but it was May, and at this time of the year it was covered with lush, pale pink blossoms. She noticed violets blooming in the shade at the base of the fence, and buds on the two rosebushes near the patio.

It was spring here, a much tamer spring than came to Quintana Roo in the Yucatán Peninsula. Her backyard looked peaceful and safe out there, pastel and pretty, with green grass and a high wall to keep the world at bay. It was all so very deceptive. There was no more safety in this place than in any other. There wouldn't be while greedy, callous criminals like Torres were loose in the world.

"Something has got to be done about that man."

She hadn't realized she'd spoken aloud until Rafe came up behind her and put his hands on her shoulders. She'd been aware of him talking on the phone and of his leaving, but didn't know he'd returned to the house until he touched her. "It will be." His tone held a steely promise. "Soon."

Leaning into Rafe's steadying embrace was an automatic gesture, a necessary comfort. She noticed their images reflected, ghostlike, in the glass. They looked right together, like a couple who'd been with each other forever, a pair used to facing the world and taking on anything the world threw their way. Though the image was only a faint reflection in a town-house window, she hoped that there was some basis in reality in what she saw there.

"Why involve my family?" she asked. "Why not have me meet him somewhere neutral? Why bring them into this? Torres can threaten me," she went on angrily before Rafe could answer, "but nobody messes with my family."

Rafe's hands came around her waist. He turned her to face him. His wide mouth was turned up in a smile. "Because Torres doesn't know how mean you are, *querida*."

"You're only saying I'm mean because I shot you."

His arm was still sore. "It wasn't your shooting me. It was the way you nursed me that convinced me how dangerous you are." He stepped back. "I think it's time we got ready to go."

Those were words Carrie had dreaded hearing, but she tried not to show it. "Sure," she said with a nonchalance she did not feel. In fact, she felt as if she would be dressing for her own execution.

Chapter 12

She couldn't go through with it.

Sometime between getting out of the shower and putting on her underwear, the impossibility of the whole enterprise finally overwhelmed her. Carrie didn't know what she was going to do, but she did know that she was totally drained of courage, of energy. Rafe had said she was mean, that she was brave and tough. She didn't feel as though she had any of those qualities. Maybe an hour ago she'd had them, but not right now. She'd been on a roller coaster for days, pumped up on excitement, living on nerves and passion. Maybe she'd been tough and brave and all those other things she'd reveled in hearing Rafe say about her, or maybe she'd just been faking it because there was no other choice.

Right now, she just felt scared. Disoriented. She wasn't even sure what she was doing standing in front of her closet, or when she'd picked out the black dress she was holding in her hands. She stared at the dress, hating the thought of putting it on and going off to meet an evil man. She hated being caught in this web that Miguel Torres had woven. She hated being Rafael Castillo's stalking horse. She hated the nasty suspicions about who the evil man she was supposed to meet might be, which gnawed at what little strength she had left. She didn't want to face those suspicions even if only to prove them wrong. She refused to let herself think about them.

She just couldn't go through with it.

"Whatever else goes down—" Rafe spoke into the cellular phone, instructing his second in command "—nothing happens to the lady. I'll be with her, but I want somebody backing me up at all times. If I have to walk away from her, somebody else takes my place. She didn't ask for this trouble and nothing is going to happen to her. Understood?" His tone was adamant, and the answer he got was a crisp, enthusiastic affirmative. "Good. Is the car here? No?" He shook his head in frustration at the logistics of driving in the D.C. area. "I don't care what they say, the traffic is worse here than in L.A." There was a chuckle of agreement from the other end of the line. "Call me when it gets here."

Rafe flipped the phone shut, pocketed it, then checked his appearance in the spare bedroom's dresser mirror. The dark slacks and elegantly draped jacket were a custom fit, not some hastily acquired formal wear sent over by the office. The tux had been among the clothes he'd kept at his friend's place, a memento from another undercover assignment. He barely recognized himself in these clothes, with his hair pulled back. He guessed he would do. He just hoped he'd pass muster with Carrie's grandmother. She sounded like a formidable old bird.

If she was as formidable as her granddaughter, it would be hard work impressing her. And just why did he feel the need to impress her? He gave a wry look at his image in the mirror. Planning on presenting yourself as grandson-in-law material? he wondered. Maybe, he thought, then forced the idea down. He'd think about it later, but this wasn't the time to consider a romantic commitment. Tonight he had to concentrate on getting Carrie safely through the evening. He had to focus on catching Torres's accomplice.

"Later," he said to the image in the mirror, then walked across the hall to Carrie's room. She didn't notice him enter. He watched her from the doorway. What he saw was not encouraging.

He took in the frightened look on her face and realized that she was half-paralyzed with nervousness. The jitters had finally gotten to her. He wasn't surprised. They'd had a couple of days in the quiet haven of her house after all the mad peril in Mexico. It was going to be difficult for her to go back out into danger.

She stood in front of her closet, clad only in underwear and panty hose and holding up a simple little black dress. She was staring at it as though it was a loathsome snake, but he didn't think she was really looking at the dress. He thought she was close to her limit, that her head was full of the grim possibilities of how the night could turn out. He knew she was brave and resilient, but she'd been through hell and was all too aware that she was going to have to go through more before this ordeal was over.

She needed something else to think about. He stepped forward and sneered, "You're wearing that?" He said it partly to give her a distraction, but also because he really didn't like the dress.

Carrie started at the sound of Rafe's voice and turned to look at him. He was wearing what she guessed was an Armani suit and a disapproving frown. She looked at the simple black dress on the hanger. She had more important

things to worry about than what she was wearing, but she
didn't like the challenge in his tone. She reacted instantly
to his belligerence. The dress was short, elegant, expensive.
"What's wrong with it?"

"It's dull."

"No, it isn't."

He took the hanger from her and put the dress back in
the closet before facing her squarely. "You're a beautiful,
vibrant woman." He put his hands on her shoulders. They
felt like warm silk beneath his hands. She was shaking a
little, but calmed at his touch. He wanted to smile and be
reassuring. Instead, he kept distracting her with a very real
complaint. He didn't realize just how much he meant his
words until he said, "The woman I met in Oro Blanco wore
shorts that showed off her legs all the way up her gorgeous
thighs, and she wasn't afraid of a tight T-shirt displaying
her bosom."

"It's very hot in Oro Blanco."

He smirked. "*Querida,* what you wore in Oro Blanco
raised the temperature."

Carrie blushed. She dressed comfortably to work on the
dig. She certainly didn't dress provocatively. Okay, maybe
she was a bit more relaxed in the informal atmosphere of
the rain forest, but that didn't mean her standards of dress
were any looser. "I dress appropriately for the situation,"
she told him.

"And this situation requires you to be dull and color-
less?"

"No! Of course not. What is your problem, Castillo?"

Warming to the subject, he looked at her closet. "Brown,
beige, tan, black. These are not the colors a Latino woman
should wear."

Carrie gave a cynical little laugh. "They are if she wants
to get tenure."

He looked sharply back at her. What had started out as

a distraction turned to real annoyance. "I thought you were proud of your heritage."

"I am."

"You don't dress like it."

Carrie wasn't going to stand for that kind of comment from him. Or anyone. "What do you want me to do, wear a ruffled skirt and a big hat with fruit on it?" She gestured at her face. "Am I supposed to do the *pintadora* makeup and hair thing just because I have brown skin?"

"No." He began to riffle through her things, rattling the hangers as he slapped them aside one by one. "Don't you own anything red?"

"Yes."

"Then wear it tonight." He gave her a look that sent her blood singing. "Wear something red for me, Carolina."

Rafe couldn't believe what he'd just said, what he was doing, but he couldn't stop. Never mind the case. This was about them. It was important.

She wanted to. She wanted to do anything this man asked—anything to please him, to arouse him, to show the world she was his woman. Except she wasn't exactly his woman, was she? First and foremost, she had to belong to herself. She shook her head. "I can't."

The annoyance disappeared from his face. He looked disappointed, and it nearly drove her crazy. "Why not?" He sounded more defeated than belligerent.

She hastened to explain. "I don't own anything that's bright red. I've only got a dark red sweater."

He touched the base of her neck, traced his fingers along her collarbone. "You'd look beautiful in scarlet."

"That's not the point." He started looking through her closet again. She crossed her arms under her bosom and sighed. Never mind what she wanted, what he wanted. There were some things she needed to explain. "You're from East L.A., right?"

"*Sí.*"

"Then you know all about colors."

He stopped searching through her clothing and looked at her. "Colors. You mean as in gang colors?"

"Yes."

He nodded sadly. "I wore gang colors myself for a year. I was fourteen. My dad sent me away to military school when he found out."

"Good for him."

"But what are you talking about?"

"Colors. We all wear them every day of our lives. If we aren't in gangs, we're in niches. We dress to fit in. I'm not ashamed of who I am, but I don't care to flaunt it too much, either. I can't be a *pintadora*. A 'pretty painted one' is not who I am. It may be where you come from, but it's not part of the culture I grew up in."

"I'm not ashamed of *my* culture." He pointed at her. "I thought you were fighting to preserve yours."

"I'm fighting to preserve the history of the place my mother came from. That's what I give back to my Mayan blood. I'm damned proud of it. I value that history and culture, but that isn't where I live. Besides," she hurried on before he could make any retort, "I'm also an associate professor of archaeology at a small university. Associate professors wear beige and brown and black and tan no matter what their gender or ethnic background. I don't think anyone, male or female, is allowed to be colorful if they want to be taken seriously."

"That's not true."

Her reply was just as adamant as his had been. "Oh, yes, it is. I don't even disagree with it. I bet you don't dress like a drug dealer when you go into the office. Wasn't that you I saw in a dark suit earlier today?" She looked him up and down. "And I think you'll fit in at my grandparents' party in that."

Rafe ducked his head and looked up at her from under his thick eyelashes. "Maybe," he conceded.

"Besides," Carrie went on, lifting her head proudly, "I get my conservative good taste from the Robinson side of the family." She laughed softly, with only a hint of bitterness in it. "If I walk into my grandmother's house in anything less than Ralph Lauren, she gives me this faintly offended 'shouldn't you be eating in the kitchen with the servants?' look." To be fair, Carrie admitted to herself, Grandmama would give that look to any grandchild who didn't meet her exacting, rigid, conservative standards, but it always seemed to Carrie that the woman was especially critical of her. Rightfully or not, she'd felt that way since her great-grandmother had stripped away much of her trust in her family with only a few words.

Rafe sighed and clasped her hands in his. "Okay. Point taken. Dr. Robinson is a serious person." He gave her a twinkling grin that threatened to melt her toes into the plush carpet. "But does Carrie Robinson have to dress so seriously for a fancy party? Don't you have civvies?" He looked at her from head to toe, his gaze so heated she would happily have stripped naked right then and there. It wasn't as if she was wearing that much anyway. Who needed clothes alone in a bedroom with Rafe Castillo?

Only she wasn't going to be staying alone in a bedroom with him. Their interlude was over. The thought left her melancholy. It also left her with the urge to make this one last evening into something very special—to celebrate what they had shared. She might grieve if the man walked out of her life, but she also might as well enjoy him while she had him. She wanted nothing more than to give herself to him tonight. To the devil with her grandmother's stuffy taste. Tonight she would be beautiful for Rafe Castillo, even if she didn't have anything scarlet to wear.

"Wait a second," she said, and went into the spare room.

She came back with a garment bag. "Bobby made me buy this last year. He was nominated for a Golden Globe and didn't have a date for the ceremony, so he talked me into going along. He wanted to show up with someone who looked more Hollywood than field archaeologist." She unzipped the bag and brought out what was no more than a few very expensive ounces of gold lace over nearly sheer gold chiffon. She held up the slinky dress by its thin spaghetti straps. She waved her hands slightly, causing the long column of lace to shimmer and catch the light. "This thing clings to places I didn't even know I had."

Rafe stared, transfixed. His heart rate was speeding up. "I can imagine."

"I can't even put on underwear if I don't want to spoil the line of this alleged dress. I'm a C-cup, darlin'. I *need* a bra."

"Not in that dress, you don't, *querida*." Rafe couldn't take his eyes off the wisp of gold she held before her. It was the sexiest dress he'd ever seen. He had no trouble picturing how Carrie would look in it. He wasn't sure he wanted to let her out of the house, maybe even the bedroom, wearing it. Even before she put it on, he was eager to take it off.

"I'm not sure I want to wear this again," she confessed. "Not after the way people stared at me the last time I wore it."

"Any man who isn't dead would stare at you in that dress."

Carrie thought that maybe she should blush in shame. Wearing this flimsy little excuse of a dress, she'd been nothing but embarrassed at the gala event she'd attended with her brother. As the seconds passed, she grew less and less reluctant to consider wearing it again. And not for a brother this time. She threw back her head and laughed.

Shamelessly. She smiled seductively at him. "You want me to wear it?"

He swallowed, then nodded slowly. "Oh, yes."

It wasn't just that he was looking at her like a starving man that helped her make up her mind. It wasn't just that he made her feel sexy and feminine and wild. She wanted to do this for Rafe, and not just because she loved him and might never see him after tonight. She wanted to do it because he had bravely gone off on a mad crusade, with guns blazing, to rescue her artifacts just because she wanted him to do it. He'd done it for her. It made her warm all over just thinking about it. It was a warmth born not of lust, but of pride in him, and joyous wonder, that this man had gone to such chivalrous lengths just because she'd asked him to do it.

Okay, she'd demanded it, hysterically, but the point was, he'd risked his life for her sake. A man like that deserved the best she could do for him in turn. If it meant wearing a silly, sexy, slinky bit of lace to please him, that was fine with her.

He was still staring. She passed her hand before his face. He didn't even blink. She laughed again. "I think I better go change clothes. Stay right there, monkey boy," she said as she turned toward the bathroom. "And try not to melt."

Fifteen minutes later, Carrie stared at her reflection in the hall mirror as she and Rafe waited to leave her town house. The woman gazing back at her hardly seemed like her at all, but she liked what she saw. It wasn't so much that she looked alluring and sexy. It was rather that she looked comfortable being that way.

Carrie knew she'd appeared ill at ease when she'd worn the dress once before, entering another glamorously dressed gathering on the arm of a man in a tuxedo. She knew the reason why, too. It had everything to do with the man who was wearing the tuxedo. Last time, that man had been her brother. She'd been awkward, embarrassed, very much out of place. This time, she felt ready to strut her stuff, dance until the sun came up and conquer the world.

The pleased, almost adoring way Rafe looked at her, the gently caressing way he touched her, the warm appreciation in his glance, his possessive nearness—all these things made her *know* that she was a desirable, beautiful woman. She knew that he wanted her, and that knowledge added a heady rush of pleasure that put an extra bit of seductiveness in the way she moved. In fact, she suspected she'd moved sexily for him all along. She'd just never been really conscious of it until now. She liked being conscious of it and knowing that she didn't look like this, move like this, for any other man, but for Rafe Castillo alone.

She found herself thinking about some of the things he'd said when he was complaining about the clothes in her closet and she remembered something that had happened on the day he had rescued her from Beltrano and his men.

He leaned close, his breath brushing her neck as he whispered, "What are you chuckling about?"

She tilted her head up. She suspected that she looked like she was waiting to be kissed. He certainly looked like he wanted to kiss her. His hand caressed her upper arm, then cupped her elbow as she reached up to stroke a finger along the line of his cheekbone. "I think I have to concede the truth of a behavior pattern you observed in me."

His brows lowered over his magnificent amber eyes. "You speaking English, Dr. Robinson?" She nodded. "What do you mean, *querida?*"

"I mean that you're right. I let myself act more naturally, not quite so much like a straitlaced New England college professor when I'm in Mexico. Maybe it's the heat," she said. "Or knowing that my grandmother isn't there to tell me to stand up straight, be demure, have a little dignity and always be sure to write thank-you notes.''

He still looked puzzled. ''That's why you were laughing?''

She shook her head. ''No. I was looking at myself in this dress and liking it. I remembered that I was mortified when I wore it before, but that I had no trouble making a joke about my—female attributes—when I was talking to Beltrano just before his men came storming in with guns.''

Rafe went from looking puzzled to looking annoyed. And was that a spark of jealousy she saw flaring in those gorgeous eyes? His voice was softly dangerous as he said, ''You made a joke—about which female attributes, Carolina?'' She looked down at her bosom. He followed her gaze. ''I see.''

''From that angle, I'm sure you do.''

''Hmm. You want to explain this joke?''

She flashed him an amused look. ''You're jealous.''

''Yes.''

''Cool.''

''I knew he wanted you. Torres wanted you. Didn't you ever notice?''

''No.''

''Thank goodness. You could have had every man in Oro Blanco eating out of your hand if you'd wanted.''

She gave him a slow, sultry smile, then trailed her hand up his arm. ''You think so?''

He groaned. ''I think I've created a monster.'' He drew her close. ''And I like it. What did you say to Beltrano?''

''He referred to my nose as a hooter,'' she answered. ''I told him that noses are called honkers and that hooters are—''

''Hush. I know what they are.'' He tsked and wagged a finger at her. ''Not that I would ever use so crude a word.''

She tried to look prim. ''Of course not.''

He would have said something else, but his cell phone rang before he could. He stepped away from her to answer it. He listened to the voice on the other end, made a comment, then folded the little phone and put it in his pocket. He held his hand out to her. "Time to go."

The pleasure was suddenly gone from the evening. The warm glow she'd been experiencing from an argument, followed by shared humor and seductive teasing, was snuffed out. The dread passed quickly. She refused to go back to the state of terror that had gripped her for a few minutes in her bedroom. It was replaced with steely determination. She even managed a smile for the watching man. Time to go. Yes, it was time this was over. Time Torres and his whole organization were brought down. She was happy to play her small part in this final phase of the operation.

"Time to go," she agreed, and trustingly put her hand in Rafe Castillo's.

"Nice house."

Carrie chuckled as Rafe helped her out of the car. "You could say that. It was built around 1820," she explained. "It's even on the list of the area's historical buildings. It used to be the main house of the Robinson estate. After the turn of the century, the neighborhood grew up around it."

He kept her hand in his as they walked up the stairs to the entrance. Traffic was heavy in front of the three-story, redbrick edifice. The street was narrow, cobbled and clogged with a long line of stretch limousines and luxury cars of foreign and domestic make. The people emerging from those vehicles were all dressed as formally as they were.

The young woman who greeted them in the front hallway wore a simple, long black dress, very nearly the twin of the one Carrie had originally planned on wearing. The woman was blond, in her early twenties, attractive, elegantly thin.

Too thin, Rafe thought as his gaze caressed Carrie's lush form. He took a step back as the blonde's face lit with a warm smile.

"Carrie!" She threw her arms around Carrie's shoulders. Carrie hugged her back. "You look gorgeous." Then she stepped away and critically eyed Carrie's dress. "But Grandmama's going to hit the roof when she sees what you're wearing." Her gaze shifted to Rafe. Her welcoming smile widened, then warmed.

Carrie recognized the stunned look on her cousin's face. She'd worn it herself the first time she saw Rafe. A woman's natural first reaction to the man was a helpless hormonal rush. She decided to intervene before steam began rising off the poor girl. She looked at Rafe. "This is my cousin Alicia. Alicia Robinson, this is Rafael Castillo, a colleague of mine."

Alicia looked him up and down appreciatively. Her tongue briefly moistened her perfectly made-up mouth. "If he's an archaeologist, I'm changing professions."

Rafe stepped forward, an imposing male presence. Carrie put her arm through his. "Actually," he said to Alicia, his voice a Latin-accented, confidential purr, "I'm a drug dealer."

Alicia's eyes widened, then her fair skin colored. Her expression changed from entranced to sheepish. She held her hand out to Rafe. "Excuse me, Mr. Castillo, I'm not normally so rude. I should have asked *you* if you're an archaeologist."

Her apology and open expression forced Rafe to reverse his instant dislike of the young woman. He remembered that Carrie had said that most of her family were very nice. He looked at Carrie and saw the amused way she was looking at her cousin. So he kissed Alicia's hand. It seemed like the sort of thing to do when wearing a tuxedo. "I'm not an archaeologist," he told her. "I'm happy to meet you, Alicia Robinson."

Carrie observed that it took Alicia just a moment longer than it should have to remove her hand from Rafe's gentle grasp, and she considered snarling at her cousin to speed up the process. But Alicia recovered and stepped back before Carrie needed to take any drastic, territorial action.

The hallway was crowded with people. Alicia took a quick look around and said, "I see Dr. Haeder. I promised Grandpa I'd hustle him into the library as soon as he arrived." She waved toward the wide doorway. Guests mingled and talked in the large room beyond. "Have a good time. And don't let Grandmama see you in that dress," Alicia cautioned as she hurried off.

Carrie laughed, then steered Rafe toward the reception room. For the moment, her nervousness was drowned in the sheer delight of being with him. Though she did blame Alicia's comments about her dress for the deliberate way she leaned against her Latin lover's arm and the way she slinked, rather than walked, through the crowd. She really didn't pay attention to where they were. Her attention was centered on Rafe.

"Drug dealer indeed," she whispered as they paused somewhere near the center of the big room. She shouldn't have been amused, but there was a merry twinkle in his eyes. She found his teasing humor infectious.

He put a finger over her lips and shook his head. "Shh, *querida,* that's our secret." He didn't mean to trace the outline of her soft lips with his finger. He was sure she didn't mean to playfully nip at the tip of his finger. Or toss her head in a way that sent a silky strand of hair brushing provocatively across his palm while their gazes locked and burned into each other. It just happened. And if there was anyone else in the room for those few seconds, neither of them took any notice.

"I'd appreciate it if you two would stop burning up all the oxygen in the room."

The speaker's tone was clipped, cultured and very cold. Rafe's attention shot to the woman who'd spoken so disapprovingly as the rest of the world came into focus. His first thought upon seeing the forbidding old woman was that Carrie hadn't gotten her dark chocolate eyes from her mother's side of the family. The woman's skin was as white and fragile as rice paper, her short hair pure silver, her dress creamy white. All this paleness made her dark eyes even more striking. He wondered how eyes that dark could be so cold.

He almost asked, but before the incautious words could slip out, Carrie said, "Hello, Grandmama." She refused to be cowed by the basilisk look that was turned her way. She forced a bright smile. "I came to your party after all."

"And decided to leave half your dress at home, I see."

Carrie started to cross her arms under her bosom, but that seemed too much like a defensive gesture. She didn't reach for the support of Rafe's hand, but his fingers slipped reassuringly through hers as she said, "I like this dress. It shows off my assets."

This comment only caused the matriarch's frown to deepen. "A granddaughter of mine should keep her assets in an investment portfolio and her bosom under cover." She relented somewhat and kissed Carrie's cheek. "It's good to have you home, dear. It really is." She looked Rafe over critically as she continued, "But do keep your private life private. All the ice was melting on the buffet table from the way you two were looking at each other. I see no need to upset either my guests or the catering staff, do you, young man?"

"No, ma'am." There was absolutely no other response he could have made. She commanded instant respect as well as something that went beyond fear and straight to awe. He was grateful that Carrie was now squeezing his hand reassuringly while her grandmother's attention was turned on him. It took him a moment to recover, but he was a man who'd faced down armed and very dangerous men. That had to count as some sort of basic training in dealing with this frail little old lady, didn't it? "I'm happy to meet you, Mrs. Robinson. I'm—"

"Rafael Castillo, who is neither an archaeologist nor a drug dealer. Or so my other granddaughter tells me. But he kisses hands quite nicely." She smiled slightly as Rafe instantly took the cue and brushed his lips across the back of her hand. "I'm Delia Robinson. Welcome to my home."

It was a tiny hand, blue veins prominent under the thin skin, the long fingers still elegant and capable. He realized that a sense of humor lay underneath her acid words, along with an unwavering sense of propriety that brooked no compromise. Would Carrie be like this when she was old? As strong as a diamond and as tough as nails? He thought that he'd very much like to be around to find out.

"Our behavior was a bit out of line, perhaps," he said. "I'm sorry."

"Apology accepted, Mr. Castillo."

Their conversation was being held quietly, their words blending in with the noise from all the other people gathered in the large room. Despite being caught up in his attraction to Carrie, Rafe was well aware of why they were there and what was going on around them. His gaze swept the room.

Against one pale blue wall, a buffet table was set up beneath large oil paintings of people in eighteenth- and nineteenth-century clothing. He guessed these were portraits of distinguished ancestors. Waiters moved skillfully through the gathering, carrying trays of drinks. Rafe noted the position of everyone in the room. He noted the discreet presence of security people other than his own, here to unobtrusively protect the ambassador the affair was honoring. No other government agency had been briefed on tonight's DEA operation. Rafe didn't want any interference. He just hoped the other security agents didn't notice. The plan was for his people to stay unnoticed and do their job so efficiently that no one but the man they arrested would know they were here. To that end, Rafe made a very careful scrutiny of the waiters.

So did Delia Robinson.

"Stand up straight, young man," Mrs. Robinson said to a passing dark-haired waiter.

A look of surprise crossed the tall man's face as his spine automatically straightened. He gave her a respectful nod, exchanged a look with Rafe, then quickly disappeared into the crowd. Carrie and Rafe both struggled not to crack a smile in front of a woman of such rigorous disposition.

While Carrie struggled not to laugh or to say anything to Rafe about the waiter, she was happy to see another family member come up behind her grandmother.

The old man who approached them was tall and thin, bald but for a corona of white hair, with outsize ears and a neatly trimmed white beard. Rafe could tell by the pleased look on Carrie's face that this was her grandfather.

"Delia, are you pestering my grandchild?"

Delia Robinson gave her husband a smiling glance that made her look decades younger. "Of course I am, Jonathan."

"It's her way of showing affection," Jonathan Robinson said to Rafe, then gave Carrie a swift hug. "I thought you weren't coming, *chica*. She tried to get me to call you," he added conspiratorially, but with a teasing glance at his wife. "But I told her that I didn't coerce my grandchildren. I'm glad you came." He held Carrie out at arm's length. "You certainly add a touch of—glamour—to this stuffy affair." He then turned his attention to Rafe, and Carrie hastened to introduce them. "Happy to meet you. Have you known Caroline long?"

Before Rafe could answer, Delia Robinson said, "There's Congressman Taylor, Caroline. You really should say hello to him. Come with me."

Carrie gave Rafe a helpless look, but before he could intervene, her grandfather put an arm around Rafe's broad shoulders. "You seem like the sort of young man who enjoys a good beer. I know I do. Let's get a couple of Robin Reds, shall we?" Without waiting for an answer, he steered Rafe toward the buffet table.

Rafe had to admire the old couple's teamwork in separating him and Carrie as they were borne away through the crowd in separate directions. A quick check around convinced him that it was safe enough for her to spend some time away from his side. His men were all over the room, most of them inconspicuously serving drinks. He didn't like their being apart, though, especially knowing Carrie was being led off by a matchmaking grandmother to spend time with a more suitable candidate for her hand.

"Don't look so worried, young man," Jonathan Robinson said. "Taylor doesn't stand a chance."

Carrie cast a glance over her shoulder as she followed her grandmother toward a knot of people standing by the fireplace. She saw Rafe and her grandfather, both holding beer bottles—her father insisted that his brew was best consumed straight out of the bottle and Granddad insisted on following his son's instructions no matter how much Grandmama frowned. Granddad had a suspiciously kindly look on his face. This was not a good sign. "He's going to drill the living daylights out of Rafe, isn't he?"

"Of course he is," Grandmama answered. "When one of our granddaughters brings a stranger into our house and they act as if they need to have a bucket of cold water poured over them, that calls for some serious questions."

Normally, Carrie would have been too flabbergasted, and
shamed, by Grandmama's comments to manage any sort of
response. Other than blushing and possibly apologizing, of
course. She wasn't feeling normal right now, however. She
certainly wasn't feeling intimidated. What she felt, at least
about Rafe, was wonderful, and she wasn't about to put up
with anyone's belittling or trying to subdue their attraction
to each other. She stopped in the middle of the room, high-
heeled shoes planted firmly in the deep, rose-patterned carpet. Her grandmother went on a few steps before noticing
that Carrie wasn't dutifully following in her aristocratic
wake. When she turned back with a commanding look and
lifted brow, Carrie laughed.

She was angry, but she laughed. She had never felt more
liberated in her life. When she didn't budge, Grandmama
came back to her.

"What is the matter with you, Caroline?"

"Not a thing." Carrie chuckled again. "Not a thing."

Grandmama frowned sternly at her. "You certainly look
as if something is wrong. If nothing else, I would guess
that you've been having a great deal of very pleasant sex
recently."

The words did not have the effect of cowing her. Carrie
couldn't keep the wide smile off her face. "I have."

"Good for you."

"No offense intended, but for the first time in my life,
Grandmama, I don't care what you think." She meant the
words from the bottom of her heart. Even if she and Rafe
Castillo never saw each other after tonight, she'd always
remember him for helping her feel the way she did right
now—a free adult woman who had to answer to no one but
herself. "I'm happy," she went on while Grandmama's
eyes widened. "He makes me happy."

The reaction she got was not the one she expected. Her
grandmother reached out and gently patted her cheek.

"Good for him. And good for you." She stepped back and sighed. "I suppose you won't be spending any time with Nat Taylor this evening."

"Not a single minute."

Carrie expected an argument, an order. What she got was a twinkling smile. "I'll have to revert to Plan B."

"Plan B?"

"Alicia isn't seeing anyone at the moment. She and the congressman might just do for each other." She peered around. "Where is the girl?"

"I saw her out in the hall, Grandmama."

Grandmama looked up at the man who'd spoken, her usual disapproving expression slipping back into place. Carrie turned at the sound of the light, pleasant voice.

He was tall and slender, blond and tan, very handsome in a fine-boned, seemingly fragile way. He was always cheerful, joking, helpful, easy to be with. She'd loved him more than any other member of her family for a very long time. As she held her hand out for his warm grasp and made herself smile, she hated him more than she'd ever hated anyone in her life.

"Hello, Jeremy."

Chapter 13

It was Jeremy.

She hoped she was wrong, but knew she wasn't. She'd suspected, really, though she'd fought thinking about it ever since Rafe questioned her about the photo over her mantel. She hadn't actually remembered seeing one similar to hers in Torres's office until Rafe asked whether anyone professional had photographed the site. She'd noticed Torres's picture at the time, but hadn't connected it to her cousin's photography. Or his visits to the Chalenque dig. Maybe she should have made the connection immediately—but why should she have?

He was a banker, in a position where he managed a great deal of money in international accounts. That sounded like the sort of position someone funneling drug money could use. He lived beyond his means. Everyone knew that. He was so insouciant about living the high life that no one but Grandmama ever paid it any mind. Grandmama had complained to her that he'd brought a great deal of luggage when he'd moved in after splitting up with his wife. Clothes were probably not the only things in his luggage, Carrie thought, and she'd been sent to pick up a suitcase. More damning, maybe more so than the photos, was the arrogant callousness of sending her an invitation to this party. Hadn't he known, or cared, how she'd react to that?

The painful irony of it all very nearly broke her heart. The man she'd thought was a monster but couldn't help but love turned out to be a hero. The man she'd always loved unconditionally turned out to be the villain. She wanted to strike back at her smiling cousin. To give him a piece of her mind.

She wanted to find out why.

Which was the reason she didn't immediately scream for Rafe and his team to collar the man they'd come here to arrest. Besides, she knew they couldn't close in on him yet. She knew enough about the law—having many a lawyer in her distinguished lineage—to know that they needed something called probable cause to make a case against Jeremy Robinson. They needed physical evidence—his handing her a suitcase full of money and telling her to take it to Torres would be the preferable scenario.

She and Rafe hadn't discussed this part of it. Maybe he trusted her to know that she had to take this thing the whole way. She did know that. Or maybe Rafe made a habit of keeping his plans to himself. She wondered how long he had suspected it was Jeremy. And why he hadn't told her. She hated Jeremy for what he'd become. And she hated Rafe, just a little bit and just for a moment, for the things he hadn't said.

All these thoughts flashed through her mind in a second, and she hoped to God that none of them showed on her face. Jeremy didn't seem to notice anything amiss as he brushed his lips across hers. He stepped back and looked at her in a way she'd never seen before. It was not cousinly, but full of masculine possessiveness. It was a look she reveled in from Rafe, but found obscene on this stranger's familiar face.

She had a role to play, so she tossed her hair and answered the look with a sultry laugh. "I think you like the dress."

"I like the whole package, Carrie. I always have. You look beautiful tonight."

"Thank you."

"It's been a long time."

"A year can be a long time," she agreed. "Grandmama says Sharon left you. I'm sorry."

He waved her condolences away. "I'm not. We have a lot of catching up to do," he said with a warm smile. "And a long night ahead of us. But first, let's dance."

"Dance?"

The house had been built in the early nineteenth century. It not only had a reception room and a formal dining room that seated fifty, it also had a ballroom. Carrie could hear the music of a live band coming from the open doorway of the ballroom and caught occasional glimpses of couples moving together across the floor when she looked that way.

She gave a puzzled frown at the buffet table and the open ballroom door. "I thought this was supposed to be a dinner party."

"Last-minute change of plans," Jeremy said. He put his hand beneath her elbow and continued to explain as he guided her toward the ballroom. "There was some sort of problem with the kitchen and the kitchen staff. Grandmama had to call in a new catering company just this afternoon. Now the formal dinner is a formal dinner dance."

"Where'd she get the band on such short notice?"

"They're some friends of Alicia's."

Carrie noticed that the music wasn't quite as staid and stuffy as she expected at a Delia Robinson affair. In fact, the music was heavy on the bass line and rather loud. "That's rock and roll."

"More or less. I think Alicia's friends are trying to tone down their normal style for the evening."

Carrie looked over her shoulder as they left the reception room, but Rafe was nowhere in sight. She disliked being alone with Jeremy at this point, but considering that the ballroom was full of well-dressed couples moving on the polished dance floor, she supposed they weren't technically alone.

She felt bereft without the comfort of knowing Rafe was nearby, but supposed she was just going to have to cope. He had to be around here somewhere, didn't he? She didn't feel any better especially when the band began playing something slow and romantic and Jeremy took her into his arms.

"That's him," the waiter said in a rough, low growl when he stopped by the table.

"I know." Rafe put his untouched beer down in front of him. He ignored the quizzical look from his host as he spoke to the waiter. "No one approaches him yet."

"I'm not an amateur, Castillo. Do we have a name?"

"Robinson."

"Another one. Every other person in this place is named Robinson. What's your girlfriend doing with him?"

"She's here to make the pickup, remember?"

"She knows that's who he is?"

"I didn't tell her, but she's a smart girl. What are you doing here?" Rafe finally got around to asking Steve Quarrels. His attention was riveted on the couple talking in the middle of the room. He didn't like the way Robinson was looking at Carrie. He definitely didn't like the way her cousin touched her. He let it go for now. He was alert, doing his job. He was at the point where nothing got in the

way of his doing his job. In the long run, his doing everything right would be far safer for Carrie than giving in to
the protective, jealous urge that gnawed at his gut.

"I had to bring those rocks to the university anyway,"
Quarrels answered. "I figured I might as well stick around
for the takedown."

"Takedown?" Carrie's grandfather echoed. "What's going on here? Young man," he addressed Quarrels,
"shouldn't you be doing something—waiterlike? Mr. Castillo, would you kindly explain your behavior?"

"You've got all the proper warrants?" Rafe asked.

"Certainly have."

Rafe turned to the man who probably wasn't going to
end up as his grandfather-in-law since he was about to
bring a major scandal down on this very highly placed,
respectable family. They'd undoubtedly try to stuff Carrie
in a convent before letting her anywhere near him after
tonight. He said what he had to anyway. "I'm about to
arrest your grandson for drug trafficking and money laundering, but first I want to have a look at his luggage. Would
you mind showing me to his bedroom, sir?"

Jonathan Robinson looked at Rafe Castillo for several
long, tense moments. The old man had blue eyes, the color
faded with age, but they were clear and full of sharp intelligence. "I see," he said at last.

"No, sir," Rafe answered. "You do not."

"Who are you, Mr. Castillo? Really? In what way are
you using my granddaughter?"

"I—" he gestured at Steve Quarrels "—we work for the
DEA, the Drug Enforcement Agency. Carolina—Caroline—is voluntarily cooperating with us on an undercover
operation. That's not exactly true," he admitted after the
old man's expression turned skeptical. "Carrie was blackmailed into meeting a drug dealer's American money contact. I was working under cover as a member of this drug

lord's organization. He sent me with her as a bodyguard, which gave me the opportunity to use her to trap the man she was sent to meet. We fell in love along the way,'' he heard himself reveal. ''But that's not important at the moment, sir.'' And why the devil had he just admitted something to this staring old man that he hadn't even told Carrie?

Because the old man's stare defied him to tell anything less than the truth. His voice was just as uncompromising. ''Is Caroline in danger?''

''No, sir. Not now.''

''But she has been?''

''Yes. She's been threatened and chased and frightened for days. She deserves better than that.''

''And Jeremy is responsible?''

Rafe nodded. He kept his gaze on Carrie as he talked. She seemed to be having a pleasant conversation with her cousin, but he recognized the tension in her. He knew she was fighting the urge not to look his way. He fought down the temptation to go to her.

''Your grandson has probably been working for Miguel Torres for over a year. I've been attempting to destroy Torres's organization. That effort has resulted in Torres needing a great deal of cash very quickly. He liquidated every asset he owns to pay off some Colombians whose shipments he's lost. If he doesn't get that cash, he's a dead man, though I plan to see that he's caught by the authorities before that happens. To ensure his capture and conviction, I need to arrest your grandson, and I need that money as physical evidence.''

''Your grandson,'' Steve Quarrels added in his cynical way, ''will be granted immunity from prosecution in return for his testimony detailing his involvement with Torres.'' He sneered. ''Your little boy won't go to jail if he cooperates, if that's any consolation to you.''

"That is no consolation." Robinson's voice was hard. Before Rafe could say anything mollifying, the old man went on. "I've always believed that a man has to pay for the things he does. If Jeremy's committed crimes of any sort, he should face the consequences." The old man sighed tiredly and looked down dejectedly. "He's never been very good at that."

Rafe suspected those words cost the old man a great deal. "I'm sorry, sir."

Robinson raised his head. "So am I." He gestured toward a doorway to his left. "You said you wished to see Jeremy's room. I'll take you there now."

"You stay here," Rafe told Quarrels. He shot one more look at Carrie, then followed after her grandfather.

"Sharon didn't leave me."

The hand on her waist held her too tightly. Carrie pretended not to notice. "No?"

"I left her." He ducked his head to brush his cheek against hers. He smelled of a citrus-scented, expensive cologne. She was reminded of the scent of Rafe's skin. Jeremy did not compare favorably.

Carrie wasn't surprised. It had been a stormy marriage. They'd split up before. The last time he'd come to visit her in the Yucatán had been during one of their separations. It only occurred to her now, as their bodies swayed together in a slow dance, that there might be something more than platonic in the affection he'd always shown her.

"You feel nice," he said, running his hand up her bare back. "You look terrific, sexy." He pressed his palm against the base of her spine, bringing them closer. "We should have danced like this years ago," he whispered in her ear. "We fit so well together."

"We're first cousins," she reminded him.

He chuckled. "So?" He looked at her, eyes sparkling

with excitement. "Don't you like a hint of wickedness in your men? A little danger? The thrill of the forbidden?"

She didn't protest, but she wasn't thinking of Jeremy when she answered, "It has its attractions."

"It's seductive."

It had always been there, hadn't it? That look of hunger in his eyes. He'd kept it banked before, hidden it with jokes and playful affection. She'd been clueless. Always happy to be with him, loving him as her cousin. He used to tease her that he was disappointed that she wasn't jealous of his wife. It was only now that she realized he hadn't been joking. She wanted to be ill, but she didn't have time for it right now.

"Is it the dress?" she asked him. "Are you being so blatant because of what I'm wearing?"

"It suits you, sweetheart. You should always dress like that."

"I know." *But not for you.* "Maybe it's not the dress," she went on. "Maybe it's the money. Money's a powerful aphrodisiac."

Jeremy stiffened slightly. Carrie let her body melt against his. He didn't relax, but the tension changed. "Money?"

"Yes. Quite a lot of money. In a suitcase." As well as being furious with him, she was grievously disappointed. She wasn't afraid of him and was driven by a strong need to know. "I believe you have something to give me."

He looked pleased, supremely so. "Why, little cousin, you guessed."

"How long have you known Torres? How long have you worked for him?"

"Three years, and I'm the one who approached him."

"You met him while visiting me?"

"A fortunate circumstance for everyone involved. He needed a new American business partner. I needed the extra income. We decided not to tell you about the acquaintance.

In fact, the fewer people who knew about me the better. We saved the possibility of using you as a contact between us for an emergency situation.''

''Like now?'' She snarled the words, but he didn't seem to notice. How could he be so casual about doing this to her? Her own cousin? How could he have been so easily tempted to go to work for Torres? Was she to blame for having put the temptation in his way?

No. She refused to blame herself for Jeremy's having succumbed to the lure of easy money from Torres's trade. She'd known about Torres. She'd met him, but never been involved with him until it was forced on her. She did blame herself for getting drawn in against her will. Like everyone else in Oro Blanco, she turned a blind eye to the activities of the lawless man who ran the district. It was supposed to be safer. Besides, she was a scientist, an outsider, a civilian. A fool. In the midst of her self-recriminations, her heart was warmed by the thought of Rafe Castillo. He hadn't turned a blind eye to the things happening in the town his ancestors came from.

''At least, it has been fortunate for everyone,'' Jeremy went on, ''until now.'' He drew her even closer. ''You are so beautiful tonight. Did you dress like that for me?''

She started to ask him why he would think such a foolish thing, but thought better of it. Instead, she gave him a look that was sultry and full of promise. Since Rafe didn't want to make an arrest in the middle of a party full of VIPs, she supposed it was up to her to draw Jeremy away from the crowd. Rafe—and just where was Agent Castillo?—had people outside. Once she got Jeremy out in the open, she could signal them to close in. First, she had to get him there. Maybe a spot of seduction was in order.

''Maybe—'' Startled, she jumped as he cupped her buttock and squeezed. ''Hey, we're in public here!''

He laughed. ''You think Grandmama's going to see us?''

"I think we ought to go somewhere where Grandmama won't catch us."

He whirled her off the dance floor. "Fine with me. How about Singapore?"

She trailed her fingers along the back of his neck and through his hair. "I was thinking somewhere a little bit closer. Besides, don't you have something you're supposed to give me?" she whispered as they eased through a knot of people to get to a door on the far side of the room.

He pushed it open. A hallway led to the house's rear entrance. After closing the door, he leaned against it, his arm around her waist. He kissed her, his mouth quite fierce against hers. It took all of Carrie's self-control to allow it, to open her mouth beneath his and pretend to respond. "There's a great many things I plan on giving you, darling. That was just for starters. Twenty-five million can buy us a lot."

"I...see." She pushed his hand away when it cupped her breast. "No, I don't. Twenty-five million what? Dollars? Torres sent me to pick up twenty-five million dollars?" Jeremy nodded, a mad grin on his face. "No wonder you brought so much luggage. I can't carry all that back to Mexico." She was rambling, half-hysterical at finding out how much Torres had at stake. "That much money has to weigh a ton!"

"It's not all in cash, darling. Besides, you're not going to Mexico." He pulled her into another tight embrace, forced another hungry kiss on her. "You and I and all that money are going to Singapore. Come on."

Carrie was speechless as he hurried her down the hall. They were outside and heading through the back garden before she got her voice back. "Where are we going—other than Singapore?" It was hard to walk across the grass in her high heels. She paused to take them off and to look furtively around in the hopes of seeing a lurking DEA agent. As far as she could tell, there was no one in the yard. Where were they? In a surveillance van out front? Or did Grandmama have the ones inside so cowed they were hustling around being waiters and forgetting they were supposed to be watching her? Had anyone seen her and Jeremy leave? Why wasn't she wearing a wire? As if she'd have somewhere to put it in this getup.

As she stood dangling her shoes in her hand and hoping for one of the good guys to put in an appearance, Jeremy got tired of waiting. He grabbed her by the hand and started off toward the back gate.

"Where are we going?" she repeated.

"To the carriage house."

Oh, great. She almost started screaming for help then and there. She hadn't told Rafe about the carriage house. She hadn't even remembered about it. It wasn't on the Robinson property, but two houses down the street. In the back across a narrow brick-paved alley. It was indeed an old nineteenth-century carriage house, part of the original estate, renovated and used as a garage. Her grandparents rented it from their neighbors and used it for storage and extra garage space. She guessed that Jeremy had a car ready and waiting inside.

A car with twenty-five million dollars in it.

"What are you planning to do?" she asked as they walked down the alley. "Take the money and run?" The old bricks beneath her nearly bare feet were cool and a little slippery.

"Take the money and the girl and run," he corrected.

Carrie stopped in the middle of the alley. "Are you crazy?"

He hurriedly put his hand over her mouth. "Don't shout."

She batted his hand away, but kept her voice level as she went on. "Torres is what they call a drug lord. What sorts of images does that term conjure up in your mind?

Lots of people with lots of guns, perhaps? International connections? You can't double-cross people like that.''

"It happens all the time."

"You can't run from them." Despite her current low opinion of the man, he was still her cousin. She worried about him. "Jeremy, you're an amateur. These people are dangerous. Killers."

He was not in the least perturbed. "I'm smarter than they are, Carrie. I know how Torres's organization is run." He laughed. It was a cold sound that echoed off the low buildings lining the alley. "I know that Torres will be dead in a few days. When he doesn't get the money, his Colombian business partners will take it out of his hide."

"Then they'll come after you."

He laughed again, a sinister sound in the darkness. "They don't know who I am." He grabbed her arms and pulled her to him. "I've thought this through very carefully. We have new identities waiting for us, and a fantastic life to get on with. I'm going to give you everything you've ever wanted, darling." He stroked his hands up and down her arms. Even in the near darkness of the alley, she could see the greed and desire plain on his face. "And I'm getting everything that I ever wanted."

It occurred to Carrie that Jeremy, her darling, ex-favorite cousin, had been very careful indeed. "You set me up. Insisted to Torres that he send me. You're giving me no choice but to run with you when you steal Torres's money. If that money doesn't go back to Mexico, I'm as good as dead."

He stroked her cheek. "That's true, darling. I'm the only one who can offer you safety. You have to come with me. I've planned this very thoroughly. I'm really quite clever."

"Except for one little detail," Rafe said as he stepped out of the shadows, moving more quietly than a cat. An amber-eyed cat with a very large gun.

Carrie very nearly fainted from relief, thankful that somebody had told him about the carriage house. She wanted to run to him, to throw her arms around him and sob out both her joy at seeing him and the horror of Jeremy's betrayal. Instead, she carefully stepped away from her cousin while he remained standing in the middle of the alley, his gaze fixed on the large gun and larger man coming slowly toward him.

"What you didn't take into account," Rafe told Jeremy, "was that Torres might send someone with his mule."

"That wasn't part of the plan," Jeremy answered, sounding utterly stunned. "She was supposed to come alone." He seemed to forget Rafe's presence as he looked toward Carrie. "You were supposed to come alone."

Jeremy looked devastated. It almost hurt Carrie to see him like this. Remembering the people in Oro Blanco whose lives were threatened because of this errand she'd been forced on killed any sympathy she might have for her cousin. As she watched the two men facing each other, lit mostly by moonlight and a light on a nearby garage, she was reminded of a meeting of archangels—one all slender, gold and seemingly full of light, the other dark, dangerous and righteous. "Rafael," she said, remembering her manners like a proper Robinson, "meet Lucifer."

"Turn around, Lucifer." Rafe's voice was low, a sinister near monotone. "Which one's the carriage house, *querida?*"

"The next building on the left." She was as puzzled about what Rafe was up to as Jeremy was. She had expected Rafe to announce that he was Special Agent Castillo, read Jeremy his rights, put handcuffs on him and take him away. She had expected it to all be over, to be able to relax, but apparently that wasn't how the scenario was going to be played out. When Rafe told her to open the carriage-house door, she obeyed, but not without giving him a worried look first.

Rafe wished he could answer Carrie's look with an explanation. She looked close to the limit of her nerves, but this had to play out for a few more minutes. If he was going to offer immunity to Jeremy Robinson, he'd have to produce an airtight case against the man. A paper trail—and there had to be one no matter how deeply buried—wouldn't be enough. He had to have proof that Jeremy Robinson was in possession of Torres's money. There had to be no question of planted evidence.

"Turn on the light," he told Carrie after she opened the door. "Now, Señor Robinson, I want you to very carefully take the car keys out of your pocket and open the trunk of your car."

Jeremy swore, but he did as he was told while Rafe waited in the carriage-house doorway, his gun poised to cover Jeremy's movements. Carrie stayed next to the light switch, leaning against the wall, her nerves and thoughts tied up in knots. Why couldn't this nightmare just end? Her attention was drawn to the flash of polished metal when Jeremy opened the trunk of his blue Mercedes. What she saw inside was a large metal suitcase.

"Take it out," Rafe ordered.

Jeremy swore, but hefted the case out of the back of the car. He turned to face Rafe. "Now what?"

"Take the suitcase and walk ahead of me until I tell you to stop." He gestured, carefully keeping the gun trained on Jeremy as they walked out into the alley.

Carrie sighed tiredly and hurried to reach Rafe's side. She wanted to take his hand, or feel his arm around her shoulders, but he was holding the 9 mm, his attention centered on the man moving ahead of them. She noticed that she was still carrying her shoes, her fingers clenched around them in a death grip.

They followed the alley past the back gate of the house and out toward the street. As they neared the front entrance of the mansion and the lights of slowly passing traffic, Jeremy asked, "Are you taking me to Torres?"

"No."

Jeremy laughed. It was not a sane sound. He turned around, walking backward, the heavy case held in both hands. He sneered at Rafe and Carrie, snarling, "You're taking it for yourself, aren't you?" The look he turned on Carrie was full of contempt. "You're running off with him, aren't you? This filthy Mexican punk's your lover, isn't he?"

She couldn't stop the triumphant smile. Couldn't fight the temptation to look at Rafe with everything she felt showing clearly on her face. "Yes," she answered her cousin proudly, "he's my lover."

"I should have known." Jeremy's sneer grew even uglier. He stopped moving, his attention and hatred focused on Carrie. "Whore."

The word hit her like a blow. The reaction lancing through her, as white-hot as lightning, sent her over the edge into a blind, righteous, liberating, vengeful fury. No one called her that. No one got away with calling her that. Never ever again.

She threw her shoes at her cousin, then herself, all fists and nails and screaming rage.

Rafe made a grab for her.

Jeremy spun around, using the metal suitcase as a weapon. The flat side knocked her sprawling. Then the corner of the heavy suitcase hit Rafe high in his healing left arm, sharp as a spear and with a lot of weight behind it. Rafe howled and went down like a stone. In a split second, Jeremy snatched Rafe's gun from his hand and ran.

The knowledge that Rafe was in pain brought Carrie to her senses. She dropped to the ground beside him. Lace ripped as she knelt, but she scarcely noticed. She called for help, knowing that his people were somewhere nearby. Remorse and worry warred with guilt. If she hadn't overreacted...

If she hadn't shot Rafe in the first place, he wouldn't be on the ground writhing in agony. "It's my fault."

Rafe heard Carrie's voice through the shocking wall of pain. He didn't have breath enough to answer. He had to get the pain under control. He had to get moving. It shouldn't hurt this bad. Shouldn't didn't matter. He had to work through what was.

He felt Carrie's hands on him, patting and searching. "You're going to be okay. I have to fix this. I know where he went, but... You've got to have... Where *is* that? Ah!" The sound came out on a cry of angry triumph. He felt her hand pushing up his trouser leg. She barked a word, then was gone. He heard her bare feet slapping against the pavement as she ran.

He heard other running footsteps and people shouting in the distance. He managed to get to his knees, then to his feet, and open his eyes. No more than a few seconds had passed, but the situation was wildly out of control. He had to get back into it. He had to stop Carrie before she got herself killed. Rafe ran after her. He knew exactly what his crazy woman was doing.

Carrie's guilt urged her on. It was her fault. Completely her fault. She'd stupidly overreacted, and now the situation was out of control. She had to do something to make it right. While Rafe struggled to sit up, Jeremy was getting away. Not into the night, not toward the men he must have seen rushing toward him from the street, but back toward the house. She knew where he had to be going.

There was another part of her grandparents' property she'd forgotten to mention to Special Agent Castillo. Of course, if he'd told her he suspected one of her relatives of being the contact, *she* might have been more prepared. Then she wouldn't have forgotten.

A lot of things shouldn't have happened lately. They were both at fault. They'd talk about it later. Right now, the .22 she'd found in Rafe's ankle holster weighed heavily in her hand despite its relatively small size. Jeremy was only a few yards ahead of her. She was ahead of the DEA men who'd been on the other side of the busy street when the shouting started. Jeremy reached the steep front steps and barreled up them two at a time. He pushed an elderly man leaving the house out of his way as he reached the door.

The old man stumbled down the stairs and bumped into Carrie. She steadied him, preventing him from falling but slowing her down. She was at the front door when a hand snagged her arm from behind. She whirled, bringing the gun up without thinking. Then down again instantly when she saw who it was.

"Thank God, it's you!"

"Give me that!"

"He's in the house!"

"No guns!" Rafe shouted as two other agents crowded up the stairs behind him. He tried to snatch the pistol from her hand. "Not in a house full of people!"

"He's got your gun!" Carrie shouted back.

"I know." Rafe swore inventively in two languages. The next thing she knew, he had another pistol in his hand. Where he carried all of them without spoiling the lines of his tuxedo, she did not know, but she wanted to. Later.

Right now, she blocked his way just long enough to explain about the tunnel entrance in the library, a feature of the old house left over from the last century and the Underground Railroad. The entrance to the library was off the reception room.

"We used to play there when we were kids. The other

end opens in the woods in the park two blocks from here. It's very well hidden—because Robinson kids keep stealing the historical marker that says it's there.''

On hearing this, Rafe sent the men behind him to find the tunnel exit in the park. After giving the order, Rafe dashed into the house. The pain in his arm was forgotten. He didn't have time to deal with it at the moment. It didn't even occur to him to tell Carrie to stay outside. It wouldn't have done any good. The most important thing was to keep Jeremy Robinson from making it to this tunnel at all.

Carrie's armed and dangerous cousin was now loose in a house full of people. Rafe knew that his DEA team was inside the house along with security people assigned to the VIPs. Jeremy was walking into a trap, but he was a frightened, desperate man, capable of turning the situation into a bloody one. Rafe prayed that Jeremy was smart enough to make his way quietly through the room with the big gun tucked away under his jacket.

It was a prayer that wasn't answered.

They heard the screams from the reception room when they were still in the hall. The sound of a gunshot rang out, followed by more screaming. They were slowed by a panicked rush of people out of the room, but Rafe's broad shoulders plowed a way through, with Carrie following close behind.

Jeremy was not the only one in the room holding a gun. He was the only one with a hostage. Carrie remembered the joke she'd made to Steve Quarrels about a group of undercover cops all drawing their weapons on each other. The scene in the reception room looked like that now, but there was nothing funny about it. There were men dressed as waiters, men in tuxedos, two women in evening gowns—all of them had guns aimed at her cousin. Jeremy was in the middle of the room. The metal suitcase was on the floor. He held the gun in one hand while his other arm was around a terrified girl's waist.

Steve Quarrels was kneeling amid the remains of a spilled tray of drinks a few feet from Jeremy and his hostage. Quarrels was hunched over, struggling to stand, his blood staining his white waiter's jacket.

Rafe stepped forward, trying to get on top of the situation before somebody was killed. He caught Quarrels pained gaze and waved him to stay put. It looked like the man had a chest wound. He ought to be flat on his back, but he was too stubborn to fall down when he ought to. At Rafe's signal, Steve stopped trying to get up. Very slowly, he bent sideways. No one but Rafe noticed the silver tray lying on the floor at Quarrels's side.

Rafe turned his attention to Jeremy. "I think we should talk."

"Put down the gun," Jeremy demanded. His gaze shifted nervously around the room. "All of you put down your guns."

"That isn't going to happen," Rafe responded.

"Isn't it?" Jeremy's voice was too calm. When he looked directly at Rafe, however, the expression in his pale blue eyes was far from calm. The man was going to lose it. Something had to happen fast. "You put down the gun." Jeremy placed the barrel of his weapon at his hostage's temple. The girl whimpered. "Do it."

Rafe obeyed, slowly setting the pistol on the floor. He kicked it aside before Jeremy ordered him to. He knew the drill. "There." He raised his hands, holding them out before him. "I'm unarmed. Now what are you going to do about all the others?"

"I'm going to leave," Jeremy answered. "And I'm taking her with me."

"Oh, no, you're not."

Rafe was not surprised when Carrie spoke. Or when she

stepped out from behind him. He wished she hadn't, but he was not surprised. *"Querida,"* he whispered warningly.

She didn't look at him as she took a step in front of him, putting herself between him and her cousin. He could tell that she was shaking, but she held her ground. She also held her right hand behind her, the gun grasped tightly in her fist and hidden by her long skirt.

"Let the girl go," she said to Jeremy. "Take me with you instead." Her voice was low, with a sultry undertone that was believable enough to send a flash of jealousy through Rafe. She took a step closer to her cousin. "It's all right, Jeremy. We'll do it your way. Didn't I always do things your way when we were kids? Let the girl go. I know you're mad at me, but I'll make it up to you. Just let the girl go."

"You want to come?"

"I want to."

Rafe noticed that the thin straps of Carrie's dress were down over her arms. It made him wonder what sort of view Jeremy had of her cleavage. He knew how distracting that view could be and hoped the man was crazy enough to pay more attention to a woman he desperately wanted than to the situation.

Jeremy hesitated for several seconds. Then he sighed. He lowered the gun from the girl's temple. "All right, Carrie. We'll trade. You for her."

"Good."

Rafe looked at Quarrels. The man was still conscious; he nodded. What happened next happened very quickly.

Rafe shouted, "Now!"

Carrie ducked and turned. She tossed the .22 to Rafe and dived for the floor. Quarrels threw the serving tray, spinning it edgewise like a Frisbee. Rafe caught Carrie's gun as Jeremy raised his hand to fire at Rafe. The tray hit Jeremy's hand, making the shot go wild. People screamed and ducked as the bullet ricocheted around the room. Quarrels lurched forward, falling, but snagged the hostage around the knees and covered her with his body as they landed on the floor. Rafe ran forward and kicked Jeremy's gun out of his hand.

Rafe raised his gun. This scene was so familiar. The setting was a mansion instead of a barroom, that was all. He looked down the short length of the barrel. It was aimed at the spot right between Jeremy Robinson's eyes. The world stood still for a fraction of a second as their gazes locked. Rafe was high on a surge of fury and adrenaline, poised on a dagger's edge, all too aware of holding the power of life or death. He hated Jeremy Robinson's guts. The man was a vicious, nasty, cowardly thief. The world would be better off without him. Rafe had already killed a man in Oro Blanco. Killing was easy.

This wasn't Oro Blanco. Despite all his warring emotions, his training held. Even more importantly, the civilized man Carrie helped bring back from the edge of evil was able to control those dark emotions. Rafe sighed, relieved to know that killing was really the hardest thing in the world. He knew he would have pulled the trigger again if it had been necessary, but he had no inclination to kill Jeremy just for the pleasure of ridding the world of the man. Rafe's fear that he was no different from the criminals he'd lived among vanished in that long moment. It happened so swiftly that no one but he and Jeremy Robinson noticed it.

He smiled coldly as he stepped up to Jeremy and said very softly, "Because you took a hostage, because you shot my friend and, most importantly, because you called my lady a very bad name, I am going to see that there is no way you are granted immunity."

Chapter 14

"Does your arm hurt?"

He rubbed it. They were alone for the first time in hours. He hadn't let himself think about it before now. "Yes."

She bounced on her toes. Outside the open library door, she heard someone ask the whereabouts of Special Agent Castillo. She heard her grandmother answer that she had no idea where the man was. Carrie was certain Grandmama had seen her take Rafe by the arm and tug him into the library. Then again, there was still quite a crowd out there though the guests were mostly gone. Steve Quarrels had been taken away by paramedics. Jeremy had been handcuffed and led to a van parked nearby. Local police had arrived and DEA people were answering their questions. Representatives from other government agencies had also arrived. Camera crews and reporters had showed up outside, as well. Everybody wanted to talk to Agent Castillo, but not as much as she did.

He'd frowned when she'd interrupted his conversation

with a uniformed officer in the hall and insisted it was her turn. He hadn't argued, though. But once they were alone inside the library, Carrie suddenly found it difficult to talk to this serious man with the closed expression.

As he looked distractedly toward the half-open door, she said, "We made quite a team, didn't we?"

"*Sí.*"

"As if we'd worked takedowns together for years."

He nodded.

Carrie found herself staring at the carpet, feeling like a schoolgirl in trouble. "You're mad at me, aren't you?"

"I'm very proud of you." Rafe grasped her by her upper arms and hauled her close. When they were nose-to-nose, he said, "Don't ever put yourself in danger like that again. Do you hear me? That stupid stunt took ten years off my life."

She brightened at this evidence of concern. "It worked."

He kissed her. What else could he do?

That kiss sent Carrie's pulse racing. She slipped her arms around his neck, opened her lips under the insistent pressure from his. They melted together. When it was over, she found that the kiss raised as many questions as it answered. She deliberately stepped out of the circle of his arms.

Hugging herself tightly, she looked at him as steadily as she could, considering that she was terrified of what he might answer. She asked the question anyway. "Where do we go from here, Castillo?"

Rafe wanted to hold her. Like Carrie, he kept the distance between them. He took a deep breath, then ran his hands through his hair. He began with the truth. "I want to be with you." He added, "I never say the things I should say soon enough."

Carrie looked down guiltily at Rafe's admission. "At least you say them eventually." She shrugged. It was a small, restrained gesture. "I haven't said a word to you about how I really feel."

He couldn't stand being separated even a short distance from her. Stepping forward, he brushed the back of his hand across her cheek. "Do you know how you feel? Really?"

It annoyed her that he could question the reality of emotions she hadn't even voiced yet. "Do you know how you feel?" she flung back. "Really?"

"It isn't just passion, *querida*," he told her while he touched her, running his hands lightly over her neck, her shoulders, her back, her arms. "I know that."

His touch, light as a feather and completely possessive, left her shaken to the core. "It's hard to breathe when you do that."

He put his hand on her waist and drew her closer. "It's hard to think when we're like this."

Carrie looked up at him and found breath enough to laugh. "Then maybe we should stand across the room from each other and shout. If we want to have a logical conversation."

"I don't want logic."

"Me, either."

"I want you."

"I want you." She paused and her smile widened. "There. I said it."

He pulled her closer, and she could feel the heat of his body all through her. She felt the hard-muscled flesh, felt how perfectly her softness molded against that strength. It isn't just passion, he had said, but passion always rose so quickly between them. Passion got in the way of reason. Did they need reason? Should they just go on as they had? There was a great deal of satisfaction in mutually fulfilling passion.

A great deal of physical satisfaction, but that wasn't

enough. Deep down—no, all the way through—she wasn't the sort of woman her great-grandmother had accused her of being. She needed more than hot and heady desire to get her through life. She needed commitment. To give it and to get it. She needed someone to share her life with.

"You want me," he said, interrupting her thoughts. "But do you need me?"

"Do you love me?" she blurted in response. "You said you wanted to be with me—but you didn't say anything about love."

"I love you," he said.

And kissed her until her head was spinning and she was half-tempted to drag him down on the carpet in her grandfather's library and... No. She recognized that once again passion was threatening to get in the way of a very important conversation.

It was Rafe who stepped back this time. He put his hands firmly at his sides. "We aren't doing this the right way. We need to be reasonable, practical. We need to think this through logically." He forced himself to be realistic for her sake. "We met under the wrong circumstances. We don't really know each other. I don't belong in your world, and I'm not even sure where my world is right now." *Other than with you,* he thought, but didn't say. "We come from different backgrounds, different places. We have different ambitions. I'm a career cop, you're a college professor. You're rich, I'm not. We don't have that much in common. Don't look at me like that, *querida.* You know what I'm saying is true. We have to consider that we might not really be in love."

Carrie listened, growing more shocked and hurt with every word. To cover her pain, she managed to say, "We both like beer." It was the only thing she could think of when he was done.

"What?"

Their lives had intersected for a while. Now they had to part, maybe never to come together again. He hated thinking that he might not see her again, but maybe it was for the best.

Carrie kept very still and hid her pain. "You're going?"

"I have to."

"I see."

"I'll call. I promise I'll call as soon as I can."

She forced a smile, a small, stiff gesture. "Of course. I'll see you when you get back," she returned tightly. She found herself motioning at her ruined dress. "Alicia says she has something I can change into. Excuse me." She fled before he could say another word. Certainly before he could say goodbye.

Delia Robinson stepped in front of Rafe just as he reached the library doorway. He did not want to meet the stern look in her eyes as he approached, but forced himself to give the matriarch a polite nod. She did not let him get by.

"A word with you, young man." It was not a question or a request.

Rafe had been a marine. He knew how, and when, to take orders. Small as she was, this woman had the bearing and presence of a general. He couldn't help but respond with respect. She rather reminded him of his own grandmother, actually.

This wasn't going to be pleasant, but he knew there was no escaping the inevitable scathing lecture he was about to receive. He didn't think charm would work with her. He decided on sincerity. "I'm sorry about tonight, Mrs. Robinson," he said. "I'm sorry about disrupting your life. I'm especially sorry about what happened with your grandson. I deeply regret the scandal."

Delia Robinson took a step forward, forcing Rafe to back

up a little. After she closed the library door behind them, cutting off any semblance of escape before she was done with him, she said, "We will cope with Jeremy's disgrace. That young man is getting what he deserves."

"But the scandal—"

"The family has weathered scandals before." A faint wisp of a smile momentarily softened her flinty expression. "Back in 1812, Daniel Robinson was executed for treason. Now *that* was a scandal. Jeremy has always been wild and foolish. No one we know will hold the family responsible for his behavior."

"Unfortunately, there's going to be a lot of media coverage of his arrest," Rafe reminded her. He wished he hadn't. He hated the thought that she might blame Carrie for the inevitable media feeding frenzy that was about to surround this prominent family.

She pressed her lips together in a thin, disapproving line. "I am well aware of what passes for mass entertainment in this day and age. People do not seem to understand that notorious and notoriety are not the same word, and that neither is something to wish for." She touched Rafe on the arm. It surprised him. She didn't strike him as the sort of person who was comfortable with casual physical contact, certainly not with a stranger whom she could easily blame for the evening's events. "I," she went on, "am perfectly capable of dealing with any media intrusion." She gave him a genuine smile, and Rafe saw the resemblance between this woman and Carrie.

"*Señora*, I think you're capable of dealing with anything."

"I certainly am, young man. Especially since I plan to spend the next few months visiting friends in Sri Lanka." She gave a decisive shake of her head. "No, young man, I'm hardly worried about my fate, or how most of my family will deal with the inevitable fallout from Jeremy's crimes. It's Caroline I worry about. She was in the thick of this and she's the one who is most vulnerable." She leveled a very critical look at Rafe. He found it difficult not to stand at attention and salute. "I trust you are aware of just how sensitive she is, Mr. Castillo?"

"Yes, ma'am."

"And special."

He certainly agreed with her on that point. "I'm glad you've noticed, Mrs. Robinson."

Rafe cringed under her frown of disapproval. "I shall take that comment as a sign of protectiveness and tender feelings toward my granddaughter, young man."

"Yes, ma'am," he answered. "It was meant that way, ma'am." He didn't know why he was putting himself through this confrontation with the autocratic matriarch of the Robinson clan. He did have places to be and things to do. "If you'll excuse me, Mrs. Robinson, I am needed—"

"You most certainly are," she interrupted. "By Caroline."

"I..." His voice faltered under her stern look. "I..."

She backed him farther into the room, into a literal as well as an emotional corner. "I know it isn't politically correct these days to say that a woman needs to be taken care of," she went on. "What nonsense. Everyone needs an emotional anchor, someone who makes them whole and happy. I believe you are just the sort of person Caroline needs to truly be happy."

"Me?" He was completely flabbergasted. "I'm a Chicano cop, and she's—"

"A princess? Yes, I know. Beautiful, sensitive, brilliant. Only she's quite uncomfortable being all those things."

Rafe tactfully refrained from commenting that Mrs. Robinson might have had something to do with Carrie's attitudes. Not that silence did him any good.

"I know what you're thinking, young man, and to a certain extent you are quite correct. It took a while to accept Caroline's mother into the family. In our defense, I should point out that it also took the family quite a while to accept an Irish in-law a few generations back, and he became a senator. We're a staid lot, and Carrie's great-grandmother was no help. She gave us no end of trouble when her favorite grandson married 'that foreign woman.'"

Rafe gave a noncommittal nod. "Carrie's mentioned her great-grandmother."

Delia Robinson's expression brightened. Her voice warmed. "Really? That serves to illustrate my point." Her mouth drew down into an even thinner line. "I've always suspected Caroline had some issues with her. Which isn't difficult. I am over eighty and I still have issues with that woman. She was very hard to please and both blatant and quite subtle in showing her disapproval. But the psychological damage inflicted by her is not what we're here to discuss, young man."

Rafe hated to be impolite, but he gave Delia Robinson a hard look and asked, "Just what are we here to discuss?"

"I overheard what you said to Caroline," she stated bluntly. "Yes, I was listening at the door. I heard you tell her that you don't belong in her world. I want to let you know that you are dead wrong. Caroline's world, and yours, are what the two of you choose to make it."

"Is that what you told Carrie's parents when they got married?" He didn't regret the question, impolite though it was.

Mrs. Robinson wasn't taken aback in the least. "Of course not," she answered. "I was outraged when they eloped. I thought it was the worst mistake my son could possibly make. That was also nearly forty years ago. Times, and people, change, young man. Caroline's mother is a wonderful woman and I've come to love her dearly. I admire the way she put herself through college while raising three children and helping my son start his business. Hard work and education mean a great deal in this family. In the end, they matter far more than shade of skin or country of origin or family background. Individual accomplishment is what counts.'' She leveled a witheringly assessing look at him. ''I trust you have attended a university, young man?''

''Yes, ma'am,'' he answered.

''You are also employed in a worthwhile occupation.''

''Thank you, ma'am.''

''Though I would appreciate it if you behaved in a less flamboyant manner—and stopped encouraging my granddaughter to dress like a drug dealer's girlfriend. She was quite shameless this evening.''

Rafe smiled reminiscently as the warm memory spread through him. ''She was beautiful.''

''Oh, I quite agree, but I believe that sort of lack of inhibitions should be saved for the bedroom and not exhibited in public. It distracts my guests.'' She smiled, then added with a devilish twinkle in her eyes, ''I was afraid that several elderly gentlemen were going to suffer fatal heart attacks at the sight of Caroline in that dress.''

He ran his thumb along his jawline. ''I almost did,'' he admitted.

''I noticed. I noticed quite a bit about the way you react to my granddaughter. And having noticed these reactions, what I fail to understand is why you are planning on walking out on her at a time when she needs you. I saw how you looked at her, and what I saw encompassed far more than lust. You love Caroline, don't you?''

He couldn't stop the honest answer. ''With all my heart and soul. But...'' He shook his head. ''We don't live in the same world, *señora*.''

She laughed. The sound was full of genuine, affectionate amusement. ''Young man, no two people live in the same world when they meet. If there is one thing I've learned from Carrie's parents, it's that two people who love each other create their own world." She pointed toward the door. "Now you get out there and create a world with my grand-daughter. Right now."

It took Rafe only an instant to think about what she'd said and find that he agreed with every word. Not just because they were things he wanted to hear. Different worlds combined to make new ones, cultures clashed, and people changed and grew. He'd changed since meeting Carrie. There would be no more nightmares for him because of her. He hoped he'd done her some good, too.

He hoped she'd have him.

Rafe kissed Delia Robinson's cheek. "Thank you for the advice, Grandmama."

She patted his cheek. "Welcome to the family, young man. Now, go propose to my granddaughter."

She couldn't bear the thought of wearing black. Or beige. Or gray. Carrie tossed another dress onto Alicia's bed and wiped the tears out of her eyes before turning back to the closet. She heard the door open behind her. "Don't you have anything red?" she asked without turning to look at her cousin.

The answer came as a soft, masculine chuckle. "You'd look beautiful in scarlet, *querida.*" Carrie whirled to face Rafe, then instantly wished she hadn't when he said, "You've been crying."

"What did you expect?" she answered, embarrassment making her belligerent. She hated his seeing how vulnerable he made her feel. Hated his seeing how much she was hurting after agreeing to be logical and practical and conservative. She forced down her temper, but couldn't help sounding petulant when she asked, "What are you still doing here? Don't you have to go and arrest Torres?"

"Later." He shrugged. "Maybe I'll let them send somebody else."

"No, you won't."

"No," he agreed. "But I'll be very careful."

"You better be."

He crossed his arms across his broad chest. "And then there's PBS."

She wiped away more tears and half choked on emotion as she asked, "What?" She hated that her feelings were so raw and ragged. As he stood in the doorway, she thought he was the most beautiful thing she'd ever seen, all gorgeous muscle and panther grace and warm amber eyes. She'd been trying to get used to the idea of never seeing him again since she'd rushed out of the library. Looking at him, she knew that she'd never be able to.

"I couldn't leave," he told her. "Not yet."

"Oh. What about PBS?"

"We both subscribe. It's something else we have in common. Malt beverages and Public Broadcasting. Maybe I was wrong in the library. Maybe we have a lot in common."

She lifted her head as hope shot through her. "Maybe we have everything in common." She took a step toward him. He came toward her. There was no way she could keep her voice calm. She meant to ask him why he couldn't leave. What she said was, "Don't leave me."

He held out his arms. "Never," he vowed. "Never ever." They stood a foot apart, pain and uncertainty ebbing away. A slow smile gradually tugged at Carrie's lips. A matching smile slowly appeared on Rafe's face. Familiar warmth spread through her.

"Maybe we should stop talking and just make love," she suggested.

His arms were still open wide. "Come to me, *querida*. Stay with me forever. Marry me."

"I'll marry you," she answered. "I'll love you forever. I think I've always loved you."

"I've loved you since I almost shot you."

"I've loved you since the day I did shoot you."

"No guns on the honeymoon, okay?"

She laughed. "Fine with me, Castillo." It was going to be all right. She didn't have to worry about never seeing him again. Happiness flooded her, and with the joy came an unbearable urge to tease. "I'll marry you if you promise me two things first."

"Anything," he agreed. "Everything."

She held up her hand. "Just two. For now."

He tilted up one brow. "And those things are?"

She raised a finger. "One, talk to me. Don't make me have to drag every scrap of information out of you. Don't try to protect me with silence."

He ducked his head and crossed his heart. "I promise. I'll never keep you in the dark about anything again."

"Good."

A smile played around his lips. He held his arms out to her again. "And the second thing?"

She came into his strong and welcoming embrace, into the circle of his arms where she intended to stay. Just before they kissed, she said, "Call me Carolina."

* * * * *

She found herself glancing toward her grandfather's desk, where a couple of empty bottles of Robin Red rested on the wide oak surface. "We like beer," she said. "That's something we have in common."

Rafe laughed softly. "This isn't a commercial, *querida*. People don't build lives together because they like the same drink."

"It's a beginning."

He nodded. "Maybe what we should do is start at the beginning." He didn't want to start over. "Maybe we should take this slowly." Maybe they didn't belong together at all. He didn't want to say that. Didn't want to believe it. He didn't want to draw her into a relationship that wouldn't be any good for her. She deserved the best. A few wild, romantic days together didn't mean that she'd still love him a year from now. "The glamour might wear off," he told her. "I could easily turn into a frog."

Carrie wanted to kick him, but the part of her that had been emotionally cautious most of her life stirred within her. Along with an analytical turn of mind, she had a wide, practical, conservative streak. These insidious parts of her told her that Rafe's arguments made sense. She did not like that part of herself very much, but she listened to it.

A part of her was afraid that he was gently trying to tell her goodbye. It was as much defensiveness as practicality that made her answer, "Maybe you're right. Maybe we need some time to think things through."

He nodded slowly. His whole body was stiff with the effort to control his feelings. His heart weighed a ton. "I have to go now," he told her. "I'll be out of Washington for a few days." He shrugged. "Maybe longer."

He didn't want to tell her that the operation wasn't completed yet. His next move was to lead the raid on Torres's headquarters in Oro Blanco. Then he might end up in Los Angeles for debriefing as well as working on case reports.

Welcome to the Towers!

In January
New York Times bestselling author

NORA ROBERTS

takes us to the fabulous Maine coast mansion
haunted by a generations-old secret and introduces
us to the fascinating family that lives there.

Mechanic Catherine "C.C." Calhoun and hotel magnate
Trenton St. James mix like axle grease and mineral
water—until they kiss. Efficient Amanda Calhoun finds
easygoing Sloan O'Riley insufferable—and irresistible.
And they all must race to solve the mystery
surrounding a priceless hidden emerald necklace.

Catherine and Amanda

THE Calhoun Women

**A special 2-in-1 edition containing
COURTING CATHERINE and A MAN FOR AMANDA.**

Look for the next installment of
THE CALHOUN WOMEN with Lilah and Suzanna's
stories, coming in March 1998.

Available at your favorite retail outlet.

CWVOL1

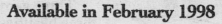
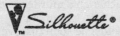

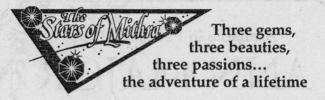

**Three gems,
three beauties,
three passions...
the adventure of a lifetime**

SILHOUETTE·INTIMATE·MOMENTS®
brings you a thrilling new series by
New York Times bestselling author

Nora Roberts

**Three mystical blue diamonds place three close
friends in jeopardy...and lead them to romance.**

In October
HIDDEN STAR (IM#811)
Bailey James can't remember a thing, but she knows
she's in big trouble. And she desperately needs private
investigator Cade Parris to help her live long enough to
find out just what kind.

In December
CAPTIVE STAR (IM#823)
Cynical bounty hunter Jack Dakota and spitfire
M. J. O'Leary are handcuffed together and on the run
from a pair of hired killers. And Jack wants to know
why—but M.J.'s not talking.

In February
SECRET STAR (IM#835)
Lieutenant Seth Buchanan's murder investigation takes
a strange turn when Grace Fontaine turns up alive. But
as the mystery unfolds, he soon discovers the notorious
heiress is the biggest mystery of all.

Available at your favorite retail outlet.